D0484394

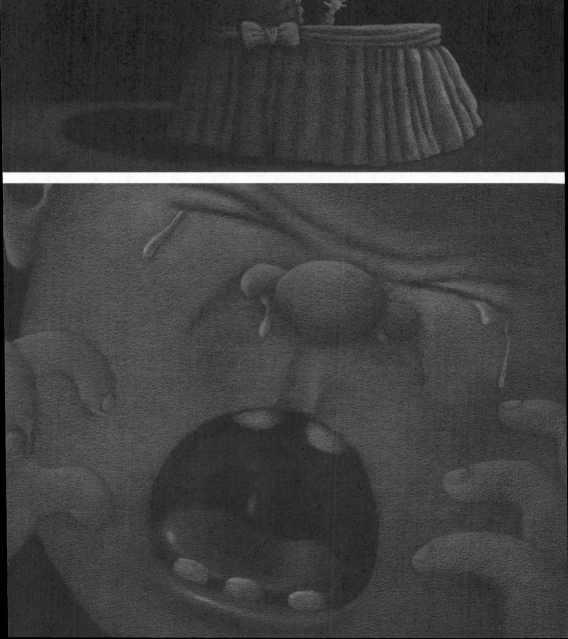

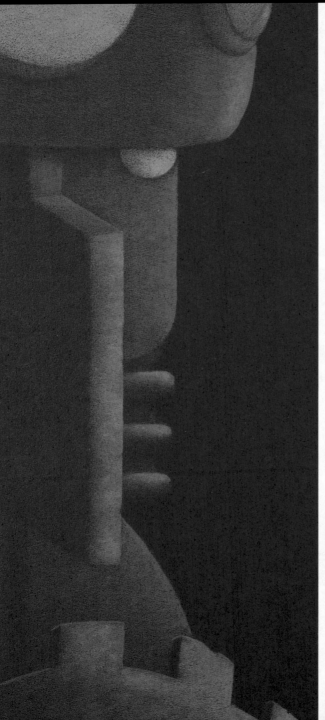

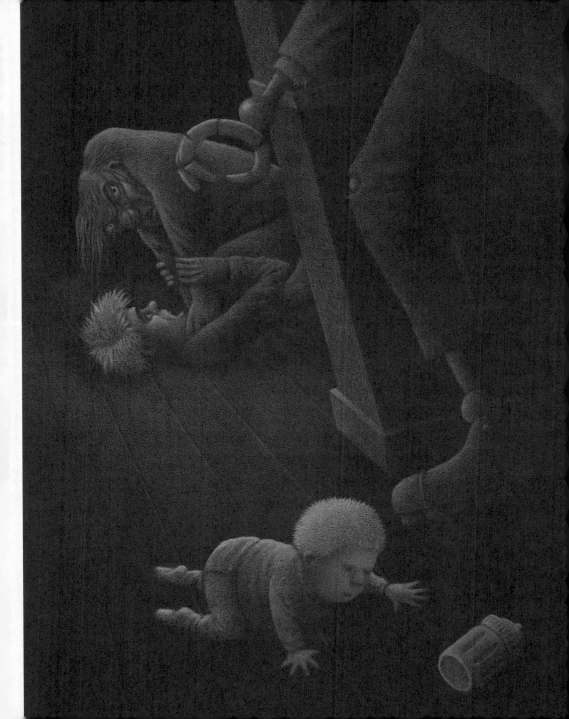

To Boris and Mel

💀 💀 💀

the ORPHAN of AWKWARD FALLS

KEITH GRAVES

chronicle books · san francisco

CHAPTER 1

The little town of Awkward Falls was known for two things: its canned sauerkraut and its insane asylum. Both had achieved notoriety for their repulsiveness. The canned sauerkraut contained cabbage, vinegar, and other appalling ingredients, the smell of which prevented most sane people from actually attempting to eat it. The Asylum for the Dangerously Insane contained insane murderers. Both were to be avoided at all costs, as one was likely to cause gas, and the other, death.

The asylum, despite its name, was anything but a safe haven for its inhabitants. Although it was listed in the phone book under "hospitals," and the criminals locked inside were referred to as "patients," the Asylum for the Dangerously Insane was actually a maximum-security prison. It was like a black hole for the criminally crazy, swallowing mad killers by the hundreds, their deranged faces never to be seen again by the outside world.

Even at its grand opening nearly a century ago, the asylum looked ancient and gray, like an enormous tomb. Only a few small windows dotted its bleak façade, and most of these were criss-crossed with iron bars. Its walls were constructed of thick granite, so as to allow nothing, not even a sound, to escape from inside.

Deep within the asylum, a team of surgeons marched down a dim corridor, their shoes squeaking like frightened mice. In black rubber gloves and white cloaks buttoned up to their necks, the surgeons looked more like slaughterhouse workers than men of medicine. The hallway was lined with identical cell doors, distinguishable only by the numbers stamped into their rusty steel plating.

"Here we are, gentlemen—number one-six-six-five-three," said the team leader, as the group stopped in front of one of the doors. "Mr. F. Stenchley."

Like all the other cells in the asylum, this one was windowless, no larger than a closet, and inhabited by a single patient. The surgeons dutifully consulted their clipboards to make sure this was the correct cell, but there was really no need. They had visited this cell so often they could have found it with their eyes closed.

"Are we really going to take the little monster out, Dr. Penrose?" one of the surgeons asked the team leader, nervously eyeing the bright red C stamped at the top of Stenchley's chart. "I mean, given the patient's violent history, it seems . . . unwise." The group all murmured their consent with this assessment.

Penrose nodded. "I understand your concern, Dr. Smoot. But you must admit the patient has made great progress since we began the new round of Treatments. There have been no biting incidents in weeks, and we rarely need to use the muzzle on him anymore. According to the Cell-Cam tapes, he has even stopped eating bugs and rodents, for the most part."

"Still, sir, asylum policy clearly says—"

"I know what the policy says, Smoot, yet our orders are very clear! As you can all see on your charts, Dr. Herringbone himself has signed off on the whole thing."

The sensitive ears of Mr. Fetid Stenchley, the notorious killer inside number 16653, heard every word of their discussion. His scrambled egg of a brain buzzed with sinister ideas at the thought of finally being taken out of his cell. For ten years he had not set foot outside this cold iron room, except to receive a Treatment.

In an institution packed to the rafters with vile, repulsive criminals, Stenchley stood out. He was a crooked little humpbacked man with apelike arms that hung nearly to the floor. Much stronger than most men his size, he had knotty hands capable of snapping a bone or wringing a neck so quickly his victims barely knew they were in danger before they found themselves taking their last breath.

Though short for a murderer and so remarkably ugly that he almost inspired sympathy, Stenchley was regarded by both the doctors and his fellow inmates as something of an all-star in the world of criminals. Like the others, of course, he was a homicidal maniac whose instinct for murder was built into his very genes. But Stenchley brought a little something extra to the business of taking lives that even the most brutal of his peers could never have even contemplated. It was the reason for the ominous red C at the top of his psychiatric chart. Fetid Stenchley was a cannibal.

☠ ☠ ☠

The peephole in the heavy iron door of Stenchley's cell slid open, and a surgeon's eyeball looked in at him.

Stenchley sat on his plank bed, the cell's only furniture, counting on his fingers. "You're one hour and six minutes late," he mumbled. His voice seemed to come from his nostrils as much as from his mouth, a result of a nasal infection he had suffered from most of his adult life. For the last ten years, the surgeons had come like clockwork, at the same time every day, seven days a week, 365 days a year. Even with no clock or windows to tell the time, Stenchley had learned to predict their arrival to the minute.

The eye blinked, and the peephole snapped shut again. Next came the familiar jangle of keys, which caused Stenchley's pulse to quicken instinctively. Keys meant that he was about to receive the Treatment.

The Treatment was based on the theory that searing heat applied directly to certain regions of the brain would curb the subject's desire to stab, choke, shoot, shove out of windows, drown, gag, poison, bonk repeatedly on the head with heavy objects, or otherwise exterminate his fellow man. In simple terms, the surgeons believed that a roasted brain was a peaceful brain.

The asylum required that each of its patients receive the Treatment at least once, which was usually more than enough. The Level One Treatment combined microwave heating of the brain's frontal lobe with spinal cord microelectrocution and could be counted on to reduce even lifelong criminals to whimpering blobs of obedient flesh. For those rare few killers who emerged from Level One with their desire to be naughty still intact, there was Level Two. Using intra-ear laser-probe insertion to deliver over three hundred degrees of heat to the patient's brain, followed by a complete flushing of bodily fluids using a patented system of pressure hoses, Level Two always worked.

Except in the case of Fetid Stenchley.

The Level Three Treatment had been developed solely for the mad hunchback and required a special generator to create the enormous electrical voltage. Few other human beings could even survive a Level Three. But Stenchley had received one each day for nearly a year.

Recently, this intense regimen had begun to show positive results. Stenchley's taste for flesh seemed to have been curbed, and he no longer required a team of linebacker-sized orderlies to drag him from his cell for his daily Treatment. Still, experience had taught the surgical team to enter Stenchley's cell with extreme caution. Many of them had scars in the shape of the madman's teeth scattered around their bodies from past visits, and regarded him as only slightly more evolved than a pit bull.

But today the little man-eater sat quietly in his straitjacket, watching the surgeons tiptoe in.

"Hello, Mr. Stenchley!" said the team leader, with a tense smile pasted on his face. The surgeons all kept as far away from the madman as the tiny cell permitted. "As you correctly observed, we have indeed come for you a little later than usual. You are a very perceptive chap!"

"Am I gettin' my Treatment now, sir?" Stenchley asked, innocently.

"Yes, don't worry, Mr. Stenchley. You will have your Treatment just like always, I promise. But today we have some special visitors who want to meet you. The mayor himself is making a special appointment just to see what a nice fellow you've become! Isn't that exciting, Mr. Stenchley?"

Stenchley was unsure exactly what a mayor was, but if it meant that he was going to be let out of his cell, then it was definitely exciting. He drooled and nodded, imagining what a mayor might taste like.

CHAPTER 2

The Cravitz family, who were peaceful vegetarians, not murderous cannibals, were at that moment driving into Awkward Falls for the first time. They had noticed the massive Asylum for the Dangerously Insane from the highway as they neared the exit for the town, but had mistaken it for a factory of some kind. After all, what kind of asylum had smokestacks?

Josephine Cravitz slouched unhappily in the backseat of the little family's old Volvo. She was tired, cranky, and hungry after the long trip from Wisconsin. The wheatgrass-ginger smoothie and oat bran muffin she'd packed for lunch were long gone by now, and the dull throb of a headache was building in her temples. If she hadn't been an only child, she probably would have chosen this moment to pick a fight with the nearest sibling.

Josephine had been sulking since her father, Howard, loaded the car the day before, huffing and puffing as he tried to pack as many of the family's belongings as possible into and onto the car, including his favorite sofa, which was strapped to the roof. Around and around the car he went, with his silly Packers hat on backward and a giant roll of duct tape in his hand. Josephine had looked anxiously at the houses nearby, hoping no one was peeking out the windows.

"Do we have to put the sofa on the roof again, Dad?" she asked. "Couldn't we hire a moving van this time like other people?"

But she could see that her father could not have cared less how ridiculous the overloaded car looked. She knew that, for Howard, packing the car was a scientific challenge, a Rubik's Cube to be solved, and he took the job very seriously.

"Nonsense, Jo!" He beamed proudly, tugging on ropes and adding extra duct tape here and there. "This is a 1978 Volvo station wagon. It's a classic! This vehicle was made for moving a small family like ours. Everything fits perfectly if you know what you're doing."

Howard was a professor of microbiophysics and had just been transferred to Awkward Falls University. This meant that for the fourth time in three years, the family was moving again. Josephine did not want to move at all, and even if she had, a small town in northern Canada was the last place she would have picked. When she checked the atlas to see where they were going, she found that the town was so far north, it was almost off the top of the page. It gave her a queasy feeling to think of living so close to the edge of the map. Every time she turned around, it seemed, her parents were packing boxes, tying the sofa to the car, and dragging her off to some new so-called "home."

This place took the cake. Now that they had arrived in Awkward Falls, Josephine was even more disappointed than she had expected. The town was old, drab, and smelled like sauerkraut. The people she saw on the sidewalks looked old and drab as well, and there wasn't a bookstore or juice bar anywhere in sight. Unlike most other places they'd lived, she saw no cyclists or joggers, or even speed walkers on the sidewalks here. Had these people never heard of exercise?

According to banners draped in store windows and from street-lamps, the town was celebrating S.A.D., which stood for Sauerkraut Appreciation Days.

I'm dead, she thought. With no friends within a thousand miles and two long weeks to go before the sauerkraut holiday ended and school started, Josephine was certain she was doomed to face excruciating new levels of boredom. She pulled her old purple knit cap, which she called Eggplant, down over her eyes and slid lower in her seat.

"What a quaint little village," said Josephine's mother, Barbara, scanning the shops as Howard drove slowly along the main street. "It'll be fun exploring all the shops, Josey!" Barbara was a nurse, expert at giving painless shots, and loved antiquing on the weekends.

As a tyke, Josephine used to enjoy joining her mother on all-day bargain hunts. She didn't even mind tagging along with Howard when he attended science lectures at the university. Josephine probably knew more about antique lamps and genetic biology than any kid on the planet. But she had turned twelve a week ago, and was vastly more mature than the doting kid whose best friends were in fact her parents. Her needs were more complex now.

Crammed in between stacks of moving boxes in the backseat, Josephine rolled her eyes at her mom's obvious attempt to make her feel better.

"Hmmph," she grumbled. "Don't try to cheer me up, Mom. I prefer being incredibly grumpy right now. And don't call me Josey. It's cute, and you know I hate that."

The trend among some girls in Josephine's class lately had been to give themselves cute nicknames, their real names no longer being stylish enough to go along with their snazzy new haircuts and sparkly accessories. A few of the more adventurous girls were even beginning to dabble in makeup, which Josephine found most puzzling of all.

Josephine was not one of the cute girls, and she worked hard to stay that way. She made it a point to wear clothes that were as unstylish as possible, Eggplant being her only nod to fashion. She and her small circle of friends dressed for comfort, not style.

She fished an organic carrot stick out of her backpack and bit it irritably. "And, Mom, this is not a 'quaint village,'" she went on, griping freely now that she had admitted her crabbiness. "Villages have horses and carts and peasants and stuff. This is just a smelly old town in the middle of nowhere. I'll bet they don't even have a natural foods store here. We'll probably all get liver disease or something."

Her mother gave her an annoyingly understanding look. "I know you didn't want to leave Madison, dear. We all liked it there. But your father's research requires him to spend time at lots of different labs. We don't get to choose where we go. Once we settle in here, I bet you'll be fine."

"That's just it. I don't want to be fine here," Josephine said. "Every time I start to feel at home somewhere, we move again. We're like nomads of the Sahara or something."

"I suppose we are a bit itinerant, Jo," Howard relented, with a glance in the rearview mirror. "But someday you'll be glad to have lived in so many different places growing up. It gives you a greater worldview."

"Dad . . ." Josephine vigorously rolled her eyes in a you-just-don't-get-it way. "I'm sure a great 'worldview' will come in handy when I'm forty-seven or whatever, but right now I have other things to worry about, things that you and Mom don't understand. I'm missing out on important stuff because we move so much. Do you realize I'm twelve years old and I've never even been invited to a slumber party?"

Barbara looked puzzled. "But Josephine, you've always said slumber parties were—"

"Lame. I know, and they probably are. But what if I'm wrong? What if slumber parties are great? I'll never know for sure, because no one ever gets to know me well enough to invite me. I mean, doing things with you and Dad is okay, but sometimes I wonder how my real life is ever going to get started if we're always moving to these weird places. I never have time to find my people."

Josephine was sure there were girls, and maybe even a boy or two, although that was a stretch, out there in the world who were a lot like her, just waiting for her to find them. She was willing to bet they weren't in northern Manitoba, however.

Her father nodded sympathetically. "By golly, Jo, I think you're absolutely right. It's high time your mother and I stepped out of the way a bit and let you discover your own genetic tendencies. Test your chromosomes, so to speak."

"I agree," said Barbara. "In fact, I have an idea. When we get to the new house, you can have first choice of the rooms and fix it up any way you like!"

"Paint the walls orange if you want!" added Howard.

Josephine just shook her head and groaned. "That's not what I mean," she said, barely loud enough to hear. What was the use? The idea of yet another new house, another new room, another school where she was the new girl was depressing.

"Speaking of houses," said Howard, "I wonder what sort of abode we'll get this time." Whenever Howard was transferred, the new school always provided a furnished house for the family.

"Something old, I hope," said Barbara. "With lots of charm!"

"Say, where is that street, anyway?" asked Howard. "Shouldn't we have come to it by now?"

Barbara scanned the map she had spread across her lap. "I think you're right, dear. Let's stop and ask someone." Barbara spotted a man in a huge overcoat walking down the sidewalk and had Howard pull over. She rolled down her window and waved him over.

"Sir, could you help us please? We're a bit lost. Are you familiar with the area?"

The man took a slug from a small brown bottle and hobbled over to the car. He stuck his craggy, unshaven face too far into the window, eyeing the Cravitzes as if they were some strange new species he'd never seen before. As politely as she could, Barbara slowly leaned away from him. Josephine's nose twitched as the strong smell of alcohol and cigars wafted into the car. What kind of person still smoked? She pulled Eggplant down over her eyes and nose and tried not to breathe.

"Americans, are ye?" He squinted up at the conglomeration of goods on top of the car.

"Yes. We're moving here from Wisconsin," said Barbara proudly, if a bit nasally from trying not to inhale.

"Americans don't get this far north too often." He turned his head and spat. "Don't like Americans m'self."

"Yes, well, my husband has a new job here. We're very excited about living in Canada."

The man frowned. "You won't like it. Awkward Falls ain't like balmy Wisconsin, ya know. We have real winters up here. In a coupl'a months, the nights'll be so long, you'll think they'll never end."

"I'm sure we'll get used to it," Howard broke in. "But do you know where we might find Oleander Alley?"

The man's forehead wrinkled up like a prune. "Aye, I know it. You're not goin' to live out that way, are ye?"

Barbara smiled politely. "Yes, of course we are. Why wouldn't we?"

"I wouldn't live there if ye paid me," the man grunted. "Some bloody goings-on thereabouts years back. Used to be real high-society folk up that way, but not no more. Some say Death himself walks the woods out there. I'd turn around and go back where I came from, I was you."

Josephine peeked out from under her cap at the mention of "bloody goings-on."

"It's easy to find, though, if you're set on it," the man said. "Turn left at the sauerkraut works at the top of the hill, go to the end of Birch Road, and there'll be Oleander on your right." From the alley a couple of boozy voices called to the man, and he began to shuffle away.

"Wait!" called Josephine. "What do you mean by bloody goings-on?" The man seemed not to hear her and disappeared into the alley. "What do you think he was talking about, Dad?" she asked Howard.

He chuckled. "Who knows? I wouldn't worry about it, though. I think maybe he'd had a few too many."

"I should've taken his photo," said Barbara. "He was our first Manitoban!"

CHAPTER 3

A wet fog began to drift in as the Cravitzes turned into Oleander Alley. It was one of the oldest streets in town, lined with dripping, black-trunked hemlock trees and old-fashioned street lamps that did not work anymore. Josephine gazed out at the houses sitting atop the large lawns that sloped up from the street. The houses had a dignified air about them. It was obvious they had once been grand, but they were now slumping and careless in their old age. The entire neighborhood had a dank, soggy look, as if the place had spent a century or two sitting on the bottom of the sea.

Howard leaned over the steering wheel, looking up at the houses. "Can you see the addresses, dear? We're looking for twelve-twelve. It's called Twittington House."

"The house has a name?" Josephine asked. "Weird."

"We just passed twelve-oh-eight," said Barbara. "There's twelve-ten . . ."

But there didn't seem to be any more houses on Oleander Alley after the one at 1210, only dark forestland on either side of the potholed road. They drove farther down Oleander, a half mile or so, until they came around a curve and saw a lone house in the distance. As they got closer, Barbara leaned across Howard's lap to read the address.

"Oh, here it is!" said Barbara excitedly.

The Cravitzes' new home appeared to be the last house on the street. Beyond the shaggy shrubs that bordered the side lawn, the fog was an opaque wall of gray, obscuring all but the tops of the tallest hemlocks and black spruces. The fog was so thick that if there had been a forbidding old mansion next door—which there was—they wouldn't have seen it—which they didn't.

Howard pulled into the cobbled driveway and brought the car to a shuddering halt. They all flung the doors open and jumped out for a look.

Barbara hugged Howard enthusiastically. "Oh, it's perfect, dear! It must be a hundred years old!"

"More like two hundred. George Washington's grandma probably slept here." Josephine was determined to remain sullen and bored, though secretly she found the house intriguing. The lacy, rotted trimmings around the windows and eaves made the place look like a gingerbread house for ghosts.

In its heyday, Twittington House had obviously been impressive. Even now, in its advancing years, the house was far grander than any the Cravitzes had ever lived in. It was a Victorian-style structure, tall and many-gabled, making it hard to tell how many stories there were. Josephine guessed that there were at least two floors, possibly as many as four. And she loved "upstairs houses."

A little wooden sign next to the front door read TWITTINGTON HOUSE in gold lettering. The door key was unnecessary, as the lock was worn out from a hundred years of use. As Barbara led them in excitedly, Josephine noticed the sweet piney smell all the best old houses had. The interior of the house was a maze of rooms of all sizes and shapes, with unexpected alcoves and big bay windows. Some rooms were large and open, with ancient chandeliers dangling from the ceiling. Some were small and cramped with walls and ceilings at odd angles. There were doors everywhere. The house was full of dilapidated charm, a fixer-upper's dream. Before they had even brought in the luggage, Barbara was already talking about paint colors for the kitchen.

Josephine found the house attractively creepy and liked it instantly, though she pretended not to. She immediately stomped up the stairs to the top floor, opening the old creaky doors and looking into each room to see which one she wanted for her bedroom. She settled on one of the smaller ones because it felt cozy and had a window seat that looked perfect for reading. Also, there was a small bookcase containing several dusty, identically bound editions of Edgar Allan Poe, an author she had recently taken a liking to. The room was furnished with a soft, lumpy old feather bed with carved posts at each corner, a huge dresser with squeaky drawers, and an antique vanity with an oval mirror attached.

She sat down at the vanity and stuck her tongue out at her own reflection, disappointed that her bad mood had almost completely disappeared. She tried making really ugly faces at herself, something she considered herself expert at, but that made her feel even better. Then she noticed something wedged in the corner of the mirror. It was a scratchy old photograph of a man and a woman. Josephine picked the picture up for a closer look. They were a striking couple and reminded her of Hollywood stars she had seen in old black-and-white films. The woman, wearing an elegant evening gown and feathered hat, was very beautiful, while the man was dashingly handsome in spite of his wild mop of white hair. They both looked very excited, as if something wonderful was about to happen.

She turned the picture over and saw something scribbled on the back: *My dear Sally, can you ever forgive me? Forever yours, C.* The picture was dated 1936.

How sad, she thought. *They look so happy in the picture, but something bad must have happened afterward.* She wondered who Sally and C were. The picture was so old, they were probably dead by now. She looked at the man's face and tried to guess what the C stood for. Charles? Nah. He didn't look like a Charles. Calvin? No. Cole? Cameron? With that hair, it was probably something too unusual to guess. As always when Josephine's curiosity was piqued, she began to nibble on the nail of her pinkie finger. Since this was a common occurrence, the poor nail was tiny. She decided to make it her mission to find out who the people in the picture were. She had two entire weeks to kill in this outpost before school started, and heaven knew she needed something to keep her busy.

"I call this room!" she yelled down to her parents. "I'm on the top floor." She hurried back downstairs to get her suitcase and officially moved in.

CHAPTER 4

The head of surgery at the Asylum for the Dangerously Insane, Dr. Herringbone, had tried his best to discourage the governor's visit to the institution. The cautious doctor could easily imagine many a thing that might go wrong in such a hastily planned event featuring his most notorious patient. But, once the mayor had gotten wind of the wondrous new procedure pioneered by the doctors at the asylum, he had called to arrange a visit right away. A demonstration was scheduled, complete with photographers and lots of fanfare. The mayor was anxious to claim credit for a groundbreaking achievement in criminal rehabilitation during his administration. Dr. Herringbone had been left with little choice but to grant the request. A mere doctor did not say no to the mayor, after all.

Preparations for the event began when aides from the mayor's office arrived and began setting up the asylum's drab old surgical theater as if it were going to host a Broadway musical. Programs were printed featuring Stenchley's ugly mug shot on the front. Fancy red and blue letters above the picture read "See insane killer receive amazing new treatment!" The press was notified. Festive bunting was draped here and there. A buffet of questionable snacks, utilizing several tub-sized cans of the local sauerkraut, was set up in the rear of the surgical theater.

Since no one would willingly have chosen to come to the Asylum for the Dangerously Insane for an afternoon's entertainment, the mayor's staff had had to use their influence to fill the theater. A number of prominent doctors from other mental institutions were whisked away from their duties and put on a bus to the asylum, as was a chemistry class from Awkward Falls University. A group of vacationing orthodontists from Florida, lured by the promise of free food and a show, piled into the bus as well, and they all made their way to the outskirts of town, where the asylum loomed ominously.

The uneasy crowd, now wondering what it had gotten itself into, was ushered into the dismal gray fortress. Inside, smiling hostesses handed them each a program and a paper cup of punch. An adventurous orthodontist picked up a sauerkraut hors d'oeuvre and tossed it into his mouth, realizing his mistake too late to do anything about it.

The mayor entered next, smiling as if he couldn't imagine being anywhere more fabulous than an insane asylum. Photographers' cameras clicked and flashed to record the moment. The governor's wife, who never missed anything that took place inside a theater within three hundred miles, had come for the presentation as well, along with Lulu, her hairless Egyptian spaniel. After the mayor had shaken a sufficient number of hands, he and the first lady made their way to their seats, which was the cue for everyone else to do the same.

The seating was arranged in a steep semicircle above the stage, allowing everyone a perfect view. The house lights dimmed, and a spotlight shone down on center stage. Unsure what to expect, the audience gaped when Fetid Stenchley, strapped to a wheeled gurney, was rolled into the circle of light. The little man, with his enormous bug eyes and hunched body, was so oddly repugnant as to be almost comical. Surely this wasn't the infamous murderer they'd heard so much about. Was he wearing some sort of costume? Several students giggled at the absurd figure, munching popcorn as if they were at the movies. *Maybe this will turn out to be an interesting afternoon after all*, they thought.

They had no idea.

☠ ☠ ☠

Fetid Stenchley had never been on a stage before. In fact, he had been inside a theater only once, as a boy, when he had paid a stolen penny to see a man wrestle a bear. To the audience's delight, the bear won the contest by tossing the man into the fifth row and eating his hat. But this stage, and whatever show was about to take place, was clearly of a different sort. Stenchley was not a mighty bear and was strapped down so tightly he could scarcely breathe, much less wrestle. Surgeons and hefty orderlies surrounded him and were watching him closely. If this was a contest, careful precautions had been taken to ensure that the madman did not win.

Stenchley had little choice but to lie still as the masked surgeons of the asylum milled about, prepping him for the Treatment. It was just as well, since he had learned the hard way that fighting the surgeons was useless and only prolonged the horrid ordeal. Instead, he had developed the helpful habit of imagining a buffet table crammed with platters of roast doctor, fried doctor, sautéed doctor, curried doctor, doctor puree, doctor pie, and doctor tea. His jawbone worked back and forth busily now, as he grazed through the medical smorgasbord in his mind.

Stenchley's intelligence was more on a par with that of the simian race than the human one. As a child, even the third grade had proved too advanced for his scholarly abilities. Yet his addled brain was somehow capable of almost photographic recall. As a result, he had memorized every step of the Treatment process down to the smallest detail and could predict exactly what would happen next. This had the odd effect of allowing the madman to think he was actually in control. *Shine a light in my ears,* he thought, and a surgeon shone a light into his ears. *Take my pulse,* he thought, and another took his pulse. *Temperature,* he thought, and a third stuck a thermometer into one orifice or another.

Behind him, a complicated-looking machine the size of a Dumpster made whirring and hissing noises, its rows of small important-looking lights blinking off and on. Technicians made final adjustments to various knobs and dials, plugged in hoses, and arranged trays of gleaming tools near the gurney, all in perfect accordance with Stenchley's "orders." When everything was ready, the surgeons took their places and waited as Dr. Herringbone stepped onstage.

"Good afternoon, ladies and gentlemen," the doctor began. "Welcome to the Asylum for the Dangerously Insane. Ten years ago, the patient you see before you, Mr. Fetid Stenchley, entered our institution a cold-blooded murderer. He was known not only for killing but, pardon me for saying it, for consuming portions of his victims as well."

The audience became very quiet.

"As many of you may recall, Mr. Stenchley was responsible for the death of one of Awkward Falls's most famous natives, Stenchley's own employer, the renowned Professor Hibble. Obviously, the patient was a perfect candidate for the advanced rehabilitation treatment pioneered here at A.D.I. Through the miracle of modern science, he has become a model patient. His violent nature and taste for human flesh have been virtually erased."

Stenchley's wide, bloodshot eyes roamed the auditorium as the doctor spoke. The madman hadn't been in the same room as this many people since entering the asylum.

It was true that he had not indulged his appetite in a while, but it had very little to do with the Treatments he had been receiving. In fact, a rotten tooth had kept him from feeling much like biting lately. He was much better now, however, after having wrenched the throbbing cuspid out of his mouth with his bare hands several days ago.

"And now," Dr. Herringbone said, clasping his hands together, "we will demonstrate for you the innovative procedure responsible for the transformation of Mr. Stenchley. It is known simply as the Level Three Treatment."

With that, the surgeons and technicians began bustling about the stage like ants at a picnic. One eagerly stuck a tube down Stenchley's throat, while another attached an array of wires to various points over the length of his body. A third filled a long hypodermic needle with the contents of a bottle of blue liquid. Stenchley jerked as the needle was jammed into his neck.

"Observe," Dr. Herringbone said. "First we lift the scalp flap to access the skull-release panel."

A surgeon ripped back a large flap of scalp from Stenchley's forehead, which had been held in place with Velcro. Then, with a power drill, he loosened two small screws at the hairline and lifted open the top half of the skull, as if he were opening the lid of a charcoal grill. The madman's brain was now fully exposed.

"As you can see, there is some minor discoloration of the patient's temporal lobes," Dr. Herringbone said, using an ink pen to point out the areas. The brain was greenish with fuzzy black blotches, like a moldy avocado. "Just a bit of bruising here, a harmless side effect of daily treatment," he said, reassuringly. While the doctor spoke, another surgeon inserted wired spikes into Stenchley's putrid brain, plugging the loose ends into a flashing console.

Stenchley, having endured the procedure hundreds of times, looked only mildly uncomfortable, as if he were getting an extremely vigorous haircut.

"Now we simply bring the generator up to speed and let the device work its magic." A surgeon pushed a fader switch up the face of the console as high as it would go. The machine kicked into a higher gear, rattling noisily.

Dr. Herringbone and the team of surgeons stepped back from the gurney. Stenchley's body began to twitch and jerk. Little wisps of smoke curled up from the connection point of each wire on the madman's quivering body. A smell not unlike Gorgonzola cheese filled the theater.

In the audience, one of the orthodontists fainted into the lap of his neighbor, but the students and visiting doctors, who were less queasy by breed, leaned forward, watching even more closely.

A surgeon shifted gears on the machine once more, and Stenchley's cerebellum began to glow from within. His brain was now pulsing in and out like a slimy green lung, and his eyes looked as if they were going to blast right out of his head.

The doctor lectured on blandly. "To the untrained eye, the patient may appear to be experiencing some discomfort, but I can assure you the Treatment is not only painless, but even somewhat soothing."

After ten more minutes of this, the machine began to cycle down again. The brain's pulsing slowed, and it gradually settled back into its cavity. Stenchley's body went limp on the gurney as the contraption hissed and jerked to a stop, steam shooting from its joints and connections. A colored lightbulb blew out and shattered on the floor.

Applause broke out across the theater. The mayor and first lady stood and led the crowd in a standing ovation. The unconscious orthodontist came to, looking relieved that the whole thing was over.

"Most impressive, doctor," called the mayor, in his booming politician's voice. "But I wonder if we might hear from Mr. Stenchley himself? I'm sure we'd all like to get his perspective on this wonder cure."

"Yes, Dr. Herringbone," agreed the mayor's wife. "Unstrap the little fellow and let him speak!" The pampered spaniel in the plump woman's arms gave a little yip.

The audience applauded the suggestion enthusiastically, but the doctor waved them off, shaking his head.

"I'm afraid that's out of the question, madame. You see, Mr. Stenchley has never been without restraints since being admitted to the asylum. It's standard policy. If anything were to go wrong—"

"Oh, come now, doctor," said the mayor. "What could possibly go wrong? You just told us your procedure has rendered the man harmless. Does the Treatment work, or not? If your program is all it's cracked up to be, prove it, man!"

"Well, I, I . . . that is, we . . ." He looked around at the other surgeons for support, but found them all suddenly staring at their shoes.

The doctor squirmed for a moment, the color rising in his face, then finally shrugged and gave in. "Very well, Your Honor. Gentlemen," he murmured, "release the patient."

The static fizzing and popping in Stenchley's ears had kept him from hearing the doctor's words. As the technicians went about disconnecting the probes and screwing his skull shut again, Stenchley was just starting to return to something like a normal state of consciousness. With stars still blossoming in front of his eyes from the enormous electrical current that had been coursing through his brain for the last twenty minutes, he had no idea that his restraints were about to be removed. He assumed he would now be straitjacketed and wheeled back to his cell as always. He was already looking forward to his usual post-Treatment reward of protein paste, delivered via a tube in his nostril.

The last thing Fetid Stenchley expected was what happened next.

Members of the surgical team unstrapped him, lifted him off the gurney, and stood him up next to Dr. Herringbone. For a moment, he thought the surgeons were preparing to inflict some new torture, but they just stood there holding his arms. The muscle-bound orderlies with the straitjacket and leather muzzle, standing off to the side, made no move toward him. He felt oddly naked without the jacket's belts cinched tightly around him.

For the first time in a decade, Fetid Stenchley was outside his cell with no restraints.

CHAPTER 5

Stenchley eyed the audience in the seats above him. They all looked so lovely and plump. He tipped his head back and sniffed the air, his nostrils quivering at the rich scent of so much live flesh.

The hump on Fetid Stenchley's crooked spine began to throb. It was this deformity, this bowling ball of gristle atop his shoulders, that held the madman's darkest secret. Stenchley was convinced that a large black python named Cynthia lay coiled inside his hump. The snake had been there for as long as he could remember, whispering in Stenchley's ear, telling him to do awful things. Cynthia craved blood and flesh, and demanded that he kill for her. The madman had learned long ago that Cynthia was not to be disobeyed.

Stenchley felt the python begin to stir now for the first time in years, uncoiling from a long hibernation brought on by his solitary confinement. The lack of available victims had sent Cynthia into a long, starved sleep. Slowly, her head now slithered up into his throat and peered hungrily out of his open mouth.

The madman's purple lips curled into a tiny smile.

The mayor smiled back at Stenchley. The man's face was soft and round, like a pie, and as red as an apple. It was the kind of face a cannibal could love.

"Hello, Mr. Stenchley! We're all curious to hear your feelings on this whiz-bang new treatment you have received here at the asylum."

The mad hunchback's tongue, parched and swollen from the Treatment, lolled out of his mouth. *We're thirsty, love*, whispered the python. *Get us a drink.*

"Water," he grunted. Someone handed him a paper cup, which he quickly emptied down his throat. He realized everyone was waiting for him to speak.

Pretend to be nice, Cynthia said. *Fool them.*

Stenchley obediently clasped his hands together and held them to his chest. He bowed his greasy head and rolled his bulging eyes up toward the mayor, like an innocent schoolboy.

"The doctors has all been quite kind and gentle with me, sir," Stenchley said in a nasaly croak. "They has kept me from doing evil and bloody deeds."

Very good.

"Do you feel that you have been cured, Mr. Stenchley?" asked the mayor.

Yesss.

"Oh, yessir. I assure you I has tasted no creature's blood since I come here. Other than bugs and wormies, that is." *We really are getting hungry for something more filling, though.*

A ripple of laughter spread through the audience.

"If you were ever to be released from the asylum, what do you think you would do, Mr. Stenchley?" asked the mayor's wife.

She looks delicious. I'll bet she's slow as well.

"Well, missus, I think I would probably get myself something to eat first." *Exactly.*

More laughter.

We don't like being laughed at!

"No, I mean what would you do with your life?" The chubby woman spoke to him more slowly, as if he were a child. "Would you turn over a new leaf?"

Stenchley was confused. "I don't rightly know, miss. I ain't seen no leaves in a long time."

The audience was now roaring with laughter. Stenchley wondered what was so funny.

That is quite enough! Cynthia hissed angrily. *Are you going to let them make fun of us like this?*

Dr. Herringbone nervously raised his arms to quiet the crowd. "All right, ladies and gentlemen. I think Mr. Stenchley has had enough excitement for one day. Let's all give him a hand."

I want more than a hand.

The audience stood, clapping and cheering enthusiastically for the seemingly sweet and harmless murderer.

Dr. Herringbone quickly turned to the surgical team. "Let's get the patient back into his restraints, gentlemen, immediately."

I don't think so.

At the sight of the orderlies approaching him with the strait-jacket, its belts and straps dangling like tentacles, Fetid Stenchley's hump began to burn as if it were filled with molten lava. At that moment a fundamental change occurred inside him. Whereas only a second before he had been a small unattractive criminal with an imaginary snake inside his shoulder, he now became a murderous python named Cynthia. Cynthia was not amused by the idea of being wrapped up like a burrito and returned to that cold little cell for more brain-pulverizing sessions. Dinner was finally being served!

No one was aware of this deadly change, however. Stenchley looked the same as before. It was therefore all the more surprising when he suddenly yelled in a loud, menacing voice, "I AM CYNTHIA! AND I AM HUNGRY!"

The audience began laughing again, but stopped short when Stenchley grabbed the necks of the two surgeons holding his arms and slammed their heads together. The men fell to the stage floor, out cold. With insect quickness, the madman pounced on Dr. Herringbone, pinned him to the floor, and began to bite at his arm.

The orderlies rushed over and tried to pull Stenchley off the doctor, but they were no match for the incensed hunchback. Stenchley turned on them with the wild, Animal Channel fury of a dingo attacking a pair of marmosets.

The terrified audience screamed in unison and stampeded for the exits. The students, being young and fast, were the first ones out the door. Sauerkraut hors d'oeuvres splatted on the floor when the buffet table was overturned by the fleeing doctors, leaving the floors slippery with stringy goo. The orthodontists from Florida beat a hasty retreat, nearly trampling the mayor's wife on their way out. The poor woman stood frozen, clutching Lulu, and gaping with horror at the carnage taking place on the stage. The mayor tried in vain to lift his hefty spouse and carry her out of the theater, but finally abandoned this strategy and ran for the doors.

Lulu, the hairless Egyptian spaniel, and the mayor's wife were left completely alone with the snarling creature on the stage below. Stenchley, having whetted his appetite on a rather unsatisfying chunk of the doctor's arm, now turned his attention to the plump, quivering entrée in the seats above. The manic hunchback bounded on all fours up the aisle and over several rows of seats toward the first lady.

In a daring move that was lucky for the mayor's wife, but not so much for the dog, Lulu leapt to her mistress's defense, locking her jaws onto Stenchley's bulbous nose. The madman swiped and swatted at the dog, which only caused it to dig its teeth deeper.

Howling and disoriented with pain, Stenchley stumbled through the exit doors and out into the lobby with the spaniel firmly attached to his face.

Doors slammed and deadbolts slid into place all around the now-empty lobby, trapping the mad killer. Stenchley looked around desperately for a way out. A tiny shaft of dusky light from the lobby's lone window gave the room a wan glow, but to a prisoner who had been kept in a dark cell for so long, the light was blinding. Instinct told Stenchley that light meant freedom.

Like a gazelle clearing a rail fence, the wailing hunchback bounded across the hall and launched himself and the lock-jawed Lulu through the glass.

Outside in the asylum's parking lot, frightened students, orthodontists, and dignitaries had packed the tour bus, which gunned its engine and fishtailed toward the entrance gates. Looking back, the passengers were treated to one last startling scene. They gasped as they saw the crazed madman with a dog dangling from his nose come crashing out of a window in a spray of shattered glass. Stenchley yelped as he slammed to the ground with a bounce, then ran to the nearest wall and clawed his way straight up its face.

The first lady then staggered out into the parking lot, the tear-smeared mascara around her eyes making her look like a two-hundred-pound raccoon. She looked up just in time to see Stenchley and her pet disappear over the asylum wall.

"Lulu!" she whimpered. "Lulu, my cupcake, come back!"

CHAPTER 6

During the time it took Fetid Stenchley to receive the horrible Treatment, inflict numerous nasty wounds on people inside the theater, crash through the window with the First Dog locked on to his nose, and escape from the asylum, the Cravitzes finished unpacking their Volvo. Howard brought in some kindling from outside and lit a fire in the living room fireplace, while Barbara made her famous tofu chili with gluten-free cornbread on the side. They all sat on floor pillows in front of the fire and had dinner by candlelight.

Josephine had planned to give her parents the silent treatment at least through dinner as the first phase of ongoing punishments for ruining her life, but her excitement over the mysterious picture she had found weakened her resolve. She couldn't resist showing them the photo and the inscription on the back. Howard thought the man's face looked familiar, but couldn't recall where he'd seen him before.

"What an interesting-looking couple," said Barbara. "Haven't we seen them in an old movie? They must have been sweethearts. I wonder what he wanted forgiveness for?"

Josephine told her parents about her plan to find out who Sally and C were.

"I think that's a great idea, Jo," Barbara said. "How can I help?"

"You could let me borrow your laptop for starters." Josephine was already heading for the kitchen to fetch the computer. This was something her parents would not normally have allowed, but since they were probably feeling guilty about the move to the Arctic Circle, she figured it was worth a shot. "I want to see if I can find anything on the web."

Howard picked cornbread crumbs from his sweater and flicked them into the fire. "Sorry, dear, we're not connected yet. The satellite guy is supposed to come out next week."

Barbara brightened. "We could try the library in town, Josephine. They may have records of the house and its former residents."

"Good thinking," said Howard. "Sometimes nothing beats a good old-fashioned library."

"We'll go first thing tomorrow morning, Jo, as soon as your father is off to work. Maybe we'll find a nice yoga studio in the village while we're there. It'll be fun!"

Josephine nodded casually, careful not to appear as if she had had forgiven them for their recent transgressions. "Whatever."

She stared at the old brown photo, biting her pinkie nail. What had started out as a lousy day had ended much better than she had expected it to. If she had to live in the boonies, she guessed, at least she had the puzzle of the photograph to sink her teeth into until school started. It annoyed her to realize she was actually looking forward to tomorrow.

☠ ☠ ☠

After dinner, Josephine left her parents discussing wallpaper and climbed the stairs to her new room. She was tired and planned to read herself to sleep. She put on her flannel pajamas (hand-me-downs from Howard) and selected one of the Poe books from the bookshelf. She got comfortable in the window seat and wiped the dust from the cover of *The Raven and Other Poems*.

It was late when Josephine finally closed the book and turned off her light. Outside in the foggy darkness, the moon glowed like a flashlight with dying batteries. She watched the black trees as wisps of fog crept slowly through their upper branches. Then the fog thinned slightly and the moon revealed a building next door, just beyond the line of hemlock trees. The structure seemed far too large to be a house, although she could not imagine what else it might be. It had the blocky shape of old courthouses she had seen, and there was a widow's walk on the roof.

A flickering light, the kind created by a candle, appeared in an upper window of the building, outlining the silhouette of a man. Josephine sat up straight, recognizing a good spying opportunity. She noticed right away that there was something odd about the man,

a curious awkwardness in the way he moved. The candle gave her a quick glimpse of his face just before the building disappeared again behind a thick fog bank. Maybe it was a trick of the light, or maybe she was imagining things, but the face seemed vaguely . . . inhuman.

She waited and watched intently for another look, but the fog did not reveal the building and its strange inhabitant again.

CHAPTER 7

When a mosquito sees a light in the darkness, it is drawn to it by an urge too powerful to resist. Even if the light is a bug zapper, caked with the carcasses of all the mosquito's electrocuted relatives, the poor insect will still use the last flap of its wings to fly to its death. It simply can't help it.

Part of Josephine's brain, though much larger and more complex than a mosquito's, functioned similarly. If she became curious about something, this part of her brain jumped into the driver's seat and took control. When Josephine saw the strange person in the window, the reckless-driver part of her brain grabbed the wheel. She was absolutely tingling with curiosity and badly needed to know what she had seen in the fog, to know whether it was real or not.

She pulled on Eggplant and put her sweater on over her pajamas, mumbling to herself the whole time that this was a crazy idea and she really should have her head examined, but she didn't pause for a second. She eased downstairs as quietly as possible on the squeaky old staircase. At the door to her parents' room she paused and considered telling them about the house and the man she had seen, but decided against it when she heard their gentle snoring. Her parents were open-minded about her curious nature, but even they would have nixed the idea of prowling around at this hour in a strange new place. *Let them sleep,* she thought. *I'm just going to have a little look around. No big deal. I'm practically a teenager now, I should be doing things on my own, right? Right.*

Josephine stepped out the back door of the kitchen and buttoned her sweater up to her throat against the damp chill of the night air. The fog seemed to swallow up all sounds. She walked toward the line of trees along the edge of the yard and pushed through the evergreen branches. The boughs closed behind her like a door, leaving her standing in pitch-darkness. As she wound her way through the huge black trunks, an owl hoo-hooed softly when she passed under its perch.

The trees ended abruptly at an old stone wall too high to climb. She walked up and down the path beside the wall, but could find no way around it. A low-branched fir tree provided the perfect solution. She scrambled up to the low branch, pulled herself up on top of the wall, then dropped down into the tall weeds on the other side.

She had landed in some kind of formal garden gone to seed. The trees and bushes were arranged in geometric patterns, but they were shaggy and overgrown with weeds and vines. There was a small cluster of stone pediments to one side that she was startled to find that were tombstones. The chipped and cracked grave markers leaned this way and that. Beyond the little cemetery was a hedge maze that led to the house. She stepped into it and made her way down a curving alley formed by the towering hedges on either side until she came to a large crumbling statue of someone on a winged horse. The building, even larger than she had expected, loomed just beyond. She quickly scampered across a weedy lawn, past more crumbling statues and fountains.

Once she was close enough to see it more clearly, Josephine realized the building was indeed a house: a mansion, in fact. The gargantuan, crumbling structure was the gloomiest of gloomy places. Gloom hung over its black, crumbling roof like a cloud. Gloom clung like a fungus to its cracked, vine-strangled walls. The twisted, leafless trees that stood on either side of the massive front door cast gloomy shadows in the moonlight over the house's façade.

Next to the front door, a window glowed. She tiptoed over, crouching low as she went, and hid behind a rosebush below the sill. Taking a deep breath, Josephine slowly raised her head and looked into the window. The room inside was dimly lit by some unseen light source. Nearest the window was an antique armchair—French, she was sure—with a side table and lamp. A half-finished glass of something sat on the table, along with a fraction of a cookie. Across the room was an empty fireplace flanked by two tattered sofas. Mounds of debris littered a coffee table in the center. The place was a wreck. It was too dark to see much, but there appeared to be a box of cereal—those disgusting Frosted O's, she noted—spilled on the floor.

Josephine gasped as something suddenly jumped up on the chair back no more than a foot from her face and looked her right in the eye. Her heart leapt into her throat.

Then she realized what it was.

"Breathe, Josephine," she told herself. "It's only a cat."

The cat and Josephine stared at each other through the window. The cat was a gray tabby with large green eyes. Then Josephine noticed the cat actually had one green eye and one yellow eye. In fact, as she looked more closely, she also saw that only the cat's head was that of a gray tabby. Its body was black. The tail and its left rear foot were white, with bits of stitching visible between the different sections. And she wasn't sure, but one of the ears looked like it belonged on a bat instead of a cat.

The strange cat narrowed its eyes at her, then hopped down and disappeared into the darkness. It returned a moment later, followed by a very tall man in a tuxedo. The man looked straight toward the window, as if he knew someone was there. It was the same man she had seen from her room, she was sure. Josephine knew she should have ducked out of sight at that point, but she couldn't resist keeping one eye in position to get a better look at him. As the figure came closer, Josephine was horrified to realize that it was not a man at all. It was a robot with glowing red eyes and steel pincers sticking out of its sleeves. And it saw her.

Josephine panicked and ran off into the fog the way she had come, dodging statues that now seemed to be watching her. A spotlight suddenly lit up the lawn around the house. Josephine sprinted between the hedges, afraid to look back. She hurdled over the tombstones in the cemetery and made it to the wall, panting for air. She tried to dig her fingers into the cracks between the masonry but could not get a handhold. A sound like the swinging of a rusty gate came from the direction of the house. The robot was coming. Each of its heavy footsteps crunched into the grass with a dull thunk. Josephine ran back and forth, desperately searching for a way over the wall. The robot was close now, coming straight toward her. Finally, she found a tangle of vines that had grown up to the top of the wall. She grabbed the thickest and began to haul herself up, hand over hand. Then, with the grip of a steel vise, the robot grabbed her ankle.

Josephine screamed and kicked at the robot, but he was much too strong. He plucked her down as easily as if she were a grape on a vine and stuffed her into a sack. Josephine continued to fight, clawing at the sack and screaming at the top of her lungs.

"Hey, let me out! Help, somebody!" she yelled, even though she knew her voice was now too muffled to be heard by anyone. The robot ignored her and tied the sack shut. He slung it over his shoulder like a bag of laundry and began trudging back toward the house.

Brilliant, she thought. *I could be home in bed sleeping right now, like a normal person. Instead, I'm caught like a rabbit by a robot, for Pete's sake, probably never to be heard from again. Just brilliant.*

She took some consolation in the fact that when her parents woke up in the morning and found her missing they would probably feel guilty for moving here. "Oh, Josephine was right!" they'd say. "We should never have left Wisconsin. If we'd only listened to her!" Of course, Josephine wouldn't get to enjoy it, being dead or whatever, but that was beside the point.

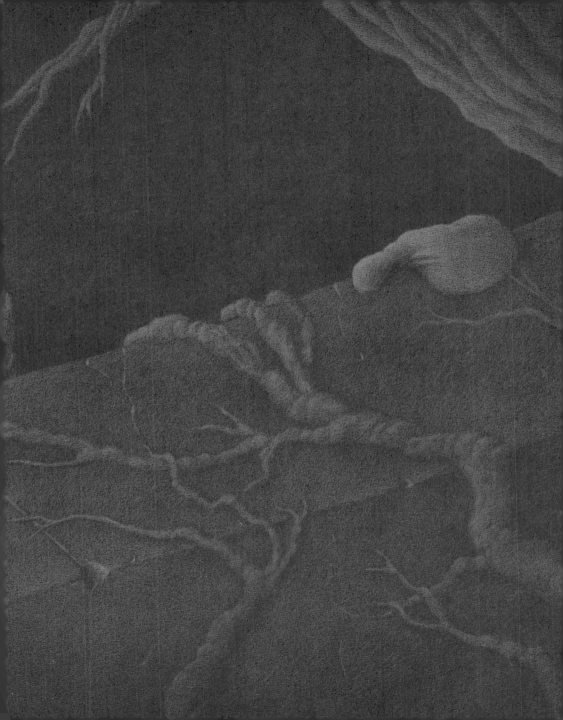

CHAPTER 8

Josephine finally stopped trying to fight her way out of the sack. It was only a waste of energy, and she might soon need all her strength to escape. She could hear the robot open the front door, step inside, then lock the door again. He dropped his bundle on the floor unceremoniously.

Josephine twisted around inside the sack until she found a small hole she could see through. A few sputtering candles did little to illuminate the room, but she could tell she was in the foyer of the house. The smell of rat droppings permeated even the coarse material of the sack.

The robot's steel feet clanged past her and out of the room. She heard the rattle of plates and silverware from the next room as the machine man banged about. After a few minutes, the robot clunked back into the room carrying a covered silver tray, which he set on a side table. He untied the sack and dumped Josephine onto the floor. Her immediate instinct was to run, but a quick glance around showed no clear way out. The door was locked, and the windows looked as if they hadn't been opened in years, if ever.

As she looked around, she could see that the cavernous foyer, with its enormous dangling chandelier dripping with shards of shattered crystal, its crumbling marble floor, and its gold-framed paintings hanging crookedly on the walls, must have once been breathtaking. A massive staircase, coated with cobwebs and looking as if it might come crashing down at any moment, ascended three stories in a graceful arc. Even in its dangerously decayed state, the staircase made Josephine think of Cinderella. Or maybe Cinderella's skeleton.

"Good evening, Madame Prisoner," said the robot. His voice crackled with static, as if it came from an old radio. His red eyes beamed down at her like lasers. "Welcome to Hibble Manor."

Hydraulics huffed and hissed inside the robot's mechanical body as he bowed slightly, steel scraping on steel. Now that she could see him up close, she got the impression he could squash her like a bug if he really wanted to. Still, as scary as the robot was, there was something a little goofy about him as well. His ratty tuxedo hung on his steel frame like a cheap Halloween costume. The sleeves and trouser legs were too short for his long limbs, and his clip-on bow tie was crooked. He was like a cross between a waiter and a dump truck.

"I do hope you will not try to escape," he continued. "Running would be futile, since I am rather speedy and would undoubtedly catch you again. I should warn you that I once won a race with a 1932 Oldsmobile. A red one, as I recall."

She quickly scanned the room again, hoping she had overlooked a handy exit. Nope, no chance. She was Madame Prisoner for the moment, whether she liked it or not.

The robot kept its eyes on her as if it were waiting for an answer. She nodded slowly. "Okay," she said. "You got me. I won't run." It felt strange talking to a machine. She wondered if it could tell she was lying.

A dusty cuckoo clock on the wall suddenly came to life. Josephine recognized the clock as a replica of the cathedral at Notre Dame. When its tiny doors swung open, a live mouse wearing a red and gold robe and a tall pointed hat scurried out onto the toy cathedral's balcony. The mouse looked out at the room and gave a solemn little wave, then took hold of a string that hung down from the belfry and tugged. With each pull, a miniature bell tinkled. When the mouse had rung the bell twelve times, a morsel of cheese dropped down from the tower, which it snatched up greedily. The doors opened again, and the mouse ran back inside with its reward.

The bell-ringing mouse was nothing compared to what came next. A small door hidden in the baseboard near Josephine swung open and out rolled a toy train. On closer examination, Josephine saw that the train's engine was made from a dented old teakettle fitted with wheels. Tooting and puffing white smoke from its chimney, the engine pulled several cars made from pots and cookie tins.

When the train chugged past Josephine, she did a double take at the sight of two small furry legs attached to the kettle that were furiously pedaling the engine's wheels like a bicycle. There did not appear to be an animal attached to the legs. The little appendages were part of the engine itself. Also, on the front, where the headlight is usually found on a real train, was an eyeball built into the kettle.

Okay, that's a real eyeball, she thought. *And unless I'm hallucinating, it's guiding the train around the furniture! What kind of place is this?*

The train made a circuit once around the room and stopped at the robot's feet. He set the silver tray on the train's tin-pan freight car, then it started up again and rolled across the floor toward a very dark corridor.

"Please follow me, madame," he said to Josephine as he flicked on a spotlight built into his forehead.

Josephine got to her feet, but was hesitant to follow the robot into the darkness. She could hear things scratching around in there.

"Where are we going?" she asked.

"To meet the master of the house, of course. It is time for his midnight meal, a perfect opportunity to introduce you."

She didn't move.

The robot locked his iron claw pincer onto Josephine's wrist like a handcuff. "I'm afraid I must insist."

"Hey! That hurts!" Josephine protested as the robot effortlessly pulled her behind him into the hallway.

"A necessary discomfort, unfortunately," he said. "But it is for your own good. The closer you follow, the less likely the rats are to bite."

The bizarre little train rattled and tooted along the dark corridor, leading them deep into the musty heart of the mansion. Like a shackled convict, Josephine stumbled along behind the robot, staying as close on his heels as she could manage. They turned left, right, then left again, at one point rounding a corner and sending a few dozen rats who had been feasting on what looked like a box of jelly doughnuts scurrying for cover. She tried hard to create a mental map in her head of each turn they made. If she was able to get free at some point and make a run for it, she wanted to be able to find her way out of this place.

When the train neared a pair of tall doors in the darkness ahead, an unseen mechanism that sounded as if it were located inside the walls whirred into action and the doors swung open with the screeching moan of old hinges. The robot led Josephine into the room and released her wrist, allowing the blood to begin circulating in her hand again.

This was her chance. As the robot went about the room lighting numerous candelabras, she turned and dashed for the doors. But before she had taken two steps, the doors slammed shut and the clunk of a deadbolt followed. She frantically twisted the knobs anyway, but it was no use.

The robot's small red eyes beamed at her. She cringed, expecting him to come and grab her again, or something worse, but he did not. The machine man patiently finished lighting the last of the candles and pinched the match out between his steel fingertips.

"I had hoped you wouldn't try to escape, madame," he said. "Hibble Manor can be quite treacherous in the dark if one doesn't know where one is going."

Josephine jumped as something furry skittered past, brushing her ankles. "Oh! What was that?"

"A rodent of some kind." The robot's eyes tracked the animal's movement along the baseboard. "The larger ones tend to congregate near the doors for some reason."

Josephine moved quickly toward the middle of the room, praying nothing else would touch her. With dozens of candles now flickering, she could see they were in a once-grand dining room. Shadows danced over an impossibly long table lined with big, fancy chairs that could have passed for thrones. Framed mirrors on the walls created the odd illusion that the room was even larger than it was.

The robot opened a door on one side of the room revealing a stairway that descended into what she guessed was a basement.

"I should warn you, the master is easily perturbed by interruptions, even for meals. When he enters the room, you should be prepared to dodge any objects he may fling," the robot said as he brushed off the lapels of his tuxedo jacket and picked flecks of lint off his cummerbund.

"Right. . . ." Josephine was unsure what to make of such a warning. She moved closer to the table, figuring she could duck behind it if she had to.

The robot pulled a velvet cord hanging from the ceiling. A gong sounded from somewhere in the darkness downstairs.

"What do you want?" a voice grumbled.

"Good evening, Master," the robot called down the stairs. "Your twelve o'clock meal is served, sir."

"Oh, for Pete's sake, Norman, just leave it! I'm in the middle of an operation!"

"As you wish, Master. But there is a disturbing matter that requires your attention."

The voice became more impatient. "What is it?"

"I'm afraid we've had an intruder, sir. Naturally, knowing your desire for privacy, I gave chase."

"An intruder? Drat! Was it the man in the black suit? I told you we should never have filled in the tiger pits, Norman. Perhaps we should install a high-voltage fence."

"A first-rate idea, sir. In any case, I am happy to report," the robot said proudly, "that I was able to apprehend the culprit. I am rather speedy, you know, having once outrun an Oldsmo—"

"You caught the intruder, Norman? Excellent work! Ran him off, did you? Tossed him over the wall?"

"Actually, sir, I have the intruder right here."

"Here?" An angry snort was followed by footsteps stomping up the stairs.

Josephine saw the silhouette of a very short, round man, who arrived at the top of the steps and began yelling up at the huge robot towering over him.

"Norman, you ninny!" he wheezed, out of breath from the climb. "I've told you a BILLION times, outsiders are never allowed inside! That's why they're outsiders! If we let them inside, they become insiders!"

"Your logic is flawless as always, sir."

"Well, let's have a look at the perpetrator, as long as I'm here."

The little man barged past the robot toward Josephine. As he stepped into the light, her jaw dropped.

"The master" was not a little man at all. He was a boy.

CHAPTER 9

The boy glared at Josephine suspiciously. "Who are you, and what are you up to? Are you a spy sent by the orphanage? Did the man in the black suit put you up to this?"

He was the unhealthiest-looking kid Josephine had ever seen. His marshmallow-pale skin made her wonder if he had ever been outdoors in his life. She winced at the boy's neglected teeth, which were badly in need of a patient dentist. His uncombed white hair showed no evidence of having been shampooed in recent months. His unclipped fingernails were dirty, his thick glasses smeared with fingerprints, his too-large white jacket and trousers spotted with stains from numerous sloppy meals. The boy was overweight, under-exercised, and smelly.

Josephine found him repulsive, yet somehow interesting, like some long-forgotten cheese discovered at the back of the refrigerator.

"Of course I'm not a spy!" said Josephine. "And I don't know any man in a black suit."

He snorted. "A likely story!"

The boy hurried over to a small stepladder near the wall, climbed to the top step, and pulled a lever. A crude periscope made from rusty pipes and telescope parts slid down from a tube in the ceiling. Like a submarine commander, he squinted into the eyepiece, rotating the periscope in every direction. "I know he's out there!" he said. "I've spotted him before, you know, skulking around in his black suit, hiding in the trees outside the fence. I'm fully aware of what you people are up to."

"I am *not* a liar. And please make this . . . this *thing* let go of my arm." She glared up at the robot. "It hurts!"

"Norman is not a thing," he declared. "He is an ingenious creation, built by my grandfather, Celsius Hibble, one of the greatest scientists of the twentieth century."

"I don't care who built it. Just make it let me go!"

"You *should* care!" The boy ignored her pleas, instead removing his smudgy glasses and wiping them with his coattail. "Grandfather was no mere tinkerer. He won the Nobel Prize in science, a feat I hope to match someday. He was very famous. This estate was his, in fact. He did much of his groundbreaking work here, prior to his murder."

Josephine gasped. "Murder! That's terrible!"

"Terrible, indeed." The boy became somber. "Ten years ago, Grandfather was killed in this very room by his lifelong assistant, a terrible man named Fetid Stenchley. The fiend strangled him with his bare hands."

Josephine gulped and instinctively touched her throat at the thought of it.

"Why would your grandfather's assistant murder him?"

"No one knows. The man was a lunatic. He's been locked inside the Asylum for the Dangerously Insane ever since, serving a life sentence. A fitting punishment for killing one of the world's top geniuses in cold blood, I'd say."

Finally satisfied that no one else lurked outside, the boy pulled the lever again and the periscope slid back up to the ceiling. He hopped down from the ladder and walked right up to Josephine, looking into her eyes suspiciously.

"If you are lying, and you really are from the orphanage, I swear you'll never take me alive."

"I'm not from the orphanage, I promise," she said. "My name is Josephine Cravitz. I just moved in next door. I'm your new neighbor." She smiled and stuck out her hand to shake.

He looked at it as if it were a dead fish. "Neighbor? Urgh! I despise neighbors almost as much as I despise spies. How many of you are there?"

"Just my parents and me."

"Drat! An entire clan," he fumed. "Throw her in the dungeon, Norman!"

"We don't have a dungeon, Master."

"The torture chamber, then!"

"What?" gasped Josephine. *Was this kid some kind of psycho?* she wondered.

"Sadly, we lack one of those as well, sir."

"Bother! Where do we put prisoners, then?"

"I don't know, sir. We've never had one before."

The boy and the robot thought it over for a moment, then the robot said, "How about the broom closet, sir?"

"Good idea!" The boy slapped his knee enthusiastically. "It's dark and uncomfortable, though not as cold as I'd like. We'll keep her in there until we decide on something better to do with her. Tie her up, Norman! And use lots of ingenious knots. Spies are expert at untying things."

"As you wish, sir." The robot found a rope and began coiling it around Josephine's body, pinning her arms to her sides.

"Hold on a minute!" Josephine squirmed as the robot pulled the ropes tight. She had to stop this craziness, before it got out of hand. "You really don't have to do this, I'm pretty harmless."

"I'll be the judge of that." The boy jutted his chin out defiantly. "Into the closet with her, Norman!"

"Right away, Master."

"And I'll have my dinner now. All this ruckus has stirred my appetite."

CHAPTER 10

Inside the broom closet, Josephine sat on an overturned bucket surrounded by long-unused cleaning supplies. She squirmed and strained against the ropes and quickly found that there was nothing very ingenious about Norman's knots, after all. Having gone to yoga classes with her mom every Saturday for years, Josephine could twist her body like a pretzel into impossible poses. She dropped her shoulders and folded her arms behind her, rotating her torso and sucking in her belly at the same time. The ropes fell slack, and she was soon able to free her hands. In no time, the ropes were off, which was nice, but she was still locked inside a closet inside a locked room, which was a problem.

She held her ear to the door and listened as the boy and the robot discussed her as if she were some diabolical villain.

"She is obviously a spy from the orphanage, Norman." The boy chewed as he spoke. "This whole 'neighbor' business is just a clever ploy to trap me, I suspect. Don't you agree?"

"It seems she was peeping, sir, which is very similar to spying, though not exactly analogous in the strictest interpretation of the word. So in that sense—"

"Or maybe she and her 'parents,' as she calls them, are some kind of elite commando force, sent here to infiltrate our stronghold!" A loud slurping sound followed this speculation.

"I can only hope," ventured the robot, seriously, "that she is not an alien assassin from the planet Mars. I saw a very interesting report on television just last evening in which Los Angeles was being invaded by female Martians armed with quite fearsome weaponry. I'm afraid the city has been completely destroyed."

The boy smacked his forehead. "That was a movie, you dolt, not a report! I've told you a TRILLION times, Norman, movies are fictitious."

"Oh, what a relief," the robot sighed mechanically. "I've been so worried all day."

"So who is she, then? She was up to something devious, I'm sure of it. Why else would she have been sneaking around here in the dead of night? She knows our secrets now that she has been inside. She has sensitive information!"

As the discussion went on and their ideas of what to do became increasingly outlandish, Josephine began to worry. Her parents did not have the slightest idea where she was, so rescue was impossible. Screaming would also be a waste of time, and it might cause her captors to become even more agitated. Though the boy and the robot were naive and a bit silly, they seemed to be truly paranoid and capable of doing who knew what. At one point, she heard the boy suggest the possibility of Norman driving her far out into the tundra and dropping her off, like some terrible people did with unwanted kittens. Luckily, the robot answered that the car was low on gas and they dropped the idea. Then the robot suggested there might be some simple surgery that could be implemented to erase her "memory circuits," since he had seen that done on television also. Chillingly, the boy actually liked the surgery idea, but decided against it, citing a lack of the proper drilling tools.

Hearing all this, Josephine tried desperately to come up with an escape plan. Just as she began looking for air vents in the ceiling, the closet door opened and Norman's strong claws reached in for her. The robot lifted Josephine out of the closet and plopped her into a chair at the dining table.

The boy noticed that the ropes were gone. "Hey! You're supposed to be tied up. Norman, didn't you tie her up properly?"

"Yes, Master. My knots were quite elaborate."

"Then why is she not tied up?"

The robot looked Josephine over closely. "Perhaps she chewed through the bindings, sir. She does appear to have exceptionally sturdy teeth."

"I untied myself," she said. "It wasn't that hard."

"So, you are a professional!" The boy shone a toy flashlight in her face, eyeing her suspiciously. "Very well, Ms. 'Cravitz.' If that is your real name. We will interrogate you without ropes. You will tell us everything . . . or ELSE! First, who are you really working for?"

"I'm not working for anyone!"

"An obvious lie." He wiggled the flashlight inches from her face. "We'll make you sweat. Are you a foreigner?"

"No. Well . . . sort of. I'm from Wisconsin, but—"

"AHA! So, you are a foreign spy from Wisconsin! A country known for its many cruel orphanages." The boy gulped the rest of his candy and flung the wrapper.

"Actually, sir," said the robot, "I believe Wisconsin is a state, not a—"

"Shush, Norman. She may be wearing one of those tiny recording devices all the top spies have. Our enemies in Wisconsin are probably listening to every word we are saying."

"Look," Josephine said, as calmly and sincerely as she could, "I admit I was snooping around. I'm a naturally nosy person. But I didn't mean to cause any trouble, and I definitely don't work for any orphanage. I don't even like orphanages. I think they're depressing."

"You do?" The boy looked perplexed. He bit off a chunk of the candy bar he held in his chubby fist.

"Yes," she said, looking him in the eye to get her point across. "I would never want to be put in one of those places. They're like prisons for children."

"A perfect analogy!" he said. "I wish I'd thought of it. With their evil wardens and disgusting bowls of gruel. They're inhuman!"

"You're right." Josephine had never seen an orphanage, but, like all children, had very strong ideas about them nevertheless. "The truth is, even though you tied me up, I wouldn't want you to be sent to one."

"You wouldn't?" He clicked off the flashlight. "I'm pleased to see we share the same opinion on the matter, Ms. Cravitz."

"I'm very antiorphanage," Josephine said.

"Hmmm. If a spy from the orphanage said those things, she'd be banished, if not assassinated. Perhaps you're not a spy after all."

"I've been trying to tell you that. And you don't have to call me Ms. Cravitz, you know. I'm not an old lady. Just call me Josephine."

"Fine. Josephine, then."

"That's better. Now, what about you?"

"What about me?"

"Aren't you going to tell me your name?" she asked.

He tipped his head back and pointed his chin at her. "You may call me Master Hibble," he said.

"But you're a kid."

His face was blank. "Your point is . . . ?"

"Come on," she said. "I told you my first name, now you have to tell me yours."

"Oh, bother! If you must know, it is Thaddeus, though no one calls me that."

She smiled. "Of course. You look like a Thaddeus."

"I'm glad you approve." He hopped up onto a chair across from her and ripped the paper off another candy bar.

"Would you care to join me for a bite, Ms. Crav—er, I mean, Josephine?" Thaddeus offered. "Norman has laid out more than I can eat, as usual."

Josephine could not imagine a less appetizing place to eat. The smell of rodent droppings was enough to make her stomach turn. Dunes of crumpled candy wrappers, empty soda cans, overturned cereal boxes, cookie crumbs, ice cream tubs, and many other unidentifiable clumps made the table's surface look like a landfill. Still, she could see he was being generous in his own way, so she did the polite thing and nodded and smiled.

When she turned her attention to the items laid out on the dishes between them, she immediately wished she could take it back. There was a pot of brown sludge that she guessed was supposed to be hot cocoa, an enormous bowl of dusty sugar cubes, a plate of ChocoChewy Nut Logs, and a family-sized sack of mini doughnuts.

The robot tied a bib decorated with blue teddy bears around Thaddeus's neck. With the grace of the finest butler, he daintily topped off the boy's mug of cocoa/sludge and filled a cup for their guest.

"Where are my marshmallows, Norman?" The boy used a stubby finger to search the depths of his cocoa.

"My apologies, Master, but I'm afraid we're a bit short on cash again," Norman explained. "Marshmallows are rather expensive, you know."

"Vexation! Perhaps we could sell another piano. The one in the conservatory should be worth something."

"We sold that one last month, sir. There are no more pianos."

"Urgh. Cocoa without marshmallows is barbaric."

To Josephine's shock, Thaddeus plunked six lumps of sugar into his cocoa/sludge and stirred. She grimaced. Her teeth hurt just watching him.

"Refined sugar is extremely unhealthy, you know," she blurted out before thinking. "I mean, so I've read."

He slurped from the cup. "Nonsense. Sugar is delicious! Here, try this and see for yourself," he said, plucking a lump of sugar from the bowl and handing it out to her.

She recoiled as if the sparkling cube were radioactive. "No, no, I can't. It's not good for my teeth," *Or anything else, for that matter,* she thought. "Don't you get lots of cavities?"

He looked at her as if she were loony. "I can assure you that the majority of my teeth are in perfect condition! In fact, I find that drinking five or six cups of sugared cocoa per day is quite beneficial to my system." He peeled the wrapper off a ChocoChewy Nut Log and bit off a hunk. "Especially when accompanied by just the right entrée."

Josephine felt as if she had discovered some new species of creature. She had never seen anyone cram so much unhealthy food into his stomach at one sitting in her life. She badly wanted to snatch the candy from Thaddeus's hands and replace it with a celery stick or anything from the vegetable or fruit family, though the likelihood of finding such a thing in this house seemed remote.

The mere thought of all the unhealthy things going on inside his body made her woozy. His triglyceride levels were probably off the chart, not to mention his adrenals. And she didn't even want to think of his spleen.

"Why are you so worried about being sent to an orphanage, Thaddeus?" Josephine asked, as he licked imitation doughnut dust off his fingers. "Are you an orphan?"

He bristled at the suggestion. "Certainly not. I have parents. In fact, I expect their arrival any time now." He slid down from his chair and headed for the far end of the table, followed by Norman. "Come with me."

The robot set a candelabra at the other end of the table, where three formal place settings had been laid out—complete with china plates, soup bowls, and crystal goblets, plus multiple forks, knives, and spoons. Cone-shaped party hats and paper horns sat on each plate. The settings would have been festive if not for the shroud of dust and spiderwebs covering them. A board game, also coated with dust, was set up in the center of the table, as if a game were about to begin.

Thaddeus went over to the place settings and began blowing the dust off them. "We're going to have a homecoming party in their honor, the moment they return. Mother will sit here, and Father over there, with me right between them. We'll have a huge feast, then play games until bedtime!" He beamed, as if he were seeing the reunion playing out before him. "First we'll play Candyland, my personal favorite, then perhaps Monopoly or Chinese checkers, if Mother prefers. All the best families play games together."

"Looks like you've been expecting them for a while," she said. "How long have they been gone?"

"I don't know." Thaddeus set a faded party hat on his head that read HAPPY PRESIDENTS' DAY. He absently hopped one of the little plastic gingerbread men game pieces across the Candyland board. "A long time, I expect."

"Don't you remember when they left?"

"No. It must have been when I was very young. A toddler perhaps."

"A toddler! But that's awful. Why would a mother and father leave a toddler all alone?"

He seemed to be offended by the question. "I don't know, but I'm sure they had a very good reason. They are brilliant, highly educated people, of course. I wouldn't be surprised if they've been on an important mission of some kind for a head of state. They've probably been working in some remote corner of the globe, like Antarctica or Madagascar, and are steaming home to rejoin me at this very moment! In the meantime, I am living in the lap of luxury. Besides, they didn't leave me alone, did they? I've had Norman with me the entire time."

Josephine tried to make sense of what he was saying. "Thaddeus, have you ever seen your parents?" she asked gingerly.

"Seen them? Of course I have seen them!" he insisted. "Just because I can't recall the details doesn't mean I haven't seen them.

You can't remember everything you saw as a toddler, can you?"

Josephine could see that the subject was a sore one. Though she was dying to ask more questions about these mysterious parents, she didn't have the heart to continue. "I guess you're right. I'm sure they will be back soon."

"Of course they will. All I have to do is avoid the thugs from the orphanage until then, and all will be well."

He took the party hat off his head, placed it carefully back on the plate, then drained the cocoa from his mug.

"Enough of this idle nattering," he announced with a scowl, his chubby face mustached and goateed with dripping cocoa. "I must get back to the lab. I have a weasel to repair!"

"What should I do with Madame Prisoner, sir?" the robot interjected. "Shall I lock her in the closet again?"

"She's no longer a prisoner, Norman, merely a meddlesome neighbor. You may see her out."

"Wait!" Josephine said, as the robot loomed over her. "I can't leave yet!" She had barely scratched the surface of this puzzle of a boy, and now he was talking about repairing weasels? Questions were piling into her head by the dozen. If she left now, she'd go nuts with curiosity.

But Thaddeus had already turned and started toward the door to the stairs. "I have work to do." He made little sweeping motions with the back of his hand toward her, as if he were brushing away a mess of cookie crumbs. "You are released."

"But . . . couldn't I stay just a little longer?" Josephine couldn't believe what she was saying. She suddenly had no interest in escape. Her brain's reckless driver had taken over again and thrown caution out the window. "My parents won't be getting up for a few hours. Maybe I could watch you repair the weasel."

"Unthinkable. My work is top secret, spy or not. Besides, I tire of your chatter."

The robot's claw seized Josephine's arm firmly and led her toward the double doors.

"But I won't chatter."

Thaddeus did not look back.

"I promise!" She tried a new strategy. "Please, I've never watched a true genius work before. I could learn so much from a great scientist like you."

This time he hesitated. His posture improved slightly.

"It would be such an honor. After all," she continued, piling it on now, "you're so much more brilliant than my father. He's a microbiophysicist at the university."

Thaddeus stopped and looked back at her. "I suppose I am a rather singular talent, though few are aware of it, due to my seclusion."

"I saw it right away," Josephine said. "You've got that genius twinkle in your eye. Kind of like Einstein."

A small, cavity-dotted smile creased his face. "He is my idol. How perceptive of you to notice the similarity."

She had him now. Simple flattery was often all it took to get what one wanted. "Oh, yes, you're very similar. Though Einstein, of course, loved an audience. But," she sighed dramatically, "if you're not up to it, I certainly understand. I'll just go away and let you work your magic all by yourself." Josephine turned to leave.

Thaddeus's brow wrinkled as he took the bait. "Well . . . I suppose I could allow you to watch, just this once, if you promise not to bother me again."

"I promise." But she knew it was a promise she would never be able to keep. Bothering Thaddeus Hibble was about to become Josephine's primary occupation.

CHAPTER 11

Fetid Stenchley sloshed through a bog in the foggy darkness, deep in the forest that stretched beyond the Asylum for the Dangerously Insane. He had been running steadily for hours, fleeing from the wailing sirens and thumping helicopters that were hunting him. The police had badly underestimated the mad hunchback's speed, however, and he was miles farther away than anyone would have thought possible. Loping swiftly through the forest on all fours, leaving barely a footprint behind, Stenchley ran like a creature born to the wilderness.

Since clearing the asylum wall, the madman had stopped only once, and then only long enough to remove Lulu, the hairless Egyptian spaniel, from his nose. The little dog's viselike jaws had remained clamped stubbornly to the madman's face after his escape, and it had somehow held on as Stenchley tore through the woods. At the first opportunity, the madman had crouched in a gulley and wrung the pooch's neck, carefully detaching its teeth from his swollen and bleeding nose. He made a quick snack of the pampered pet, then ran on, not daring to stop again until after nightfall.

Feeling his way through the murk of the bog, Stenchley found a grotto beneath a fallen hemlock tree where he could rest and feed. Wild-eyed and panting, he lapped water from a black puddle at the foot of the tree, jerking his head up nervously every couple of seconds to scan the area for any sign of his pursuers. After he drank his fill, he crawled under the curtain of dripping roots and munched on beetles plucked from the mossy underside of the tree. As Stenchley crouched there in his muddy hooch, enjoying the crunch and pop of the bugs' exoskeletons between his teeth, it dawned on him that after so many nightmarish years of captivity, he was finally free. No more surgeons. No more Treatments. No more walls. Even a cold, damp hole under a tree and bugs for dinner were vastly preferable to life in the asylum.

But just as he had begun to relax, his hammering heart finally slowing down to something like normal, Stenchley heard the sound that all creatures on the run dread more than any other. Echoing through the woods somewhere in the distance came the yelps and whoops of bloodhounds. Though he enjoyed the mild flavor of the smaller canine breeds, Stenchley had a deep-seated fear of anything larger than a dachshund. The thought of the fanged, slobbering jaws of a pack of hounds snapping at him sent a jolt of terror through his brain. So he set off again, fear driving him faster than before. He leapt and dodged through the dense bramble of the woods, circling back many times to cover his trail, splashing through streams for long stretches, making it hard for the hounds to follow his scent.

In the wee hours of the morning, he found a tall tree and clawed his way to its highest branch. He took the opportunity to feed again when a squirrel, no doubt surprised to find a drooling killer squatting just outside its nest, scurried out onto the branch at his feet. The hunchback chewed swatches of the squirrel and listened for the hounds. Their baying was farther away now and heading in the opposite direction.

He slid down the tree to the forest floor and ran on at an easier pace. An occasional police helicopter passed overhead, invisible in the soupy fog, but the noise of their engines gave him plenty of time to hide. Stenchley could easily have spent the rest of his life like this, prowling the woods by night, hunting and scavenging for food, then disappearing into holes or trees by day. In the vast wilderness, which stretched northward for thousands of miles, all the way to the edge of the Arctic, he would have been impossible to find. In time he might simply have become another legend of the great northern woods, like Sasquatch, never to be seen again, except by unfortunate hikers who would not live to tell the tale.

But Cynthia had other plans for Stenchley. There was a score to settle, now that he was free. The vile, white-haired child who had come between Stenchley and his beloved master, who was the cause of all Stenchley's suffering in the horrible asylum, had to die. No more than a useless, babbling toddler at the time, the pathetic thing had escaped the python's coils ten years ago. The robot had intervened and hidden the child away before Stenchley could get at it. Cynthia vowed the child would not be so lucky this time. This would be a meal she would truly savor.

Though Stenchley had no conscious idea of where he was going, his filthy bare feet ran steadily on, guided by the whispering python inside his hump. If one were to look at a map of Awkward Falls and draw a line following Stenchley's path, it would begin at the Asylum for the Dangerously Insane, travel out into the forest where it would scribble around crazily, then turn back toward town again, heading straight for Oleander Alley.

CHAPTER 12

Josephine followed Thaddeus and the robot down the long flight of narrow stone steps into chilly darkness. At the bottom they entered the lab through the kind of heavy steel door one normally saw on a meat locker or possibly a nuclear waste facility. When Norman closed the door behind them, it became a virtually seamless part of the wall. Thaddeus flicked a switch, and the room's lone light source, a bulb dangling at the end of a wire, flickered and came on. The room looked nothing like the immaculate modern labs where Josephine's father worked. This place was filthy. Dust and grime coated everything in sight.

All around the room stood a collection of odd machines, some refrigerator-sized, some smaller than a toaster oven, most somewhere in between. All were very old and heavy looking, made of thick steel held together with bolts and rivets. Crisscrossing the walls and ceiling was a mad jumble of pipes, valves, and gauges reminiscent of the

boiler room of a steamship. A workbench crowded with beakers and glass tubes from neglected experiments extended along one wall.

The only part of the lab that was even remotely clean was a steel table in the center. There, under the lightbulb, was the most grotesque thing Josephine had ever seen in her life (though that record would fall in less than twenty-four hours). It was a dead animal, its organs exposed.

"Is that the weasel you were talking about?" she asked, feeling one of her own organs lurch sideways at the sight.

"Yes, this is Coco. She belongs to the widow Gladstone." Thaddeus snapped on surgical gloves. He had to stand on a chair to reach the work area. "I think the beast is looking rather good, considering."

"Considering?" The mess of fur, bone, and gristle looked hideous.

"Considering it was hit by a speeding Zamboni at the ice rink a week ago," he said.

"But isn't it . . . dead?"

"Obviously."

"So how can you fix something that's already dead?"

"I use a microwave oven, of course," he said, as if only an idiot would ask such a thing. He licked a spot of chocolate off his top lip. "The widow Gladstone is our best customer. We repaired her Chihuahua when it fell off the roof last year, then a month later, her parakeet flew into a fan. She's particularly hard on her animals."

"You mean people pay you to fix their dead pets?"

"Yes, and a good thing, too. The Hibble fortune is not what it once was, and we need cash. After our success with Felix, Norman suggested we offer the same service to others. He is very entrepreneurial, for a robot."

"Wait, who's Felix?"

"See for yourself," Thaddeus said. "Here he is now."

The same scruffy, mismatched cat Josephine had seen earlier strolled into the lab, carrying something in its mouth. It hopped up onto the worktable and dropped what looked like a dead rat in front of the boy.

"A fine specimen, Felix." Thaddeus poked at the rodent's half-flattened carcass. "It looks like the tires missed most of the useful parts. The digestive system should be of adequate size."

"I aim to please," said the cat.

Josephine recoiled in shock.

"Whatsamatta, girly?" the cat said, in a gritty voice straight out of a gangster movie. "Never seen a talkin' cat before?"

"Y-you can talk!" She couldn't believe what she was seeing and hearing.

"What a bright kid," he said. "You oughta go on a game show or somethin'."

Thaddeus scratched the animal's bat ear. "Impressive beast, isn't he? Felix is my greatest achievement so far."

"You did this? You made a cat talk?"

Thaddeus nodded proudly. "Norman assisted, of course."

"That's amazing! You're like some kind of mad scientist."

Thaddeus did not think this was funny. "I am well versed in the sciences, Josephine, but I assure you I am perfectly sane. My work on Felix was an act of compassion. He'd be deceased now if I hadn't repaired him."

"The kid's tellin' you straight," said the cat. "I had a little run-in with a pair of honkin' big pit bulls who nearly ate me for lunch a couple years ago. I was down for the count when the boss and ol' Rusty over there came along and saved my hide."

"Norman and I were out on an errand and discovered him just in time." Thaddeus paced casually as he talked, clearly enjoying the chance to brag. "We brought him back to the lab and repaired his parts, where feasible, and replaced the bits that were too badly mangled to fix. Not an easy task, mind you, but a noble one, if I may say so. He's quite handsome now, don't you think?'"

Handsome was not the word Josephine was thinking of. "I've never seen anything like him. But how'd you manage the talking part?"

Thaddeus rolled his eyes as if a toddler had just asked how a rocket engine works. "Let's just say I made certain improvements to the parietal lobe of Felix's brain and adjusted his larynx. After that, it was a simple matter of tutoring. I've charged Norman with teaching him proper English, though the results have been somewhat spotty." He stroked the cat's grizzled fur affectionately. "He was a denizen of the street, after all."

"I ain't no powder puff," gruffed the cat as he gnawed a hooked claw. Josephine found it hard to imagine this cat losing a fight to any dog.

"Did you build the little train, too?" she asked.

"Of course."

"Very nice. But I was wondering about those legs on the train . . . are they real?"

He nodded proudly. "Rats' legs. A nice touch, I think."

"Yes, but it's kind of . . . well . . . icky. I mean, how did you . . . get them?"

"Ah, I see what you're thinking. Not to worry. The various parts I use in building my little toys are from creatures that are already deceased. Felix finds them and brings them to me."

"But I don't kill 'em no more," the cat added defensively. "I quit eatin' rat a long time ago. Too much cholesterol. I'm hooked on the canned stuff now, anyway. I just deliver the stiffs to the kid." The cat shrugged. "Keeps him happy."

"Our pet-repairing enterprise is dependent upon Felix's scavenging. We have a short list of loyal clients, mostly elderly women from the widow Gladstone's poker club, but they keep us busy."

"Isn't that kind of risky? What if somebody tells the police—or the orphanage—about you?" she asked.

Thaddeus waved off her concern. "A minimal risk. Our rendezvous point is elsewhere, and the widow has only met me once or twice. Norman primarily conducts our business with her. I believe she rather fancies him, actually."

"But she knows he's a robot, right?"

He shrugged. "The woman's vision is not keen. Besides, Norman does have a certain charm."

"How have you managed to stay hidden for so long?"

"It helps that I sleep in the daytime and do my puttering about at night. I'm quite stealthy."

"You must get really lonely, not to mention bored."

"My work keeps me busy," said Thaddeus, "and I have Norman and Felix for company. Besides, Mother and Father will be home soon."

CHAPTER 13

The early morning sky was at its blackest when Fetid Stenchley finally emerged from the forest. Creeping through the cold fog on all fours, he found himself at the stone wall behind Hibble Manor. He opened the rear gate and entered the familiar grounds cautiously. Spackled with mud and twigs, the surgical gown he still wore now ragged, he looked like something from the underworld.

As Stenchley looked out at the familiar silhouette of the stately house, fragmented memories began pricking his damaged mind. Inside the mansion's moldy stone walls, Stenchley had once experienced something like happiness. There, he had spent almost his entire adult life living and working side by side with the famous Professor Celsius T. Hibble.

Long ago, the professor had found Stenchley starving and homeless, begging on the streets of Awkward Falls. The great scientist had taken the deformed man into his home, fed and clothed him, and unlike anyone else in Stenchley's miserable life, treated him like a human being. Stenchley's grateful devotion to the professor had been boundless. No labor was too difficult, no hour too late, no burden too heavy, if the good professor asked it of him. Fetid Stenchley had loved the professor with all his twisted heart.

Ironically, it was the power of this love that would eventually drive the madman to kill his master. Stenchley coveted his status as the professor's closest companion, and deeply mistrusted any others whose relationship with the great man became too close. After Hibble's near marriage to the Twittington woman, the hunchback took it upon himself to protect his master from the devious influence of outsiders.

Stenchley was diligent in his task. One spring morning, a certain French ambassador, whose visits to Hibble Manor Stenchley had deemed suspiciously frequent, mysteriously hanged himself in his room before breakfast. No one noticed that the rope was the same one the hunchback had been fooling around with the previous evening.

On another occasion, the glamorous daughter of an oil magnate, who had begun to spend more evenings than Stenchley would have cared for attached to the professor's arm, slipped and fell to her death from the third-floor balcony. Everyone agreed it was a tragic accident.

Then one of the professor's favorite nephews came to spend his summer vacation at Hibble Manor, but disappeared after only six weeks. The police deduced that the boy must have wandered into the forest and been attacked by wolves, who probably carried him off to their den. Such incidents were not unheard of in northern Manitoba in those days.

Coincidentally, at the time of each of the mysterious deaths, Stenchley's gardening activities increased. He seemed to always be digging a new hole, planting yet another pear tree. Visitors often commented on the hunchback's green thumb, as the trees consistently produced surprisingly large fruit. When they asked what fertilizer he used, Stenchley only grinned.

Now, as the mad hunchback wandered through the grounds of the manor, there was an entire orchard of pear trees, all as healthy as that first one. Stealthily, he made his way from the fruit trees to the overgrown hedge maze, which he had planted as well, avoiding the house itself, for fear of being seen. He crawled under the hedge, within sight of the front door of his old home, and scratched out a shallow nest in the dirt. Exhausted from his long night of running, he spun around in the nest once, then curled into a tight ball and fell asleep.

CHAPTER 14

In the dim light of Thaddeus's lab, Josephine watched with a mixture of amazement and disgust as Thaddeus meticulously sorted through the gnarled body parts of the widow Gladstone's dead weasel. Felix nibbled happily on a discarded bit of lung that fell on the floor. From a walk-in freezer, Norman fetched various replacement parts sealed in jelly jars and Ziploc bags. He placed the frozen liver of a raccoon, a pig's spleen, a fox's eyes, a rat's tail, and some other things Josephine did not recognize in a bowl of water to thaw. The boy periodically reached into the bowl, fished out what he was looking for, and deftly stitched it onto the carcass. His stubby fingers handled the scalpel like an experienced surgeon, and worked so quickly, Josephine could barely follow what he was doing. Norman seemed to read his master's mind, handing him the appropriate tool just when he needed it. Only occasionally did he snap, "Not that one, Norman—the one with the hook on the end!"

Josephine was amazed at Thaddeus's skill. "How did you learn to do that?"

He shrugged, without looking up from his work. "Genius runs in the family, I suppose. I've spent a lot of time studying Grandfather's notebook, at least the few parts that I can understand. Most of it is in some kind of code that I can't decipher."

"Why would he write in code?"

"Obviously he wanted to keep his experiments secret. Judging from his diagrams, it's clear that Grandfather was working on far more complex things than the simple procedures I piddle around with. I suspect that a genius of his stature was onto something really big."

"Can I see the notebook?" she asked, casually reaching for it.

The boy snatched the book off the table and looked at her as if she were mad. "Don't touch it!" he said. "This book is the most valuable possession I have. It is written in Grandfather's own hand. If it were to be damaged, I could never replace it!"

Josephine held her hands up and backed off. "Okay, okay! I won't touch it, I just want to look. I won't even breathe on it." She gave him her most innocent smile. "Please?"

The boy squinted and pushed up his spectacles thoughtfully. After a moment, he set the book back down and opened it to the page he had been working from. "I suppose it will be all right if you only look. But you must be careful!"

Josephine tried to make sense of the hieroglyphic-style symbols and equations scribbled across the page. Carefully drawn diagrams were crammed into the margins and on top of the text, with little care for legibility.

"A daunting puzzle, as you can see," said Thaddeus.

"Yeah," she nodded. "The diagrams look sort of like the stuff in my dad's books, but in some weird language. Like this one here." She pointed to one of the larger drawings. "It reminds me of a genetic sequencing diagram, except it's written in Martian or something."

"I have heard of the genome work being done of late, but I unfortunately lack the resources to delve into it. I wonder what creature was being sequenced?"

"Is this the only notebook your grandfather left?" she asked, noticing the number twelve written on the upper corner of the cover.

He shrugged. "It's the only one I've found. There must be others, probably volumes of them. Perhaps they will turn up someday."

"Did anyone else know about your grandfather's work? Friends or other scientists, maybe?"

"His early work was widely published, of course, due to his winning of the Nobel Prize. He was an international celebrity. Then he abruptly retreated from the public eye after writing an article for a scientific magazine about a theory concerning the aging of cells. I've read and reread the article many times, but I can't understand the details. Apparently, neither could anyone else. He was roundly criticized by his colleagues, and afterward became something of a laughingstock. He never wrote another article from that point on, as far as I can tell, and mention of his work in science journals became rare.

Grandfather became extremely secretive from that point on. No one knows anything about his work after that."

"But what about Stenchley?" she asked. "He would have been with him the whole time, right?"

Thaddeus chuckled. "He would have seen things, of course. But by all accounts, Stenchley was a simpleton, too feebleminded to make any sense of them."

"Hmm, right. Do you think Norman would remember anything?"

The boy shook his head. "I've questioned him repeatedly, but his memory circuits are corroded beyond repair. He's as dotty as a loon."

The boy stopped talking then, turning his full attention to a delicate bit of stitching.

Having extracted all the info she was likely to get from him for the moment, Josephine flopped down in a chair and pondered the situation, chewing her pinkie nail intently.

☠ ☠ ☠

When the weasel's new organs had all been attached and the repairs completed, Thaddeus snapped off his rubber gloves and clapped his hands together. "Now for the best part of the operation. Prepare the beast for reanimation, Norman!"

The robot didn't need to be told. He was already in the process of inserting various colored pins into the weasel's body. When this was done, Norman carefully laid the lifeless carcass inside the chamber of a huge microwave oven that looked more like a front-loading washing machine. He closed the hatch and sealed it using a large wrench. Thaddeus twiddled knobs on a control panel until the indicator needle rose to the correct voltage. He gave the thumbs-up to Norman, who pushed a red button. The machine began to emit a high-pitched buzz, and through the glass door Josephine could see the weasel's fur suddenly stand on end. The colored pins began to sparkle and smoke, and the weasel's muscles began to twitch. Thaddeus watched what looked like a radar screen as points of light blipped on and off, getting brighter with each blip. After a couple of minutes, he signaled for Norman to turn the machine off. Smoke and the stink of scorched fur wafted out of the machine as the robot opened the hatch. Miraculously, the weasel staggered out of the chamber under its own power onto the counter and promptly coughed up the nastiest hairball Josephine had ever laid eyes on.

"That's amazing!"

If this was some kind of trick, it was an awfully good one.

"Yes, isn't it?" Thaddeus was as proud of the bedraggled creature as a father with his firstborn child. "You may deliver Coco to the widow Gladstone at first light, Norman. Tell her that the repairs were successfully completed and she's better than ever."

"Will do, sir," said the robot. "Shall I rock her to sleep in the meantime?"

"Yes, a nap will lower her blood pressure nicely. But first let's get some fluids in her."

Thaddeus poured a fizzing puddle of soda into a saucer and patted the weasel's head as it lapped up its first post-death meal. When it was finished, Norman picked up the beast with surprising tenderness and carried it to a chair in the corner, where he swaddled it in a blanket and began rocking it to sleep in his rusty steel arms.

The lab's own cuckoo clock, a miniature carousel with little saddled models of unicorns, dragons, lions, and tigers, suddenly sprang to life. A door in the center column of its round platform opened, and a trio of mice scampered out and climbed onto three of the colorful beasts. On second glance, Josephine saw that the little creatures were only mice from the neck down. Their heads were those of parakeets. Wheezy organ music played as the ingenious gadget made five turns before stopping.

After taking a moment to digest what she had just seen, it dawned on Josephine that the creatures had just announced the time. It was five a.m.! How had six hours passed since she had left her house? It seemed as if she'd just slipped out an hour ago!

Josephine hopped out of her seat. "Oh, my gosh, I gotta go! My parents will flip if they get up and find me gone!"

"STOP!" Thaddeus stomped his foot. "Hold her, Norman!" The robot reached out from the rocking chair and clamped a steel claw onto her wrist before she could leave the lab. "What do you think you're doing? You haven't sworn the oath of secrecy. Now that you have seen my secret lab, you cannot leave until you swear the oath."

"Fine, but can we make it fast? I'm cutting it pretty close."

Thaddeus gave her a serious look. "Raise your hand and repeat after me." The robot raised her hand for her.

"I, Josephine, do swear . . . ," he said solemnly.

"I, Josephine, do swear . . . ," she repeated.

"To never blabber anything about Thaddeus to anyone who might have him sent to the orphanage . . ."

"To never blabber anything about Thaddeus to anyone who might have him sent to the orphanage . . ."

"Or suffer unimaginably dire consequences!"

"Or suffer unimaginably dire consequences."

"The end."

"The end. Can I please go now?"

"Not yet." The boy looked worried. "You do really promise not to tell, don't you?"

"I really do. Crisscross applesauce."

Thaddeus looked bewildered. "What does applesauce have to do with anything?"

"It just means I promise," she said. "Don't worry, my lips are sealed."

Josephine could see the boy was still wary, but he nodded for Norman to release her wrist anyway.

"Simply follow the train at the top of the stairs, madame," said Norman. "It will lead you safely out."

"I'll be back!" She grabbed her sweater and dashed out of the lab and up the basement stairs. The train was waiting, its engine puffing. Back through the dark corridors it led her, doors opening as they approached, until they reached the foyer. She threw back the big deadbolt on the front door, slung it open, and dashed out into the breaking dawn, hoping she could make it home before she was missed.

CHAPTER 15

Stenchley's body jerked and his eyes popped open at the sound of the front door opening. Through the leaves of the hedge, he watched a girl come running out of the house straight toward him. The madman crouched low beneath the bushes and watched her sprint past. His hump quivered as Cynthia's nostrils picked up the delicious aroma of the girl's flesh.

Breakfast, the snake murmured. The girl was just about the size of a suckling pig, which is considered a delicacy among pythons.

Stenchley silently followed the girl down the path, keeping his distance, but not losing sight of her. He trailed her out of the maze and saw that she was heading for the garden wall. She grabbed a vine and began climbing up, completely unaware that her death was moments away. Stenchley closed in, his mouth watering. Cynthia coiled tightly inside the killer's hump, anticipating the feast.

Strike now. Get her! the snake hissed.

But Stenchley stopped, suddenly distracted. He found himself standing amid the crumbling tombstones of the Hibble family cemetery. One stone in particular had caught his eye. Stenchley had never learned to read, but he was able to recognize the name of his beloved master. With the realization that the body of Professor Hibble lay somewhere beneath his feet, the madman's tiny gizzard of a heart felt a twinge of something greater than the lust for blood. Stenchley stared at the monument, forgetting all about the girl, who cleared the top of the wall and disappeared to the other side. Momentarily deaf to Cynthia's angry hissing, he ran his fingers over the letters carved into the tombstone and recalled the professor's clear blue eyes. Even the thousands of Treatments he had received at the asylum had failed to erase the memory of their beauty.

Then, as madmen often do, Stenchley became obsessed with a very bad idea. He longed to see his master again. Like a hungry worm, this overwhelming desire bored into the hunchback's mind and began to chew up all reason and logic. Stenchley rammed his hands into the earth of the professor's grave and started digging.

CHAPTER 16

Josephine had no sooner slipped into bed and pulled up the blanket than she heard her father's footsteps going down the stairs. As she lay there replaying the unbelievable scenes of the night before in her mind, she was filled with conflicting emotions. Part of her wanted to run downstairs and tell her father every incredible detail of what she had seen next door. After all, he was a scientist and would be just as fascinated by the orphaned boy and his weird companions as she was. He often said Josephine had inherited the "why" gene from him.

Her mother would find the whole thing very interesting as well, though she would definitely have some problems with Josephine sneaking out for an all-nighter at a strange house. There would be a long lecture about safety and all the disastrous what-ifs of her actions. But, in the end, Josephine was pretty sure they would understand. After all, this certainly wasn't the first time she had done something a little crazy to satisfy her curiosity.

But talking to her parents was out of the question this time. Josephine had, after all, sworn an oath not to tell, and she had no desire to find out what was meant by "unimaginably dire consequences." And even if she hadn't sworn, she was pretty sure her parents would blow Thaddeus's cover. He was an orphan kid hiding in a creepy old house with only a machine to look after him. Not even Josephine's open-minded parents could keep a secret like that. They would call the police, or whoever was in charge of stray kids, and yadda yadda, he'd be in the orphanage in an hour. Josephine couldn't let that happen. It wouldn't be easy, but she would just have to keep the whole thing under her hat somehow, at least for now.

She closed her eyes, trying to force herself to sleep, but she was still way too excited for that to be a possibility. Instead, she lay there and listened to the routine sounds of Howard banging around in the kitchen beginning to make breakfast. Josephine's dad was always the first one up in the morning, and since today was Saturday, she knew he would be making his "famous" pancakes. She hoped they would be better than his last batch.

Like any good scientist, Howard used the trial-and-error method when cooking, experimenting with unusual ingredients and odd flavor combinations. As he liked to say, "Cooking is just edible chemistry."

She heard him turn the radio to a news station to keep him company as he worked. The squeaky fridge door opened and shut as he got out the milk, and the spoon began clinking on the mixing bowl as he stirred the batter.

Suddenly, the cooking noises stopped and the only sound was the radio. She could hear the announcer's voice talking excitedly in the urgent way announcers did when there was some kind of emergency. She couldn't hear all of what he was saying, but could make out a few words here and there. Did he say something about an escaped convict? Then her heart skipped a beat when she clearly heard the words "Asylum for the Dangerously Insane." Wasn't that the place Thaddeus's grandfather's killer had been sent? Josephine hopped out of bed, slipped her robe on, and hurried quietly downstairs. She paused just outside the kitchen door to eavesdrop on the radio broadcast.

". . . I have Sergeant Finneas Cole of the Awkward Falls PD on the line now," the announcer was saying. "Fin, can you give us any details about the escape?"

"Aye, Phil." The sergeant spoke calmly, as if he were talking about a missing cow instead of an escaped killer. "The escapee busted out of the asylum yesterday afternoon during the big to-do they were having over there for the mayor's visit."

"Oh, yah? Well, how'd the fella manage that? I've always heard that the asylum is escape-proof."

"Turns out, not so much," said the officer. "Anyhoo, it appears the guy went wild during some kind of scientific demonstration. Ran around bitin' and scratchin' the doctors, then jumped right through a window."

"He sounds like a dangerous one, eh, Fin?"

"I'd say so, Phil. The man's name is Fetid Stenchley. He's been locked up for murder for the last ten years or so. He even tried to attack the mayor's wife during his escape, but her dog held him off. The little pooch latched on to his nose, I'm told, and wouldn't let go!"

"That's some dog, eh? Musta been a husky, then, eh?"

"Nah. Hairless Egyptian spaniel."

"Oh, they're tough ones, those are."

Josephine gasped at the mention of the mad killer who had murdered Thaddeus's grandfather. She shivered at the thought of him on the loose somewhere nearby.

"Now, what's our threat level here in town, then, Sergeant?" the announcer asked.

"We're at hot pink now, Phil, which is, as you know, pretty high up there," said the officer. "You'll wanna be on the careful side, keepin' both eyes open today."

"And is Stenchley still at large at this time?"

"Aye, Phil, the escapee has still not been apprehended. The first lady says she saw him hightail it into the woods after he jumped the north wall. I figure he's makin' his way up north toward the lake country wilderness, but he's not likely to get that far. A crack squad of Mounties came in last night with a couple o' helicopters and a bunch of fancy gear. They're out lookin' for him now."

"Helicopters, eh?" The announcer sounded impressed, as if the sergeant had said the Mounties were bringing in cruise missiles.

"Oh, yah, they're serious, those Mounties are."

"They get their man, eh, Fin?"

"Always, Phil, always."

The sergeant went on to advise listeners in the Awkward Falls area to report any strangers or unusual activity to the authorities immediately. He stressed that this was only a precaution, however, and that the Mounties would undoubtedly have the escapee locked up again in no time.

Josephine stood frozen outside the door, pondering the news of Stenchley's escape. She suddenly thought of Thaddeus. He could be in serious danger. What if the policeman on the radio was wrong, and the Mounties did not catch Stenchley soon? Wasn't there an old saying that criminals always return to the scene of their crime? If so, the murderer might show up at Hibble Manor. Thaddeus would be a sitting duck, with only rusty old Norman to protect him. *I have to warn him*, she thought. Maybe an opportunity to slip out and run over there would present itself.

A hand suddenly grabbed her shoulder. Josephine nearly jumped out of her skin and spun around quickly.

"Oh, Mom! I'm so glad it's only you!"

Barbara, still sleepy before her first cup of coffee, gave her daughter a confused look. "Of course it's me, silly. Who else would it be?"

"Good morning, girls." Howard jogged out of the kitchen past them. "Big news! I just heard on the radio that a convicted killer escaped yesterday from the local asylum. They've got the Mounties out searching for him."

"What? A killer?" asked Barbara, now really confused. "But they're not supposed to have killers in cute little towns like this!"

"I'm as shocked as you are," said Howard. "I think we should lock all the doors and windows just to be on the safe side. They don't expect any trouble, but there's no point in taking chances." He wedged a chair against the front door and made a note to get the lock fixed.

They went carefully through the house, locking every opening they could and closing the few curtains Barbara had put up so far. Josephine cautiously stuck her head outside the front door and scanned the street for anything that might be an insane murderer, but saw only empty, potholed Oleander Alley. This did not look like a place where escaped convicts ran amok.

Then again, it didn't look like a place where kids lived in abandoned mansions with robots, either.

☠ ☠ ☠

When Howard was satisfied that the house was relatively secure, he went back to work on the pancakes, whistling a little louder than usual and glancing out the window every few minutes.

While Howard flipped the cakes, Josephine slumped down at the breakfast table across from her mom, yawning and rubbing her tired red eyes. Her hair was a rat's nest of tangles sticking out from Eggplant's edges.

"Looks like someone stayed up reading too late last night," Barbara said. "Couldn't you sleep, sweetie?"

"Nah," she said. She didn't like lying to her mom as a rule, but saw no alternative in this case. "I guess being in a new place and everything made it hard to relax."

Barbara gave her a sympathetic look. "Aw, poor thing."

"Hungry, ladies?" Howard proudly forked a stack of cakes onto each plate and plopped a dollop of meringue on top. "I came up with a radical new recipe today in honor of our first morning in the new house: vanilla bran batter with raisins, mango, and pistachio, topped with organic guava syrup–cream cheese meringue. You're gonna love 'em, kiddo."

Josephine tried to be excited about the pancakes, which were an odd shade of orange. "Wow, Dad. They look fantastic."

Barbara's nose twitched as she sniffed her own pile. "Mmmm. They smell . . . interesting."

Howard dug into his own stack with gusto, clearly pleased with his creation. Her parents ate breakfast and talked as if it were just another morning, chatting about the house, Howard's new job, the weather. They seemed to have forgotten all about the escaped convict who was out there somewhere. But Josephine could not stop thinking about Fetid Stenchley. She finally asked Howard, trying not to let her fear show too much, "Do you really think they'll catch that guy soon, Dad?"

"Who, the convict? Are you kidding?" He grinned confidently. "With the Mounties after him, that guy's as good as caught. They're the best cops in the world!" Howard stood up and grabbed his coat from the back of the chair. Barbara handed him his Packers hat. "Try not to worry about it, sweetie," he said. "I'm sure that by the time I get home from my exciting first day of work, they'll have him back in his cell, safe and sound. Just keep an eye open for anything unusual. You can call me at the office if anything comes up. The university is only thirty minutes away by bicycle."

Howard snapped rubber bands around his pant legs to keep them from getting caught in his bicycle chain, then kissed Josephine on the forehead and Barbara on the lips. He bungeed his briefcase into the handlebar basket and rolled the bike out the front door.

Just before the door closed, he stuck his head back in and said, "Oh, Jo, I almost forgot to tell you! I remember now where I've seen the weird guy from your photo. He's a famous scientist I once did a paper on back when your mother and I were in college. His name is"—something clicked inside Josephine's brain, and she suddenly knew who it was even before her father finished the sentence—"Hibble. Professor Celsius T. Hibble, the father of biocybernetics. He was a pretty famous guy back in the day."

Of course! It dawned on her that despite his age and ample girth, Thaddeus certainly resembled the man in the photo, especially that wild shock of white hair.

Josephine watched out the window as her father pedaled off. She and Barbara put away the breakfast dishes, then Barbara went upstairs to get dressed. Josephine considered running quickly next door to tell Thaddeus about Stenchley's escape before her mom came back, but before she could make up her mind, she heard her mother hurrying downstairs. So much for that idea.

"Ready, Josephine?" Barbara called, putting on lipstick with one hand and fishing keys out of her purse with the other. "I'm really excited about going downtown! After we stop at the library, I want to browse through some antique shops to look for a floor lamp. And maybe we'll get some lunch later. We'll have a real girls' day out! What do you say?"

"Um, great, Mom." But Josephine could think only about Thaddeus at that moment.

They drove off, snaking their way down the rutted streets toward town. Josephine gazed out at the tiny skyline of Awkward Falls as they drove, chewing her nail and trying to sort things out in her mind. The initial shock of Fetid Stenchley's escape began to subside a bit, and Josephine wondered if maybe she was overreacting to the whole killer-on-the-loose business. Her dad didn't think there was anything to worry about, and he was usually right about that kind of stuff. *Don't be such a worrywart*, she told herself.

The sun was out now, and everything looked considerably happier than it had yesterday in the fog. The town was clean and homey, possibly even sort of quaint, though she would never admit it to her mom. It did not look like the kind of place where horrible things happened. Josephine decided that Thaddeus was probably completely safe.

Probably.

She let herself focus instead on the tantalizing news that the man in the photograph was actually the boy's mysterious grandfather. What was his picture doing in the upstairs bedroom of Twittington House? And who was Sally? She was suddenly dying to get to the library to search for clues.

CHAPTER 17

The O. R. MacManus Library and Bait Shop was the only library in the world where a person could check out a book and buy a bucket of minnows at the same time. Fishing for the northern pike—a toothy, evil-looking fish—was an obsession for the citizens of Awkward Falls. Their love for catching the pointy-nosed pike leaked into almost every aspect of their lives. People thought nothing of buying a box of worms at the pharmacy or picking up a pair of waders at the maternity store. It was only natural that they had also found a way to blend the sport with the borrowing of books.

Barbara Cravitz fell in love with the place as soon as she and Josephine walked in the door.

"Isn't this colorful, Josephine?" Barbara picked up a reel and turned the crank excitedly, even though Josephine was sure her mom had no idea what it was for. "Maybe we should take up fishing now that we're Manitobans. I've heard it's a very meditative sport."

Josephine hadn't given much thought to fishing before, and she was too preoccupied to get very worked up about it.

She strolled through the narrow aisles, trying to figure out the bizarre filing system. Instead of the books being separate from the fishing gear, the librarian had tossed the two enterprises together in a strange salad of books and fishing paraphernalia. Displays of rubber waders and racks of fishing rods flanked the nonfiction book section. Children's books were interspersed with bins of colored bobbers and corks. The biography collection was stacked below a wall of dusty trophy pike, shellacked and mounted on wooden plaques. Occasional open spaces on the bookshelves held clearance items, such as bags of used hooks, artificial lures shaped like frogs and crayfish, and very old packets of freeze-dried beef Stroganoff. As a unifying decorative touch, fishing nets and life preservers were draped from the ceiling, giving book browsers and fishing enthusiasts alike the feeling that they were in some bait shack on a wharf instead of in a shop in downtown Awkward Falls.

Josephine realized right away she would never find what she was looking for without help. The service counter at the rear of the room was deserted, so she rang a little silver bell next to the cash register.

A gravelly voice called out from a back room, "Hold your water—I'm comin'!"

The owner of the voice then began a long fit of coughing that sounded as if he or she might hock up an organ at any moment. Out shuffled an ancient, grizzled woman in overalls and a long-billed fishing cap pulled low over her eyes. The second her coughing fit subsided she pulled a pipe from her pocket, lit it, and began puffing away.

"What can I do ya for?" the woman asked. "I got night crawlers on special today, big fat guys for only half price!"

Josephine fanned the smoke away from her face and tried to breathe as little as possible. "Are you the librarian?"

"Yes'm. O. R. MacManus, at your service. I've been librarian, bait cutter, and chief floor sweeper for a good sixty years now. Are ya lookin' for a book, then?"

"Yes. Could you tell me where your historical reference books are?"

Barbara, who had been trying on a floppy canvas hat with mosquito netting over the brim, walked over and said, "We're looking for information about old houses in the area. We just moved into Twittington House yesterday."

"That would be in outboard motors." O. R. led the way to an aisle dominated by boat motors and gas cans. She pushed a stepladder up to the bookshelves, climbed to the top, and pulled a fat volume off the shelf.

"Let's look at this one." The woman carried the book over to a table stacked with tackle boxes. Josephine and Barbara watched over her shoulder while she sat and flipped through the pages, apparently intending to lead them in their research.

She smacked her palm on the page. "There 'tis. Twittington House, built in 1897 by Elmer Twittington, founder of Twittington Sauerkraut Cannery."

Josephine and Barbara were astonished. The page showed a photo of Twittington House in its prime. A group of well-dressed people posed on the lawn in front of the house.

"It's beautiful," Barbara exclaimed. "And those must be the Twittingtons."

Josephine bent down for a closer look. The house and the Twittington family both looked brand-new, basking in the bright sun of that long-gone day. Underneath the photo was a caption identifying each family member. Josephine found Sally in the center of the group, kneeling on the bottom row.

"That's her, Mom!" Josephine pointed to a pretty little girl of about five or six in blond pigtails, smiling happily.

"What an adorable child," Barbara said.

"Yep." O. R. wheezed out a lungful of blue smoke. "Sally was a beauty. She grew up to become a star of stage and screen. Voice like a nightingale. She was famous all over Europe."

"You knew Sally?" Barbara asked the librarian.

"Ha! You betcha. Taught her how to catch pike!" The woman's laugh was a dry, smoky cackle. "Sally used to sneak away from her mother's fancy soirees and go fishin' with me. She loved getting her lace dresses all muddy."

When Josephine turned the page, she found a series of photos featuring Hibble Manor in its gothic heyday. The mansion looked newer in the pictures, but still darkly forbidding. She gasped and pointed to a figure in one of the pictures.

"Look, Mom, it's him!" Standing at the mansion's grand entrance was the man from Josephine's mysterious photo. There was no mistaking him. The eyes, the wild white hair, even the suit was the same as in her photo. She read the caption. "Professor Celsius T. Hibble."

"He's so striking," Barbara said. "If his nose was smaller, and if he had dark hair, he'd look kind of like Errol Flynn."

"That dang fool," grumbled the librarian. "Sally should never have gotten involved with him, and I told her so from the start. She could've had her pick of any fella in town. But when Celsius came to Awkward Falls and bought the place next door, it was all over but the shoutin'. He was a big celebrity back then. Rich and good-lookin' to boot, even with that strange white hair. Once he got a look at Sally, hardly a day passed that he didn't come traipsing over with a bouquet of red roses in one hand and a box of chocolates in the other. She fell for him right off."

"You knew Professor Hibble, too?" asked Josephine.

"Can't say I knew him personally. He was a real odd duck, didn't say a whole lot." The woman sucked on her pipe and frowned. "I do know he was the worst thing that ever happened to Sally, though. Broke her heart in two. Even after she moved to Paris and married that big movie director, she still pined for Celsius Hibble. For years, she used to call me every Christmas just to reminisce and talk about fishin'."

The librarian rolled the ladder farther down the aisle and climbed up again. The woman ran her finger down a row of books under a shelf of plastic gas containers until she found what she was looking for. She slid a book out and dropped it on the table. "There's a bit about Hibble somewhere in this book, as I recall, though you might have to dig for it."

Josephine thumbed through the pages of the old book, which was titled *Geniuses of North America*. The yellowed pages smelled like mothballs and featured a different genius on each page.

"I can't believe that house is next door to us." Barbara examined the picture closely. "How could I have missed something so incredible?"

"It was hidden by the fog yesterday, Mom," said Josephine. "I actually caught a glimpse of it from my window last night when I was reading. It looked really spooky."

"Oh, no, I think it's very stately. It has a real presence."

The librarian nodded. "It was a real palace once, before Celsius went around the bend."

"You mean he went crazy?" asked Josephine.

"After Sally canceled the wedding, he disappeared into that house and was rarely ever seen in public again. Lost his mind, they say. I never thought the man was right to begin with, myself."

"They were going to be married?"

"Yep. The whole affair was to take place right there at his mansion. It was going to be the biggest wedding ever seen in these parts. Sally was on cloud nine right up until the night before they were supposed to get hitched. She left town on the last train out that night. Celsius was so broke up about it, he had 'em leave the decorations up till they all finally rotted away years later. Sally never told me why she left, never wanted to talk about it. Must've been something awful, though. She finally came back to Awkward Falls for good a while ago. Lives in the big white house down the street, if you can call it livin'. She's all alone except for her nurse, never sees anybody anymore, not even me."

"What a tragic story." Barbara sighed wistfully. "I wonder what happened between her and Professor Hibble?"

The old librarian shook her head and puffed. "Only Sally and Celsius knew for sure. It was mysterious."

"Does anyone live in Hibble's house now?" asked Barbara.

The librarian shook her head. "Just the caretaker. An automaton specially designed back in the old days by Celsius to look after the house."

Barbara looked skeptical. "Do you mean the caretaker is a robot?"

"Yep. I saw it once when Celsius was showin' it off to Sally. The contraption poured us a glass of lemonade. It was a pretty nifty gadget back then, though I'd be surprised if the thing still works. It never leaves the house, as far as I know, although some folks claim they've seen Hibble's old Rolls drivin' around in the middle of the night with something strange behind the wheel."

"Sounds fascinating," said Barbara. "I'd love to go over and have a look sometime."

O. R. waved the idea away. "Don't bother tryin'. The gates are always locked. After the murder, the house was closed off to the public for good."

"The murder?"

"Hibble was strangled some years back by his assistant, a lunatic named Stenchley. He's the nasty little booger that busted out of the asylum just yesterday."

"Oh, my gosh, that's awful! Why would his assistant do such a thing?"

"That's what everybody wanted to know. Police never figured out his motive. Stenchley had been with Hibble forever, I wasn't surprised, though. Stenchley always seemed more like a wild animal than a man to me. Followed Celsius around like a mutt, but you could tell he wasn't quite right. When the police found the body, a couple of parts were missing. There were teeth marks all over it."

Barbara and Josephine gasped. "You mean he ate . . ." Josephine could not finish the question.

O. R. nodded solemnly and sucked on her pipe.

Barbara put her arms around Josephine and hugged her close. "It gives me the creeps to think something so horrible happened right next door!"

"Yep. Pretty as it was, for a long time, that house was snakebit. Seemed like every few years somebody turned up dead there or went missing. Makes you wonder."

It certainly made Josephine wonder. "I hope they catch him soon."

The librarian shook her head. "Don't count on it. According to the news, he's heading north. If he makes it into the wilderness, they'll never see him again. The good news is there's a norther blowin' in any minute now. If Stenchley's traipsing around the north woods when that thing hits, he'll be an icicle by mornin' for certain. If that's really where he's headin', that is."

Josephine gulped. "You don't think he's going that way?"

"The man's crazy, remember. No rhyme or reason to what he does. A creature like that could turn up anywhere."

"Do you think we're safe in Twittington House?" asked Barbara.

"As long as that lunatic is loose, nobody's safe." The librarian wagged her crooked finger at Josephine and her mother. "You'd be smart to take precautions. Do you have a firearm?"

Barbara was taken aback. "You mean a gun? No, of course not! We've never owned one."

"That's too bad. I'd hate to go mano a mano with that fellow if he was to come callin'. I'd at least keep a butcher knife or a sharp cleaver handy!"

The old woman struck a match and stoked her pipe again, bringing on the early signs of another nasty coughing jag. Before the fit began in earnest, she managed to croak, "If you change your mind about the firearm"—*cough*—"I can make you girls a good deal on a shotgun. I got a twelve-gauge on sale that'll blow a hole in a moose"—*cough, cough*—"from fifty yards. You can bet I'll be sleepin' with mine cocked and loaded tonight." *Cough.*

CHAPTER 18

There is a simple reason why human corpses are often dressed in suits and ties or beautiful gowns, and their faces caked with makeup before their family and friends are allowed to have one last peek at them. The dead are not very attractive.

The primary cause of their unattractiveness is hungry bacteria, who live inside the body and consider fresh corpses to be an all-you-can-eat buffet. Within a week of a corpse being tucked into his or her coffin and lowered into a hole in the ground, billions of bacteria are having breakfast, lunch, and dinner around the clock on what were once the deceased's most delicate parts. In a surprisingly short time, a human body begins to look more like a Halloween decoration than a person.

Professor Celsius T. Hibble's corpse, aboveground now for the first time in a decade, was different. He was a dead man, but he looked a little better than most. His skin, now beef-jerky brown and shriveled, was still mostly intact, with a only few bones protruding here and there. His lips were long gone, leaving him with a bucktoothed, gumless grin, but clumps of the Nobel Prize winner's distinctive white hair still protruded from his scalp. The hole in the middle of his face where his handsome round nose used to be was unfortunate, but most of one ear still clung to the side of his head.

Miraculously, both of the professor's eyes still rested in their sockets. Their irises were paler now, but they retained remnants of the blazing blue tint they had possessed during life.

It was neither luck nor an unusually well-sealed coffin that had kept the corpse from becoming germ food in the grave. During his life, the professor had often used himself as a guinea pig for testing various procedures and vaccines, which caused certain fundamental alterations in his body's chemical makeup.

Stenchley knelt next to the grave, cradling the rotting corpse, marveling at its hideous face. He thought it was beautiful. "Look! The master is smiling at us," he whispered to the hissing Cynthia. "He sees us."

Stenchley had always theorized that the professor's eyes, the only ones that had ever looked at him with anything other than disgust, must be made of a different substance than other eyes, something rare like sapphires or ocean water. With the great man's remains now lying defenseless in his arms, the madman couldn't resist the opportunity to test his hypothesis. He carefully stuck a grimy finger in one of his master's dead eyes, but was disappointed to find that they seemed to be composed of the same rubbery gristle as the dozens of other eyes he had handled.

The pale light of dawn began to spread across the grounds, threatening to expose Stenchley's filthy deed. He needed a safe place to hide his trophy. Instinctively, he dragged the body, stiff and brittle as a piñata, to the back of Hibble Manor to a door ingeniously concealed by the mansion's masonry. His hands quickly found a certain stone in the wall and pushed it. A slab of the house's granite foundation pivoted open with a screech, revealing a dusty hallway. Stenchley carried the body inside. As the stone automatically closed again behind him, the hallway became pitch-black. Stenchley's feet knew exactly where to go, making several turns and descending a long, narrow set of steps carved into the bedrock of the house's foundation. At the bottom of the steps, Stenchley pushed a lever on the wall and a sealed door swung open, releasing a whoosh of refrigerated air. He entered a cavern filled with a dim blue light.

Once his eyes adjusted, Stenchley could see that the cave was almost exactly as he had left it so long ago. This had been the professor's secret laboratory, where his most advanced and controversial work was done. The equipment here was sleek and modern, with stainless-steel surfaces and computerized controls. Except that everything was now blanketed by a film of dust, it was almost as if Stenchley and the professor had stepped out just yesterday instead of ten years ago.

This was home. Oh, what happy days the hunchback had spent here in the lab, working at his master's side! The two of them had accomplished great things over the decades, though the madman was never quite sure exactly what they were. They had been together, and that was all that mattered to Stenchley. Only a few outsiders had even known the lab existed, and most of them were no longer living.

One half of the room was dominated by an array of huge glass columns filled with bubbling liquid, like giant cylindrical aquariums. Stenchley dropped the professor's body to the floor and stepped over the thick electrical cables that snaked out from the bottoms of the cylinders to a power grid built into the wall of the cave. He was not surprised to find the intricate machinery still running perfectly on its own after all this time. The cylinders and their valuable contents had been his master's top priority, and the professor had spent years devising an electrical generator to provide perpetual power for them using geothermal steam vents as its energy source. An automatic monitoring system ensured that this portion of the lab was completely self-sustaining.

Stenchley had always been fascinated by the surprising things that grew inside the aquariums. It amazed him that specimens that began as tiny shrimplike organisms could evolve into the incredible creatures he saw bobbing inside the cylinders now. Rows of colored lights blinked on control panels at the base of each cylinder, illuminated switches pulsed, and long trains of digital numbers crawled across lighted screens, tracking every change of the creatures' continuing metamorphoses.

Long ago, the professor had patiently taught Stenchley how to tend the sensitive equipment to keep it running at optimum efficiency. Even now, the madman could not keep himself from bustling about the columns, adjusting certain knobs and flipping switches as he had years ago.

In an alcove, he came to a group of smaller, globular containers. These were segregated from the rest and contained creatures Stenchley couldn't tear his eyes away from. Alarms went off inside his deformed brain at the sight of the plump pink things bobbing inside the vats, their white hair undulating slowly back and forth like seaweed.

These were the professor's "Friends."

He crept closer to the globe nearest him. Inside, the thing's arms floated out from their sides, the hands seeming to wave at Stenchley. Cynthia hissed and coiled angrily, causing Stenchley's hump to throb. The snake writhed with pure hatred. The madman's mouth opened, and the python's head peered out, its tongue flicking. *Kill it, love! Kill it!* the snake demanded. *That is the evil one!*

Stenchley did want to kill it. It was because of a Friend that the madman had been forced to hurt the professor. It was because of a Friend that he had been locked inside the dreaded asylum. Still, the madman was slow to act. "But the master will be angry! He forbids us to touch the Friends."

The python's head flattened and its neck swelled with anger inside the hunchback's throat, making him gag for air. *The master is dead! He cannot stop us now.*

Stenchley yelped as he felt her coils begin to squeeze his heart, sending a rush of blood to his head. His eyes bulged and throbbed.

He was sure the snake would squeeze until he was dead if he did not obey her.

"I s'pose you're right," he said. Stenchley punched and kicked at the container, but even the madman's powerful hands and feet would never be able to break the cylinder's thick glass casing. He needed a tool. Stenchley scrambled around the laboratory until he found a length of pipe. He leapt from the floor up onto the narrow catwalk that ran beside the vats and howled like a wolf as he swung the pipe with all his strength. With a thundering crack, the glass cylinder exploded, its cold fluid blasting Stenchley off the catwalk and sending him sprawling across the floor. A flood of foaming liquid sloshed across the lab.

Stenchley coughed and sputtered, spitting out a mouthful of the acrid liquid. He got to his feet and found his intended victim lying nearby. The plump, glistening Friend, its arms and legs akimbo, lay motionless on the floor of the cavern. The rubber umbilical tubes that had connected its body to the machine were ruptured and leaking.

Let's eat, Cynthia hissed.

But something was wrong. Instinct immediately told Stenchley that his prey was not alive. The madman squatted over the limp form and clawed at its chest, but it did not move. Cynthia didn't like carrion, preferring to eat her food live, or at worst, freshly killed. Stenchley leaned in close to the fleshy cheek and bared his teeth, but the chemical smell of the fluid the creature had been stored in was so overpowering even the python was repulsed. Unsated, gnashing his teeth angrily, Stenchley flung the lifeless thing aside.

This was not the Friend they had come for.

As the madman's panting gradually slowed, the burning in his hump became bearable again. Cynthia's coils released his pounding heart, and she slithered reluctantly back into her dark nest, still hungry for revenge and flesh.

With the python's spell broken, Stenchley guiltily stalked over to his master's stiff body, which lay propped up on the wet floor, and sat on his haunches next to it.

"I am sorry we tried to eat the Friend, Master," he said. "But Cynthia was hungry, and I could not resist."

The hunchback idly lifted the professor's bony hand from the puddle of liquid on the floor and held it as if it were a treasured pet. As he admired the delicate fan pattern of the bones that connected the wrist to the fingers, Stenchley noticed something curious. Patches of the hand's blackened hide had begun to fade to a lighter brown. He turned it over and saw that the palm of the hand, still moist from lying in the chemical slush puddled on the floor, had become softer and slightly more lifelike. He scooped up a bit of the sour liquid and rubbed it on the professor's cheek. The dry, papery skin reacted to the moisture by becoming lighter and more supple.

An exciting idea began to bloom in Stenchley's brain. He had helped the professor reanimate dead flesh many times in the lab. The fact that they had never brought an entire corpse back to life, just bits and pieces, did not bother Stenchley. Most of the equipment seemed to still be in working order, and the hunchback's simple mind saw no reason why he shouldn't be able to perform the same kind of procedure on the professor's body. After all, Stenchley was good with a knife and had an intimate knowledge of human organs, albeit based on their taste rather than their function. How hard could it be?

There were, of course, numerous reasons why Stenchley had no business attempting such a complex operation. To begin with, the hunchback's knowledge of the process was limited to the role of an uneducated assistant. Though his excellent memory enabled him to recall nearly every detail of the operations the professor had done, where to insert the wires and which knobs and dials to turn, Stenchley had no real understanding of the scientific principles involved in the procedure. He had no idea of the many bizarre and dangerous things that could happen if he made even the smallest mistake.

Yet Stenchley, full of hope and purpose, began hustling around the lab, gathering the tools and instruments he would need to accomplish his task. He immediately forgot all about the forlorn remains of the master's Friend lying in a heap against the wall of the lab like a broken toy.

CHAPTER 19

The librarian had been right about the approaching storm. The sky was black and blue when Josephine Cravitz and her mother walked out of the O. R. MacManus Library and Bait Shop with their books. A cold, biting wind whipped out of the north and pellets of sleet began pelting their faces as they hurried to the car. Barbara suggested they skip the other errands they had planned to do and go straight home instead. With the weather turning ugly and the escaped killer on the loose, she wanted to get back to the house, lock all the doors, and hunker down by the fire until things were back to normal.

This was fine with Josephine. The librarian had let her borrow a stack of books. She couldn't wait to get them home and go carefully through them one by one.

Thirty minutes later, Josephine was sitting in front of the fireplace back at Twittington House, wrapped in a blanket, sipping green tea with the books spread on the floor around her. She loved stormy days, the stormier the better, but she had never seen anything like this. Outside, a hissing waterfall of ice had come pouring from the sky, pounding against the roof and windows. The wind rattled the panes and whistled around the eaves of the roof, snaking its way in through every tiny crack and crevice of the old house. Still, with its antique furnace rumbling in the basement and the fireplace crackling away, the house managed to stay just warm enough.

Josephine opened *Geniuses of North America* and found two references to "Hibble, Celsius T." in the book's index. The first was devoted solely to the professor, but consisted only of a couple of paragraphs listing his accomplishments. The second turned out to be part of a longer piece about Thomas Edison. Josephine read that Hibble had been one of the "Edison Pioneers," a group of twenty-nine researchers who had been singled out for their work in electronics. The white-haired professor was easy to find in the photo of the Pioneers from the group's first meeting, which took place in 1918.

After finishing the article, Josephine came back to the photo. Something about it was not right. She pulled the photo of Celsius and Sally she'd found in her bedroom from her pocket and laid it next to the one in the book. The date in the corner of the photo from her room was 1936. She guessed the professor's age at the time couldn't have been more than thirty. But if that was true, he would have been a child in 1918. She found a magnifying glass in her mom's knitting basket and took a closer look at the picture in the book.

But he was no child. In fact, the professor looked identical in both pictures.

☠ ☠ ☠

Josephine spent the rest of the afternoon poring over the library books, looking for anything that might clear up the confusion about the professor's age, but she found nothing. It wasn't long before the steady din of the storm, her cozy nest of blankets, and her lack of sleep the night before combined to send Josephine into a delicious nap. She didn't wake up until late afternoon, when her father kissed her cheek. The university had sent everyone home early, he said, before the roads became too icy to drive on. Barbara brought in a tray of carrot cookies and chai. They told Howard all about Sally and Professor Hibble's doomed engagement and Stenchley's awful murder of the professor at the house right next door.

Howard was stunned. "Wow! I had no idea Hibble was from Awkward Falls. And what are the odds that the escaped convict would be the very guy who killed him?"

Howard went into the kitchen for more cookies and turned on the radio. He twisted the dial to the local station and carried the plate in to Barbara and Josephine. It was only a few moments before Phil, the announcer, abruptly broke into the musical program to give an update on the latest developments in the manhunt. Again, he had Sergeant Cole on the phone, the officer's slow, casual voice patiently answering the announcer's excited questions.

"So, Sergeant, do ya know where the heck the escapee is at this time?"

"Well, he's headed north, Phil, just as I expected," said the officer. "The latest report from the Royal Canadian Mounted Police says that the escapee is now in the vicinity of the lake country wilderness, which is, as you know, some pretty gnarly territory. Those boys are combing the woods like you wouldn't believe. Now they've got dogs trackin' him as well."

"Dogs, eh? That's pretty good."

"They're the best, the Mounties are, Phil. They'll catch him."

"And our threat level? Any change in that, Fin?"

"Aye, we're back down to turquoise now, which means that the prisoner no longer poses much of a threat to us hereabouts."

"Did you hear that, folks?" the announcer said. "We're back down to turquoise again!" With obvious relief, the announcer reminded listeners to stay tuned for further developments, then signed off. The soothing strains of classical music once again floated out of the speaker.

"Well, thank heavens for that." Barbara relaxed and leaned her head on Howard's shoulder. "I don't think I could have slept tonight knowing a killer was out there."

Josephine wanted to feel relieved, too, but she didn't. Now that night was getting near, she began to worry that maybe the librarian had been right, and Stenchley was still a threat. She had to warn Thaddeus as soon as possible. A surge of fear, mixed with excitement, shot through her body as she made the decision to sneak next door again tonight.

"Yes, it looks like the danger is past." Howard peered out the locked living room window at the empty frozen street outside. "I still can't believe Hibble's assistant murdered him in the house right next door. I didn't even know there was a house there."

"You can't see it from ground level because it's surrounded by a stone wall and lots of big trees," said Josephine.

Barbara added a splash of milk to each of their cups. "And now the place is abandoned, except for a robotic caretaker built by the professor himself, believe it or not."

Howard sipped his chai thoughtfully. "Interesting. I'd love to see it. I wonder if . . . no, I doubt it."

"You wonder what?" Barbara punched his arm.

"Ow. Well, it's just that there was an old rumor among some of the scientific community that Hibble was dabbling in the use of microtechnology for interfacing with live neurocircuits. But that's far-fetched."

Josephine was lost. "What does all that mean, Dad?"

"I think he's talking about cybernetics, dear," Barbara said. "Combining humans and machines."

"That sounds like science fiction."

"Biocybernetics are on the cutting edge of real science even now, Jo."

Josephine knew her father loved talking about anything that was "cutting edge." He was a true geek that way. "Modern medicine is starting to use microscopic machines to replace or regrow living tissue. Several of the big biotech companies are already doing amazing things with nanomachines no bigger than a cell."

Josephine thought of Norman. "Has there ever been a person who had so many parts replaced that they were more machine than human?"

Howard shook his head. "Not even close. The ratio of human parts to electronic parts is still very large."

Barbara shuddered. "Good. I don't think I'd want to see that, thank you very much."

"Better not look, then. It's only a matter of time before it happens," Howard said. "On the other hand, there are lots and lots of robots in use today, though none that make use of any living tissue. Automatons have been in existence since as long ago as the eighth century. Even then they were quite elaborate. The possibility that there's a functioning robotic device built by Celsius Hibble himself right next door is very intriguing."

Barbara sighed. "I wish we could get a peek, but the librarian told us the estate has been off-limits to the public since the murder."

"Too bad," Howard said. "I bet that place has some amazing stories to tell."

If you only knew, Josephine thought.

☻ ☻ ☻

After a long, cozy afternoon, the three Cravitzes enjoyed a cauliflower casserole dinner followed by a spirited game of Parcheesi. Barbara won, as usual, which meant that Howard and Josephine had to do the dishes. They didn't mind, however. They washed and dried quietly, watching the storm through the icy kitchen window.

Night fell, though you could hardly tell, since the storm had kept the sky nearly dark all day. The wind continued to howl, and the sleet turned to snow, which fell in fat clumps. Outside, Josephine heard the occasional rifle-shot crack of tree branches snapping under the heavy blanket of ice that lay over everything. Howard stoked the fire regularly, keeping their little nest in the living room warm.

The dishes were soon done, and though it was still early, Howard and Barbara were already yawning. The wintry weather made a warm bed and an early bedtime all the more attractive to the adults. Josephine was anything but sleepy, and would normally have objected to ending the evening at this hour, but on this night she said nothing. The sooner her parents were asleep, the better. She kissed them good night and hurried upstairs.

The thought of traipsing through the woods, climbing over the wall, passing through the cemetery, and creeping down the dark alleys of the maze in the middle of an ice storm would not have been an appealing thought for a normal person. For Josephine, it only made things more interesting. Nothing was going to keep her away from Hibble Manor tonight.

Once her parents had turned off their light, Josephine hopped out of bed, piled on multiple layers of clothing topped with a raincoat, and pulled Eggplant snugly down over her ears. *Okay,* she thought, *parents asleep, ice storm raging, lunatic on the loose—perfect time to go out for the evening! I really should have my head examined.*

She paused to put *Geniuses of North America* into a grocery bag, and slung it over her shoulder. Maybe Thaddeus would know something about the Edison Pioneers entry. She slipped out the back door and into the freezing darkness. When she came to the wall, she saw that it had become coated with a sheet of ice. She climbed up the adjacent fir tree and held a branch while she plopped her bottom on top of the wall. She slid down the other side and landed with a crunch in the ice-coated weeds. Josephine carefully trudged through the little cemetery as the wind and snow battered and pushed at her, holding on to the crooked headstones for balance.

Suddenly her foot slipped on the slick ground and she went down hard on her back. When she sat up, she saw that she had very nearly fallen into a deep hole in front of one of the tombstones. She gripped the top of the stone and pulled herself up. A little mountain of ice-crusted dirt was piled next to the hole.

An open grave? That definitely wasn't here last night.

At the bottom of the hole she could see a muddy coffin, its lid open and its inhabitant missing. Through the glaze of ice that covered the granite headstone, she read the name *Celsius T. Hibble*.

CHAPTER 20

The extreme cold did not allow Josephine to linger at the grave for long. The wind was so cold, it made her skin burn wherever it was exposed. She ducked her head into her coat and hurried toward the mansion's front door. Moments later, she was inside the candlelit parlor of Hibble Manor, much to the annoyance of Thaddeus.

"Should I expect that you will now come barging into my house on a regular basis, Ms. Cravitz?" he grumbled. "And you, Norman," he went on, directing his ire at the robot, "opening the door to any vagabond who rings the bell. The security implications of this situation are most upsetting!"

But when Josephine mentioned the open grave and empty coffin she had passed on the way over, Thaddeus immediately stopped his complaining. This troubling development sent his hand into his pocket, from which he pulled an unfinished candy bar. Thaddeus paced back and forth on the worn carpet worriedly as he munched the nub of a Nuttycream Crunchlog.

"Who on earth would dig up Grandfather's grave?" he pondered, chewing. "And what have they done with the body?"

Josephine sat shivering in a tattered easy chair as Norman poured her a mug of steaming cocoa. "I c-can't imagine," she said.

"It would appear," Thaddeus said, "that we have had another intruder. A body snatcher, this time! I wonder if it could be the man in the black suit again? He's bound to be up to something."

Felix, who lay curled on the rug in a tight ball, opened one eye and offered his opinion. "You're off base, kid. Why would a spook from the orphanage wanta dig up Gramps Hibble? It's too weird, even for those goons."

"The empty coffin isn't the only thing," said Josephine. "What I really came over here to tell you is that Fetid Stenchley escaped from the asylum yesterday, and he's still on the loose. I figured you probably hadn't heard."

"Stenchley?" Thaddeus chuckled. "That's impossible! No one has ever escaped from the Asylum for the Dangerously Insane! The place is a fortress!"

"Well, they have now. We heard it on the radio this morning."

"That could be a problem, boss," said Felix, scratching a flea on his ear. "If this Stenchley guy whacked your paw-paw, who's to say he might not wanta whack you too?"

"That's what I'm afraid of," said Josephine. "You could be in real danger."

Thaddeus pretended not to hear her. "There's nothing to worry about! Norman can secure the house in minutes, easily." Thaddeus walked to the window and peeked through the drapes. "Besides, if Stenchley is out of doors on a night like this, he's done for."

"The police did say they think he's heading north into the wilderness," Josephine admitted, "but the librarian in town seemed to think they might be wrong. She said she would be sleeping with her shotgun tonight, just in case."

"Then we shall take all necessary precautions." Thaddeus snapped his fingers. "Norman, implement Security Status One! Check every possible entrance thoroughly, and leave nothing to chance."

The robot hesitated. "Is that the one where I seal all the windows with glue? Or is it the one where I stack the furniture against the doors?"

"Both! And gather all our deadliest weaponry."

"I'm afraid we are running a bit low on deadly weaponry, sir. We sold the last of the antique sabers and crossbows some time ago. However, there may still be a javelin in the drawing room."

"A fierce weapon," Thaddeus said. "Fetch it quickly."

"You may depend on me, sir." The robot gave the boy a rusty salute and clanked off down the dark hallway.

"There's something else, too, Thaddeus, something strange about your grandfather." She handed him the picture of Celsius and Sally. "Look at this picture I found in my bedroom."

The boy looked it over. "It's certainly Grandfather. But who is the woman? Is she my grandmother?"

"No, her name is Sally Twittington. They were engaged, but never got married. Her family lived next door in your grandfather's time. See the date at the bottom?"

"1936. But why—"

Josephine opened the grocery bag and laid the book on the cluttered coffee table. "My mom and I did some research today at the library. Take a look at this." She opened the book and pointed out Thaddeus's grandfather in the picture of the Edison Pioneers.

Thaddeus pushed his glasses up his nose and squinted at the book. "Obviously, that's Grandfather as well. What is your point?"

"The point is, your grandfather looks identical in both photos even though they were taken twenty-five years apart."

The boy studied the two pictures closely. "Astonishing! Even taking into account the excellent genes common to all Hibbles, one would expect to see some signs of aging over such a span."

"Exactly."

The boy stared at the picture for another moment. "It's too bad."

"What's too bad?"

"That he failed to marry the woman. She might have been a first-rate grandmother."

Josephine's brain was humming with questions now. "Do you know how old your grandfather was at the time of his mur—I mean his death?"

"I don't know how old he was, but we should be able to find out." Thaddeus snapped his fingers at Felix, who had been snoozing on the rug at their feet. "Felix, get me the file on Grandfather's murder."

The cat frowned and grumbled, but rose slowly and sauntered off to a nearby room. Josephine winced at Thaddeus's casual bluntness in referring to his grandfather's violent demise.

"You need not pussyfoot with me, Ms. Crav—"

"Josephine."

"Josephine. It is a fact that Grandfather did not die peacefully in his sleep. He was brutally murdered, and it is perfectly fine to say so. I find that emotions are an unnecessary distraction."

"That's not true, Thaddeus! There's nothing wrong with having feelings," she said.

Thaddeus rolled his eyes. "Urgh. You've been here for less than ten minutes, and already I tire of your babbling. Felix! Where's that file?"

"Hold your beans, I got it right here." The cat strolled back into the room carrying a thick folder stuffed with newspaper clippings.

"Thank you." The boy patted the cat's head and snatched the folder. He began sorting through the ragged clippings, tossing the irrelevant ones aside. Finally he came to the ones he wanted, an inch-thick mess of them, stapled together.

"Here's the obituary from the *Awkward Falls Chronicle*. It reports that on the date of his death, Grandfather was . . . hmm. It says his age is uncertain, but that he was said to be either ninety-one, ninety-five, or one hundred six. Let's try the one from the *Times*." Thaddeus flipped to the next clipping.

"Professor Celsius T. Hibble was killed, etcetera and so on, the professor's age is . . . unknown." He flipped quickly through several others, each saying essentially the same thing: age unknown. Some of the other papers made guesses as to his age, the oldest being one hundred twelve, the youngest eighty-nine. None of the obituaries could say for sure how old the professor had been when he died.

Thaddeus and Josephine sorted through some of the other clippings and found a photo of Hibble in an army uniform.

Josephine grabbed the magnifying glass and looked closely at the photo. "He looks the same in this photo too."

"That uniform Grandfather is wearing is from the Spanish-American War. I happen to be a buff on that particular conflict. Therefore, we can assume that photo was taken no later than 1898."

Josephine smacked her forehead. "That's thirty-eight years before the one of him and Sally! How could he not age at all for so long?"

CHAPTER 21

As the incredible idea sank in that Thaddeus's grandfather had somehow stopped aging a very long time ago, Josephine racked her brain for a way to learn the truth. The events had taken place so long ago, everyone who knew what really happened was dead by now.

Or were they? Josephine had an idea. "We could ask Sally."

"Sally?"

"Twittington. Your grandfather's fiancée. She's really old, but she's still alive, and she lives in town now. The librarian says she's a recluse, but maybe we could try to talk to her anyway."

"And how would we do that?" asked Thaddeus.

"The librarian told me where she lives. We could pay her a visit tomorrow."

The boy frowned. "Tomorrow? I think not. I'll have Norman bring the Rolls around this minute."

💀 💀 💀

The antique Rolls Royce sped through icy Awkward Falls, the robot maneuvering the huge car down the frozen streets like a seasoned racecar driver. In his disguise of a plastic nose with glasses and mustache attached, and a bowler hat atop his steel head, Norman would have fooled very few observers into believing he was just another chauffeur. Luckily, observers were almost nonexistent at this late hour during a storm.

"Are we there yet, Norman?" asked Thaddeus, for the fifth time since they had left the house ten minutes earlier. The boy eagerly pressed his face against the window on his side of the car, then switched to the one on Josephine's side, then back again, as they drove. *This must be one of the few times he's even been outside the house,* Josephine thought. *He's as excited as a kid on vacation.*

"No, sir," the robot patiently replied. "However, our destination is now in view."

The car rolled to a stop, and Norman came around to open the door.

"Do you see anyone about, Norman?" asked Thaddeus. "Any suspicious characters lurking?"

The robot's head squeaked as it spun slowly, making a complete circle. "I believe the beach is clean, sir."

Thaddeus sighed. "It's 'the coast is clear,' Norman, not 'the beach is clean.' You stay here with the car while we go in."

"Very well, sir."

Thaddeus and Josephine ascended the steps to the door of the perfectly preserved Victorian townhouse, and Josephine rang the bell. A woman in a starched white nurse's uniform opened the door just a crack and asked what they wanted, clearly hoping the answer was nothing.

"Hello, we would like to speak to Sally Twittington, please," said Josephine, in her sweetest tone.

"It is extremely late, and Ms. Twittington does not take visitors," the nurse said curtly, and began to close the door.

"Wait!" Josephine decided to take a chance. She took the photo of the professor and Sally she had found in her room out of her pocket and handed it to the nurse. "Please show her this."

Inside the house, Josephine heard someone speak. "Who is it, Olga?" a tired voice said. "Tell them to go away."

The nurse closed the door without a word.

"Drat!" grumbled Thaddeus.

"Gee, that went well," said Josephine. "I guess it was worth a shot."

They turned and had started down the steps when the door suddenly opened again. "Ms. Twittington will see you," the nurse said, her tone clearly indicating her disapproval of her employer's change of policy. "But only for a moment. She is a very sick woman."

☻ ☻ ☻

Time had stolen every trace of the beauty that once belonged to Sally Twittington. In the dim light of the sitting room, the frail old woman looked frightening. Her wrinkled face, caked with stage makeup, was as white as chalk, her lips smeared sloppily with red lipstick. She was dressed in a glittery costume that looked like something out of an old jazz musical. A steel tank on wheels stood at her side, and a plastic oxygen mask was strapped over her nose. She gingerly held the photo of herself and the professor in her lap.

When Josephine introduced herself, Sally seemed barely interested, but when Thaddeus appeared she pulled the mask off, straightened in her wheelchair, and gasped.

Sally looked at the boy as if he were a ghost. She stretched a bony, spotted hand toward Thaddeus and beckoned him to come closer.

"Let me look at you, you poor creature," she finally whispered. She touched his face. "My God. I had hoped to be dead before any of Celsius's abominations walked the earth."

"I beg your pardon, madame!" Thaddeus pulled his hand out of the woman's grasp and stepped back indignantly.

Sally turned to Josephine. "Why are you here? What do you want with me?" The woman's voice was small and raspy. "Speak quickly. I am due onstage for the third act momentarily."

Josephine was confused for a moment, then realized the woman imagined she was still an actress. "Ms. Twittington, we just want to ask you a couple of questions about Professor Hibble, if you don't mind," Josephine asked, cheerily, hoping to improve the mood a bit.

"Professor Hibble. I have tried to forget that I was ever involved with the man, if he could be called that after all he did to himself."

"How dare you speak of Grandfather so irreverently!" Thaddeus stamped his foot indignantly. "I'll have you know he was a great man!"

Sally looked surprised. "Grandfather, you say? Oh, my. Do you have a name, young man?"

"My name is Thaddeus J. Hibble! The second, actually. I am named after my father."

The old woman shook her head slowly. "My dear child, Celsius Hibble may have done some great things in his life, long ago. But someday you will find out he was no great man."

Before Thaddeus could argue, Josephine decided to butt in and get to the matter at hand. "We found out something weird about the professor, Ms. Twittington. We checked some dates, and we think he was incredibly old when he died. It sounds crazy, but he also seems to have stopped aging when he was still pretty young. Do you know anything about that?"

Sally sighed and looked at the old photo. "Where did you get this?"

"I found it in my room, in Twittington House," Josephine said. "My parents and I live there now."

Sally raised her chin and began to speak as if she were giving a dramatic soliloquy. "I remember the moment when this picture was taken. Celsius and I were at a ball the night before we were to marry, and I was happier than I've ever been in my life. I was going to be the bride of the famous Celsius Hibble. We danced for hours, drank champagne, and were the toast of the party. By one or two in the morning, I was tired and ready to go home, but Celsius insisted I return to Hibble Manor with him, as he had something important he wanted to share with me.

"When we arrived at the mansion, he led me to a hidden room, a study I had never seen before. Celsius seemed oddly excited, but also quite nervous. He insisted I sit down as he began to babble about cells, and genetic codes, and other scientific gobbledygook I didn't understand or care about. Finally, he took my hand, just as he had when he proposed. 'Sally, if we could be together forever, would you want to be?'" he asked.

"'We will be together forever, my darling,' I answered. 'Till death do us part.' But I saw that was not what he meant.

"'What if forever really meant forever?' he asked me. 'What if I told you we could live for a very long time, longer than anyone ever has, remaining just as we are now, never growing a day older?'

"I thought he was joking at first, but the look on his face was solemn. 'I lied to you about my birth date,' he said. 'The month and day, October seventh, are as I said, but the year was not 1907.'

"'What year was it, then?' I asked with trepidation, feeling an odd tingle on the back of my neck as I sensed our conversation was about to take a very odd turn.

"Instead of answering, he handed me a photo of himself standing in front of the Ferris Wheel at the Chicago World's Fair in 1893. The man in the photo and the man holding my hand were identical. I didn't understand and thought he must be playing a practical joke on me. I looked more closely at the picture, then again at Celsius. He was not joking.

"Then my fiancé, the man I loved with all my heart and planned to marry in a few hours, told me that he was actually eighty-eight years old.

"It was impossible, and yet the evidence was plain. He begged me to join him, promising that I could become forever young like he was, with a series of injections and a small surgical operation. He said he could perform the procedure then and there.

"I pushed him away and began to weep. The whole business terrified me. I realized I did not know Celsius at all. I ran away as fast as I could and never looked back."

"And that's why you called off the wedding," said Josephine.

The old woman nodded. "Celsius was undoubtedly a genius. Unfortunately, he was willing to become a monster to prove it. I left him and fled to Europe, where I threw myself into acting. The stage became my refuge."

Thaddeus looked ready to explode with indignation at hearing his grandfather described as a monster. Somehow, he controlled himself long enough to ask, "What about my parents? Did you know them?"

The effort of telling the story seemed to have exhausted the old woman. She put the oxygen mask over her nose again and closed her eyes. "I'm sorry, I have no more answers you would want to hear. My advice to you both is to wash your hands of Celsius Hibble, just like I did all those years ago. It is one decision I have never regretted."

"This is foolery," said Thaddeus. "My grandfather was one of the top scientists of his time!"

Sally's milky eyes flashed. "Yes. But he was a dangerous man. If the truth be told, the hunchback probably did the world a favor when he took Celsius's life." Sally turned her eyes from the boy. It was becoming harder for her to breathe. "If anything, Stenchley should have done it sooner, before . . . Celsius did things . . . that could not be . . . undone."

The old woman reached for the oxygen mask and held it to her face. She closed her eyes and leaned back in the chair as she breathed in the hissing air. "Fetch the makeup girl, Olga, and alert the director. He must delay the curtain. I need a moment to gather myself."

"You must leave now," said the nurse. "Ms. Twittington needs to rest. Good night." She shooed them back the way they had come and out onto the porch.

The door closed, the deadbolt slamming into place instantly. The porch light switched off, and Josephine and Thaddeus were left standing in the dark.

CHAPTER 22

Josephine slapped the leather seat when they slid inside the Rolls for the ride back to Hibble Manor. "A hundred and fifty-three!"

"What?"

"I did the math," she said. "Your grandfather and Sally were engaged in 1936, which makes him one hundred and fifty-three the day he died! She must be close to a hundred herself."

Thaddeus stared out the fogged window, brooding. "If you ask me, the crone was unhinged. I doubt her memory is trustworthy."

"She was a little spooky," said Josephine, "but besides thinking she was about to go onstage, she sounded pretty lucid to me. I wonder why she wouldn't talk to us about your parents?"

"I found her evasiveness on the subject quite offensive. And she clearly did not understand the importance of Grandfather's work."

Josephine nodded. "The real question is, how did the professor stop the aging process? If we could find the answer to that, it would change the course of science!"

"We'd be a shoo-in for the Nobel Prize!" said Thaddeus.

"We have to figure out how to read that notebook. I have a feeling the answers are in there."

"I believe you're right," agreed Thaddeus.

In minutes, Norman had them back across the iced roads to Hibble Manor, where they hurried from the car park down to Thaddeus's lab. While drinking cups of steaming cocoa, they thumbed through the old notebook, trying again to make sense of it.

Josephine nibbled her pinkie nail, then suggested tentatively, "I think we should show this to my father, Thaddeus."

Thaddeus looked shocked. "No. I won't allow it."

"But he's a microbiophysicist, a really good one. Maybe he could decipher the code."

"I thought you said I was more brilliant than he was. Much more brilliant, you said, as I recall."

"Well, I . . ."

A dark cloud came over his chubby face. "You didn't really mean it then, did you, about me being like Einstein? You were only saying that to trick me!"

"Thaddeus, you've got it wrong. Of course I think you're brilliant. You're the smartest kid I've ever met." She paused, softening, not wanting to hurt his feelings any more than she already had. "But you are just a kid. My dad's a real . . . I mean, he's a PhD and has lots of experience in labs all over the world."

Thaddeus's lower lip slid out a bit. "You think I'm not a real scientist."

"No, Thaddeus, you're missing the point. Your grandfather's notebook could turn out to be one of the great scientific discoveries of all time. My dad could help us!"

"Absolutely not," he said. "Even if he can read the notebook, what good will it do? He'll tell the authorities about me, and I'll end up in the orphanage. I don't want to go there, Josephine. I meant it when I said I'd never let them take me alive!"

"You don't understand, Thaddeus. My father isn't like that. Once he understands the situation, I don't think he'll turn you in. I'd never do anything to get you sent to the orphanage."

The boy folded his arms and frowned. "Why should I believe you?"

"Because I'm on your side," she said sincerely. "If we're going to be friends, you have to trust me."

Thaddeus's eyes narrowed, and his forehead wrinkled with suspicion. Josephine realized she had crossed a line she probably shouldn't have. The corners of the boy's mouth turned south, his chin slid forward, and he shook his head. "Who said we were going to be friends? Norman and Felix are my friends. I can trust them." Then he turned his back on Josephine and resumed his work.

Josephine realized with a shock that the strangest kid on the planet had just rejected her. She was surprised at how much it hurt.

CHAPTER 23

Stenchley spent all day lovingly preparing the professor's corpse for reanimation. He had removed the professor's burial suit and given the body a thorough sponge bath using the noxious fluid he'd found pooled on the lab floor. This made his master's skin appear a bit less rotten. Whereas the flesh had been beef jerky-ish, it was now more along the lines of a nice catcher's mitt.

Stenchley had then strapped the carcass onto one of the lab's stainless-steel gurneys and gotten down to the gory business of installing new organs. At this point, the madman's abnormally good memory of decades working in the lab with the legendary Celsius Hibble took over. Stenchley had assisted in many reanimation operations, and his hands automatically knew what to do. From a bank of refrigerated cabinets, he retrieved preassembled system sets designed by the professor for quick insertion. The digestive system, the cardiovascular system, the spinal nerve bundle, were all stored in convenient moisturized packets, each ingeniously constructed of real human tissue combined with mechanical microcircuitry. Stenchley was so happy mucking about in the old lab, twiddling knobs, inserting needles here and tubes there, sawing things, feeling the satisfying squish of fresh organs between his fingers, that he found himself whistling as he worked.

Things went so smoothly, at least by Stenchley's standards, that by nightfall he was already at the last step in the reanimation process: raising the body from the radium infusion bath, its legs and arms twitching and jerking with something like life. Like a child with a horrifying new doll, the madman giggled excitedly as he dressed the body again in its moldy tuxedo and combed the clumps of white hair that still clung to its skull.

When the body was groomed to Stenchley's satisfaction, he stood the professor up and stepped back to admire his work. Any sane person would have regarded the refurbished corpse as hideous, with its ghoulish grin and bones sticking out of its decomposed flesh. As the thing began to stagger ridiculously around the lab, Stenchley was delighted. Instead of the souped-up mass of rotten flesh that it was, the madman saw only the great Professor Hibble resurrected. He did not mind at all that the former Nobel Prize winner was not fully conscious and could now have been outsmarted by a reasonably clever pigeon.

"Master, I have rescued you from the grave!" the madman declared proudly, his joy undiminished by the fact that he had been the one who sent the professor there in the first place. "Welcome home, sir!"

☠ ☠ ☠

Anhydrous ammonia is one of the most dangerous and smelly chemicals known to man, and for this reason it is stored in specially constructed steel tanks at 250 pounds of pressure per square inch. What that means is that far more anhydrous ammonia than there is room for is forced into the tank, then the top is sealed in place before the ammonia can escape. At that point, the ammonia is absolutely dying to get out of the tube, and will come rocketing out of any opening it can find like a poisonous, 250-pound liquid sledgehammer.

Fetid Stenchley did not know any of these handy facts about the safe handling of anhydrous ammonia. He was so focused on his grisly project that the rows of missile-shaped steel tubes standing next to his worktable barely attracted his attention. To an illiterate murderer like Stenchley, the words DANGER! ANHYDROUS AMMONIA printed on the side of the tubes may as well have said HAPPY NEW YEAR!

Since the professor had been lying dead in a coffin for ten years, his sense of balance wasn't what it had been, and he teetered and staggered first one way, then the other. Stenchley, who was busy dreaming of all the wonderful activities he and his restored master would soon be enjoying, did not notice that his master was about to trip into a row of steel tanks, each one stamped with the kind of red lettering that often meant danger. The professor lurched into the tanks, knocking them down like bowling pins. One happened to clip the side of a worktable on its way down, cracking its sealed cap. This created just the sort of tiny opening that the pressurized anhydrous ammonia inside had been waiting for. The chemical blasted out of the hole, smacking Stenchley square in the chest, and pinned him against the lab's stone wall.

A curious thing happens when anhydrous ammonia shoots out of its tank into the normal pressure of the atmosphere. The temperature of the ammonia instantly drops to minus twenty-eight degrees Fahrenheit, giving it the ability to freeze-dry anything it happens to touch, such as the skin of hunchbacked killers. Clothing is frozen onto the flesh in the process as well. Fetid Stenchley screamed in agony as the ragged gown he still wore from the asylum fused instantaneously with his chest, forming a frozen straitjacket. His bare neck and lower face caught the blast directly as well, which gave him the surprising sensation of being on fire. Stenchley was so convinced he was burning, he ran out of the lab, up the steps, out the secret door, and into the icy storm, burying his face in a snowbank for relief.

Back inside the lab, the spewing ammonia tank shot like a torpedo into the stone wall and exploded, sending a rain of rocks spraying across the room.

The professor's bumbling corpse lay murmuring amid the pile of ammonia tanks, oblivious to the chain of events he had just set in motion.

CHAPTER 24

A low, thundering boom rocked the floor of the lab just as Josephine was about to leave. Dust fell from the ceiling, and glass beakers crashed to the floor, their contents spattering around the room.

"Quick, under the table!" Josephine grabbed Thaddeus and pulled him under the heavy operating table with her.

"What's happening?" he asked. "Are we going to die?"

"It could be an earthquake. My family lived in California for a year when I was in fourth grade, and we had them all the time."

They huddled there for a few tense minutes until they were sure the danger was past.

"I think it's over," Josephine said. Then an acrid, burned-plastic odor began to waft into the room.

"What's that terrible smell?"

Thaddeus sniffed the air. "Ah, anhydrous ammonia. I'd recognize it anywhere. I think it's coming from this floor drain." The boy crawled over to a large round grate set into the lab floor and sniffed.

"Yes, this is definitely the source." He turned his ear to the grate. "I can hear something. I think someone's down there."

Josephine crawled over to the grate and listened. "Is there a basement or cellar below this room?"

"As far as I know, this is the basement," Thaddeus replied.

After a moment, Josephine was able to make out faint irregular pinging sounds, like someone using a hammer. "I can hear it too. Helloooo down there!" she called. The odd sounds continued. "Maybe it's just rats."

"We certainly have plenty of those, but that doesn't account for the ammonia. I say we investigate."

Thaddeus found a screwdriver and set to work removing the screws that held the rusty iron grate in place over the drain. Josephine helped him lift the manhole-size grate and slide it out of the way.

Josephine aimed a flashlight into the hole, but could see only a few feet down, as the pipe curved off to one side. She had an idea. The drainpipe was about three feet in diameter, more than large enough for what she had in mind.

"Hold this." She handed Thaddeus the flashlight and found a length of rope lying in a pile of odds and ends. She used several granny knots to secure the rope around her waist, then tied the other end to the sturdy leg of the operating table. "I'm going in there."

Thaddeus wrinkled his nose. "Do you think that's altogether wise? It looks treacherous."

"Nah. I'm only going to go far enough to see what's around the bend in the pipe. If anything goes wrong, you can pull me out. No prob, right?"

"I suppose not." The boy handed her a surgical mask. "At least wear this."

Josephine strapped on the mask and lowered herself into the hole, pushing her back and feet against opposite sides of the drain and crab-walking down bit by bit. The smell of ammonia was stronger now that she was inside the drain. When she came to the curve in the pipe, she saw that it was not a ninety-degree bend, but more of a gradual curve that would require careful negotiation to keep her from falling farther down the drain. She touched the toes of her left foot onto the curve of the pipe and slowly shifted her weight onto that foot. The surface was slicker than she had expected, however, and Josephine immediately slipped, sliding down the drain, past the curve, into another vertical section where she hung suspended by the rope around her waist. Below her dangling feet she saw a faint light that appeared to be the end of the drain. It could be a nasty fall if she dropped from where she was now.

"What happened?" called Thaddeus.

"It's okay, I just slipped. I'm fine. I can see the end of the drain from here."

"What shall we do now? There's no more rope."

"Pull me up a little." She figured if she could get her back and feet against the walls again, she could untie the rope from her waist and crab-walk safely down to the end of the drain. Being Josephine, she'd worry later about getting back up again.

Thaddeus pulled with all his might, which was not much. Together with Josephine's own efforts, it was enough to get her back in position. She inched her way up the drain a bit so that the rope had slack in it, then she worked at the knot, trying to untie it—her fall had cinched it incredibly tight. But she became so focused on the knot that she lost her balance and dropped down the drain again.

Unfortunately, Thaddeus had failed to let go of the rope after pulling Josephine up and he was now jerked into the drain as well. He fell on top of the dangling Josephine, who struggled to hold onto the rope. Now that she had to support not only herself but a boy who ate far too many Chocochewy Nutlogs, her hands began to slide down the rope. She lost her grip and the two fell down the drain, landing hard on another grate at the bottom of the pipe.

For a moment, they were both too stunned to react.

"Ouch. Are we still alive?" moaned Thaddeus.

"I think so," Josephine grunted. "You okay?"

"Actually, several parts of me are hurting, but I'm not sure yet which ones. Is this your elbow or mine?"

"That would be my knee."

Slowly, they untangled themselves from each other. The space inside the drainpipe was so tight, only Josephine could get in position to see through the grate that supported them.

She peered down into the room below. "Wow." In the glowing blue light she could see a shiny stainless-steel console with blinking lights and switches built into it, flanked by several monitor screens of different sizes. "It looks like some kind of control room. We have to get in there somehow."

Thaddeus wriggled around, trying to get a look. All he could see was Josephine's shoulder and his own left foot. "Oh, bother! We'll never get out of here. We'll be stuck in this drain forever. Norman!" he yelled. "Save us! Help!"

As if the rusty screws that had held the grate in place for the last hundred years heard Thaddeus's wish, they lost their ability to hold the weight of two twelve-year-olds and snapped in half. The grate dropped to the floor below, followed by Thaddeus and Josephine.

CHAPTER 25

If it hadn't been for an old shipping crate that happened to be perfectly positioned below the grate, Thaddeus and Josephine would surely have been seriously hurt in their fall from the ceiling of the lab. The crate was filled with sawdust, which had kept its contents of glass beakers and test tubes from breaking during shipment years ago. Thaddeus landed first, followed by Josephine, who fell right on top of him. The ample padding on Thaddeus's plump body cushioned Josephine's landing and kept her bony knees and elbows from doing anything more than knocking the wind out of the boy.

Josephine crawled to the edge of the crate and hopped to the floor. "Are you all right, Thaddeus?"

Only the top of Thaddeus's head protruded from the sawdust. Josephine reached into the crate and helped pull him to the surface.

"Goorrgghhh," he moaned, spitting sawdust. "I can't see! I'm blind!"

"You're not blind, silly. You've just lost your glasses." Josephine dug around for a moment and fished them out of the sawdust. "Here they are."

With a good deal of grunting and gasping, Thaddeus rolled out of the crate and plopped onto the floor. Josephine helped him to his feet and brushed the sawdust out of his hair.

"Egad! I've severed an artery!" he gasped frantically, spotting a small red stain on the elbow of his jacket.

Josephine pushed up his sleeve and found a tiny cut. "You're fine. It's only a scratch."

"Are you sure?" he asked. "It looks like an awful lot of blood!"

"I'm positive. We'll put a Band-Aid on it later, I promise."

When Thaddeus had calmed down a bit, the two began to take note of their surroundings. The room was carved out of bedrock and was bathed in a deep blue light. Ammonia fumes made their eyes sting and their noses burn.

Thaddeus carefully sniffed the air. "The ammonia content of the air appears to be within acceptable tolerances. A good thing, otherwise we'd be dying a horrible death at this moment."

"That's a lovely thought, Thaddeus," Josephine said. "I feel so much better now."

Once Josephine's eyes began to adjust to the eerie light, she was astounded by what she saw. Although everything was very dusty, the place looked like the labs her father worked in. Colored lights blinked on a large control console that sat in the center of the room in a kind of raised cockpit. Rows of numbers and letters scrolled across its three computer monitors. Banks of sleek, efficient-looking machinery built into the walls all around the lab hummed and hissed quietly. A spiral staircase led up to a series of catwalks that gave access to controls too high to reach from the floor. It seemed impossible that something like this could exist inside the creaky old mansion. Thaddeus's grungy little lab was like something out of the Stone Age in comparison.

But the most impressive thing was a group of floor-to-ceiling glass cylinders that took up half the room. Specimens of some kind were floating inside the tubes.

"Wow! What is this place?"

Thaddeus's mouth hung open as he took it all in. "I can't believe it," he gasped. "This must have been Grandfather's real lab. I always wondered how he could have made all of his famous discoveries in such a small, ill-equipped space as the one upstairs. And to think this has been right here under my feet all along!"

The two were so dazzled by the lab they didn't notice the fresh handprints here and there on the dusty monitor screens and work surfaces, or the bare footprints in the dust that covered the floor.

Thaddeus, with the excitement of a kid in a toy store, approached the nearest column to get a closer look at what was inside. "How fascinating!"

The creature inside was massive, with four legs and clawed paws like those of a bear or a lion. Its horned head was that of a buffalo, and wore a kind of metal skullcap. Large teeth protruded from its mouth, and an extra pair of legs grew from its midsection. Black rubber hoses ran from its underbelly and neck and disappeared into the murky slush at the bottom of the cylinder.

"It looks like it's alive," Josephine said.

Thaddeus pressed his nose against the glass. "I think it is. Look here." He pointed to a small monitor set into a control pad at the foot of the cylinder. On it, a horizontal line pulsed into a jagged peak every couple of seconds. "The machinery is tracking the creature's heartbeat. Quite ingenious."

Sure enough, Josephine could see the thing's breast slowly rising and falling in rhythm with the graph on the monitor. And its silver eyes, which appeared to be mechanical, seemed to be following them.

"It's watching us!" Josephine whispered to Thaddeus. She instinctively clutched his arm for comfort where his biceps muscle should have been, but felt only flab instead.

He pulled his arm away. "Ow! You're bruising me!"

The next cylinder in line held a creature whose furry body was riddled with tumors and half-formed limbs. Its front and rear legs were made of shiny steel, but there was also an extra set of appendages on the shoulders above the front legs. Spread out wide as if to

give someone a hug were a pair of mechanical arms, complete with jointed fingers. The head was scaly and earless and reminded Josephine of a monitor lizard.

"Are they robots?" asked Josephine.

"Perhaps partly. The use of mechanical components is quite interesting."

Josephine felt her stomach turn. "This stuff is really scary, Thaddeus. What the heck is it all about?"

"I'm baffled. My own piddlings seem infantile in their simplicity by comparison. This is much more than mere repair work. What could Grandfather have been trying to achieve here?"

Thaddeus and Josephine slowly made their way down the row of columns, each one occupied by something more grotesque and frightening than the last. One contained an eight-armed spider-like thing topped with the head of what Josephine thought was a baboon. Amazingly, this horrible thing, like the others, appeared to be alive.

They rounded the corner and found a new group of glass containers glowing in a dark alcove. The vessels were smaller and rounder than the previous ones. The first, which bore a plate stamped with the number one, was shattered and the floor was slick with the vat's spilled fluid. Glass shards, rubber hoses, and other debris were scattered everywhere.

Josephine held her nose. "Phew! This looks like it was broken recently." A small sound somewhere in the room caught her attention. She glanced quickly between the rows of columns, but saw nothing. She had the strange sensation that they were being watched.

Thaddeus studied the broken cylinder's gauges closely. The indicator needles were still twitching back and forth. "I'd say it was destroyed extremely recently. The readings are still in flux."

After the awful things they had just seen in the other cylinders, Josephine didn't think the horror show could get any worse.

She was wrong.

Josephine was the first to notice the crumpled body lying next to the wall. Something about it looked vaguely familiar. She went over to see what it was and screamed so loudly, Thaddeus nearly slipped and fell on the wet floor.

"What is it, Josephine? Did you injure yourself?" he asked, shuffling over as quickly as he could. But then he saw what was wrong and went whiter than he already was.

"Look!" she whispered. "It's . . . it's you!"

The pale lump on the floor was the body of another Thaddeus.

CHAPTER 26

Thaddeus's mind reeled at the nightmare of what he saw before him. Impossibly, his own corpse was lying at his feet.

Josephine knelt and pressed her hands on the glistening body's neck, then held her ear to its chest. She shook her head. "There's no heartbeat," she said, wiping her fingers on her pajama bottoms. "It's . . . he's . . . whatever it is, is dead."

"Are you sure?" Thaddeus asked.

She nodded." I have to sit through mom's CPR class three times a year. I know how to tell."

"I . . . I don't understand this at all." The boy stared at the dead thing that looked so uncannily like himself." How can this be?"

There were his own features—the messy white hair, the pudgy face with its bulbous, warty nose in the center, the blue eyes—all staring up at him from another being, albeit one that may never have been alive. To be sure, there were differences, too. Its age was hard to guess, but it was smaller than Thaddeus, and thinner, and its body was dotted with tumors. A baseball-sized one stuck out from its forehead; smaller ones pebbled its neck. And there were deformities. The fingers on its left hand were webbed, and both hands showed two nubs where a sixth and seventh digit had started to grow.

The nightmare did not end there. Thaddeus looked up to find Josephine's attention focused on the other vats behind this one. The darkness made it difficult to see what was inside them, but as he moved closer, it became clear enough.

Vat number two contained its own horrible version of the pink-skinned, white-haired creature. This one was more amphibian than human, with bulging black eyes, tiny arms, and long-toed feet. The next, floating in vat number three, was a nearly perfect replica of the boy. The only noticeable difference was its ears. They were nothing more than little curls of cartilage.

The last vat, number four, was empty and dark.

Thaddeus tried to sort out what he was seeing. He felt as if a tsunami were crashing through his head, laying waste to his entire image of who, and what, he was. He felt as if he had become untethered from the real world. Josephine caught the boy and held him up as he staggered backward.

"I'm feeling dizzy," said Thaddeus.

"I gotcha," she said. "Try to breathe, Thaddeus. If you pass out on me, we're in big trouble."

The boy inhaled several times, and the color began to return to his face.

"What are those things? And why do they look like . . . like that?" Josephine asked.

"They appear to be clones," he wheezed, trying to get back on his feet. "Of me."

"Did your grandfather really do all this?" Josephine's voice trembled.

Thaddeus did not want to answer. Certainly the grandfather he had created in his imagination, the benevolent and wise genius the boy had idolized his whole life, would never have done such things. But the real Professor Celsius Hibble, a man Thaddeus now realized he did not know at all, apparently did do such things.

The words of Sally Twittington didn't seem so crazy after all.

"It looks that way," he said, shrugging. "Who else could have?"

"But what kind of scientist makes clones from his own grandson?" Josephine asked. "That's a crazy thing to do."

Thaddeus, having just noticed a feature shared by all the clones, was one awful step ahead of her. "I'm afraid you have it backward, Josephine," the boy said. "I think the other creatures predate me. They were probably experimental prototypes too flawed to be used."

"Prototypes? What do you mean, 'used'?"

The boy's chin began to quiver and the first tears he had ever known welled in his eyes. "I know why the last vat is empty," he said.

Thaddeus unbuttoned the first few buttons on his shirt and pulled it open, exposing his chest. On his pale skin was a mark, no bigger than a nickel.

Josephine began shaking her head. "No," she gasped. "That can't be true, Thaddeus!"

Neatly centered on his chest was the number four.

CHAPTER 27

"You can't possibly be . . . one of them," Josephine said, stubbornly denying what logic told her was true. She looked back and forth from the boy to the inhuman likenesses floating in the tubes. Each one bore the imprint of a faint number on its body.

Thaddeus was in a daze, tears dribbling down his chubby cheeks. "It is not only possible, it is true. Those pathetic creatures are my brothers, my only true family. I see now that I am nothing more than a growth, an elaborate fungus whose mother was only a bunch of cells in a petri dish!"

Josephine felt tears of her own begin to wet her eyes. "Why did your grandfather do this?"

The boy shook his head. "What grandfather? That's what Sally Twittington refused to tell us, don't you see? I am no more the grandson of Celsius Hibble than Norman is, than any one of these test tube monsters are. These things may possess my features, but they are not copies of me. We are all copies of him."

"But you're still you!" she said. "Nothing's really changed."

"Blather!" he said. "Everything has changed! I am alone. I have no parents. There won't be any coming-home party now, or feast, or Candyland tournaments. I am hardly even human."

"Don't say that! You're at least as human as anybody else I know, Thaddeus. And you're not alone as long as I'm around, I promise."

The boy looked at her, his pink chubby face blotchy from tears. He nodded and wiped a drop of snot onto his sleeve. In the tiniest voice possible he said, "I wanted Mother and Father to come back."

There was nothing Josephine could say to that. Being parent-less was too big a problem to fix with words. She tried to imagine how she would feel if her mother and father were gone, if they had never even existed. As much as her parents annoyed her sometimes, a world without them in it was too terrible to contemplate. The thought made her suddenly miss them.

"We're getting out of here now, Thaddeus." She took his hands and pulled him to his feet. "This place is evil. Let's see if there's a door somewhere."

She tugged him along as she snaked her way through the forest of glowing columns. She tried not to look at the terrible things inside them as they hurried past, but it wasn't easy. At the end of a row they came to a wall of solid rock. They turned and tried a differ-ent direction and wound up at another dead end. The sharp sound of broken glass crunching underfoot made them both stop in their tracks. Someone else was in the room with them, but it was hard to tell what direction the sound had come from. Together they held their breath, waiting for the next footfall, but it did not come. They kept waiting for what felt like a long time but heard nothing more except the quiet bubbling of the tubes.

Tentatively, Josephine took another step and looked past a column down the next row. Nothing. She looked back at Thaddeus and shrugged.

"It could have been a rat," he whispered. Fear seemed to have brought the boy back to something like normal. "Felix has found some very large ones in th—"

Thaddeus's eyes widened and his mouth formed a silent O as he pointed over Josephine's shoulder. She spun around and screamed as a tall man in a ragged suit reached for her with hands that looked like talons. In the blue darkness, she could tell that parts of the man's maniacally smiling face were missing as he moaned and lunged at her. His hands were as light as papier-mâché when Josephine knocked them away. She and Thaddeus turned and ran blindly.

They dodged in and out of the rows of columns, not daring to look back until they emerged into the open lab. They saw a door across the room and started to make a run for it when it began to open. The first thing that entered the room was someone's bare foot dripping with snow. When Josephine saw the hideous man the foot was attached to, her heart almost stopped.

CHAPTER 28

The snow had finally begun to numb Fetid Stenchley's chemical burns, allowing him to think of something other than the scalding pain in his face and chest. It occurred to him that he should probably get back inside the lab and look after his master before any other accidents happened. The newly restored professor's body was still in a fragile state. The stitching around his organs could be easily torn, resulting in leaks, not to mention the fact that a stumbling corpse might knock off an arm or leg if it happened to run into something.

The hunchback pulled himself from the snowbank and staggered back to the lab's hidden entrance. He made his way through the dark passageway and down the stairs to the lab. He opened the door expecting to see his master, but found a pair of intruders instead. One of them was a girl, who screamed when she saw him. The other was a Friend. Even from where Stenchley stood, the madman's nose told him this Friend was definitely alive.

The sound of screams could always be relied upon to arouse Cynthia's curiosity. Inside the murderer's hump, the python uncoiled and slithered out for a look. Her wide, flat head made its way into Stenchley's mouth and peeked out through his ammonia-fried lips. The snake was incensed. The sight of another of the hated white-haired creatures sent her into a writhing fit. *Kill it!* she hissed. *Kill them both!*

Stenchley felt the familiar rush of blood to his head, blinding him to all but the desire to kill. He became a ravenous beast and dropped onto all fours. He bounded across the lab toward the two intruders, oblivious to the broken glass underfoot.

"Run, Thaddeus!" he heard the girl shout.

But the pair were far too slow to elude a predator like Stenchley. He pounced on the Friend, knocking it to the floor. He pinned its flailing arms with his knees and sat on his victim's chest.

"Stop!" it shrieked. "You're hurting me!"

"Get off him!" the girl yelled, hitting the hunchback with a flurry of little punches. "Leave him alone!"

Stenchley laughed. He got his hands around the boy's chubby throat and began to choke the life out of him.

"I should have done this the first time I seen you," the madman growled. "And I would have if it weren't for that bleedin' tin man buttin' in. Once the Master made you, he forgot all about me, didn't he? Only wanted to be with his pretty little Friend, didn't he? He treated me like a dog after you came. I had to kill him for it. There weren't no other way, see? Now it's time for you to pay for all them years I spent in that cell, and there ain't no robot to stop me!"

The murderer drooled as he watched the Friend's eyes bulge with fear, the pale thing struggling in vain to breathe. Cynthia's scaly head slid out of the killer's mouth and touched noses with her victim, staring into its eyes, waiting to savor the moment of its death. Then a lightning bolt of pain made Stenchley's world go black.

The killer found himself on his back, looking up at the ceiling. His ears were ringing, and his head pounded with pain. He realized the girl must have hit him on the head with something as he was about to finish off the Friend. His crossed eyes saw two of her now looming over him, each one wearing an angry look and wielding a Louisville Slugger–sized pipe. Both girls reared back to hit him again, this time as if they were swinging for the fence.

Stenchley's hand shot out and slapped the girl's ankle, dropping her to the floor. The pipe went clanging off to the side. Stenchley, still groggy from the blow, began to crawl toward the pipe. The girl dove for it ahead of him, and he cuffed her on the head so hard that she went sliding across the floor and landed against the wall. The girl lay unconscious, slumped over like a rag doll.

Stenchley could easily have finished her off at that point, but Cynthia wanted the white-haired thing to die first. The Friend lay on the floor, coughing and gasping for air, rubbing the red finger marks on its throat. It tried to scramble away when it saw Stenchley coming, but was too weak and slow.

The madman grabbed a fistful of its white hair and pulled its head close to his own scarred face. The smell of its live flesh, so unlike the pickled one he had broken out of the tube earlier, filled his nostrils and made him salivate. This was the one he'd come for.

Like most prey just before the kill, the Friend was frozen with fear. It looked as if it wanted to speak, but was too busy hyperventilating to manage it.

Let's have a taste now—we're famished! groaned Cynthia, her forked tongue whipping at the thing's cheek, sensing its texture, its temperature, its life.

Normally, the grimy cannibal would have obeyed the python's commands instantly and devoured his prey without a thought. But this time Stenchley hesitated. The sight of the Friend's white hair, so similar to that which topped his master's head, and its eyes, absolutely identical in color to the blue of the professor's, gave him pause. Even its nose had the same shape, the same wart on the left nostril, the same single white hair protruding from it like a drooping antenna. It was almost as if he were looking at a young version of the professor himself.

He wondered what it must be like to inhabit a body that so closely resembled the professor's. For Stenchley, it would have been paradise, since he couldn't imagine anyone more perfect than his master. How fine it would be to walk down the street and have all those who looked your way see the brilliant, regal Celsius T. Hibble, instead of stooped, grotesque Fetid Stenchley. More than anything, the killer longed to know that feeling.

This urge caused a fuzzy splotch of an idea to begin to grow like mold under a kitchen sink in the madman's bruised brain. Stenchley tucked the squirming thing under his arm and carried it over to the operating gurney.

"Let me go, you fiend!" it yelped. "Help! Norman! I need you immediately! Josephine! Felix! HELP!"

Stenchley only grinned.

Perhaps it was his recent success at bringing back the professor that had stirred his imagination, or maybe it was simply that he was back home again. However it came about, he decided he should not eat the Friend just yet. In a flash of inspiration, Fetid Stenchley decided he should become the Friend instead.

Cynthia, hungrily twisting inside Stenchley's hump, did not like the idea of skipping easy meals. *Kill it now, fool! While it's alive and helpless!*

When the madman ignored her, he felt the python slither into his chest cavity. He was suddenly in excruciating pain as the snake's coils found some vital organ or other and began to squeeze. Stenchley fell to his knees and cried out, but made no move to destroy the Friend. The pain inside him became so intense, he began to lose consciousness. For all the hunchback knew, the snake might kill him if he continued to deny her, but he refused to give in this time. The idea that Stenchley could become a Friend himself was so enticing, so perfect. No amount of suffering could change his mind.

At the last possible moment, when death seemed imminent, he felt the powerful grip of the serpent's coils begin to relax. Her furious voice whispered in his head: *Hear me now. When this foolishness is finished, I will have the female. Do not resist me again, or I will show you no mercy.*

Stenchley was sure she meant it.

CHAPTER 29

If only I had my javelin! Thaddeus thought, as he struggled to get away from the madman.

The boy now found his arms and legs strapped tight to the gurney. Thick leather straps across his chest and forehead left him able to move only his fingers and eyes. He shivered with dread at the helpless reality of his predicament. He could hear the mad killer scurrying around the lab, muttering to himself, gathering tools, and priming various machinery.

Thaddeus had recognized Fetid Stenchley the moment he saw him. There had been no mistaking that deformed figure he knew so well from photographs. But the pictures failed utterly to convey the raw animal menace the madman possessed in real life. It seemed almost a stretch to call Stenchley a man at all.

The real Fetid Stenchley was smaller than Thaddeus had pictured him. In Thaddeus's mind, the life of the great Celsius T. Hibble could have been taken only by an equally great villain. The truth was that the professor had been murdered by an ugly little hyena of a man.

"What do you intend to do with me, you monster? I demand to know!" Thaddeus said, with as much authority as he could muster.

With his head immobilized, Thaddeus's eyes could follow Stenchley's movements only when the hunchback was directly in front of him. The boy soon had the horrifying realization that Stenchley was preparing to perform some sort of operation and Thaddeus was the unfortunate subject.

The crazed killer paid no attention to the boy, seemingly involved in a conversation with himself. Thaddeus could not see what the madman was doing, but could hear him clearly.

"There, there, Master. Drink this," Stenchley said. Thaddeus then heard what sounded like a dog lapping up water from a bowl.

Stenchley's footsteps moved toward him again, but there was another set of footsteps as well. These dragged more than walked. Who was with Stenchley?

"Ms. Crav—er, Josephine?" Thaddeus called hopefully. "Is that you?" There was no reply. He hadn't heard a sound from the girl since Stenchley had knocked her away.

In a second, Stenchley was at his side again, the killer's burned and distorted face gazing down at the boy.

"Looky what I have here, Master," said Stenchley proudly. "It's one of the Friends! Ain't it pretty?"

Who was he talking to?

Then Thaddeus saw. A tall, unspeakably hideous figure loomed over the table. It was the man he and Josephine had encountered in the rows of cylinders. Or what had once been a man. Now the thing was little more than a ghoulish conglomeration of rotted remains that clearly belonged in a coffin. The corpse moaned quietly and cast its milky blue eyes down at Thaddeus. It appeared to smile at the boy, but Thaddeus realized this was only an illusion caused by its lack of lips.

It was the sight of the thing's white hair that triggered the boy's first inkling of recognition. Thaddeus's stomach turned as he realized what, and who, he was looking at.

"G-Grandfather!" he gasped. He found he could refer to him no other way, even though he knew the real truth. "Is it really you?"

Thaddeus could hardly have expected the thing to respond with more than a grunt, since it lacked a tongue or lips. He was filled with wonder and horror at the same time. Here was his lifelong idol, or at least what was left of him, standing close enough to touch. In Thaddeus's dreams, this moment had always been a happy one, a boy and his grandfather reunited at last. Never could he have imagined this, a mindless corpse drooling over the clone it had concocted from a test tube.

Despite the utter wrongness of the situation, Thaddeus felt a sense of awe just the same. These were the remains of the man who had constructed the house he called home, who had designed and built Norman. This zombie was Thaddeus's own creator.

The boy's eyes blazed at Stenchley. "It was you who dug up the grave!" he yelled. "What have you done to Grandfather?"

Stenchley only giggled, then brought out an electric razor and began mowing off clumps of Thaddeus's cottony hair. He seemed to regard Thaddeus as no more than a gibbering lab rat.

The killer whistled as he worked.

"Stop it, you beast!" the boy demanded. "I don't know what you're up to, but I assure you you'll never get away with it!" Thaddeus tried to jerk his head away, but the straps were too tight.

When the job was done, he was left with a nubbly buzz cut. Stenchley, grinning stupidly, then took the razor to his own head and scraped off its greasy strands.

Thaddeus lost sight of the hunchback for a moment, but could hear him rummaging around behind the gurney. Then Stenchley returned, holding two bulbous copper helmets with colored electrical leads dangling like dreadlocks from the sides and top. He smeared a cold gel onto the boy's scalp and shoved one of the helmets onto Thaddeus's head. Stenchley jerked the helmet's strap tight under Thaddeus's chin and began sorting out the leads, plugging the ends from one helmet into the jacks of the other.

Next, the madman pulled the boy's shirt open and placed a wide suction cup over his belly button. Tubes protruding from the top of the cup ran down like spaghetti in several directions.

Stenchley then reappeared with a large hypodermic needle in

his filthy hands. Thaddeus panicked at the thought of the crazed killer jabbing him with the syringe.

"Get away from me with that!" The boy's round face flushed bright red with rage as he tried mightily to pull free of the gurney's straps. "Norman will come for me shortly, and you'll pay for this. He's a robot, and he's very large! He will squash you with ease! NORMAN!" Thaddeus was certain his faithful servant would respond to his summons, just as the robot had every time the boy had ever beckoned. "I need you at ONCE, Norman!"

Stenchley was entirely focused on his task and paid no attention to the boy's cries. He gave the syringe a thump and squirted out a stream of liquid.

Thaddeus cried out when he felt the needle enter his shoulder with a sharp sting. The thick solution burned as it seeped into the fatty tissue. Thaddeus's ears began to ring faintly, and the burn in his shoulder became a tingling warmth that flowed over his body. He guessed correctly that the injection was some sort of anesthesia and that he would soon lose consciousness. He could not bear to think of what was going to happen next.

As the narcotic slowly took effect, Thaddeus gazed up at the dead professor's horrible face. He wondered if any part of Celsius Hibble's once great mind still resided inside the moldy ghoul who now hovered over him. The thing's eyes, so similar to the ones Thaddeus saw in the mirror every day, seemed to focus on his own blue eyes. Had some remnant of memory somehow survived ten years in the grave? Was it only Thaddeus's woozy imagination, or did the corpse have some tiny idea that the boy strapped down before it was its own creation?

As if he heard Thaddeus's thoughts, the dead man raised a hand and softly stroked the boy's cheek. The stiff dried fingers with their bones protruding from husks of skin felt like chicken claws against Thaddeus's delicate face.

The last thing Thaddeus was aware of before he blacked out was the professor's index finger, as it broke off like a rotten twig.

CHAPTER 30

Sometime before dawn Norman and the little freight train arrived at the lab door with his master's "Late-Late" dinner. This meal was traditionally a large one, made up of all of the master's favorite food groups. In addition to the usual staples of candy and soda, there was a fried pie for its fruit content, canned Beanie Weenies for protein, and a can of spray cheese for dairy. This feast was always the boy's most anticipated feeding of the night. It was for this reason that Norman found it troubling that the young master and his guest were nowhere to be found when he brought the platter into the lab and announced that dinner was served.

Felix had hungrily followed the robot downstairs to the lab as well, since the meal usually included a can of Kitty Gourmet for himself.

"That's weird," the cat said. "The kid hasn't missed chow in forever." Felix wrinkled his sensitive nose at the sour fumes he detected in the air. "What's that smell?"

"Though there is a protrusion of sorts between my eyes, I have no olfactory capabilities," the robot droned. Norman put the tray down and set his logic cylinders spinning in the hope of generating an idea as to where his master might be.

"Perhaps Master Hibble and his companion are playing the hiding game," the robot speculated. "When he was somewhat shorter, the master often engaged me in such an activity. I believe I was required to count to three hundred while he concealed himself in some obscure place, then I was to search for him. For some reason, the longer it took me to find him, the greater pleasure the master found in the process."

The cat, sniffing around the floor of the lab, shook his head. "I don't think they're playin' hide and seek, Rusty. They're a little old for that kind of thing now."

Felix followed the odor to the open drain under the operating table. "Hey, look at this."

The lanky robot laboriously lowered himself down onto all fours and looked under the table.

"Someone has removed the cover from the drain," Norman observed. "Perhaps this is relevant to our search!"

Felix stuck his nose down into the drain and tried to see where it went, but the pipe was too dark. "Okay, I'll make this simple. Here's what I want you to do: Hold me by my tail and lower me down into the drain as far as you can so I can take a look around. Got it?"

Norman hesitated. "Will that not be unpleasant for you? I would not like to hurt your tail."

"Don't worry about it," Felix said. "You could drive a truck over my tail, and I wouldn't feel a thing. It's all gristle at this point. Just don't let me fall down the hole, whatever you do."

"You may rely upon me, sir."

"Drop me, and you're toast—got it?"

"I have it, sir."

"Don't drop the kitty."

"Your wish could not be more plain."

"Good man." The cat crouched at the edge of the hole and raised his tail toward the robot. "I'm ready when you are."

Norman locked Felix's tail in his iron grip and lowered him into the dark drain.

"I can't see a thing," Felix shouted from below. "But I can hear something down there. Can you get me any lower?"

"I'll try, sir." Norman lay flat on his chest and extended his arm as far down the drain as possible.

"I can hear things rattlin' around, and voices. A little lower!"

Norman clung to the tip of Felix's tail with his fingertips to allow him to descend a few inches further. Suddenly, they both heard Thaddeus's voice faintly call out, "Norman! I need you at once!"

The robot's rusty old circuits sparked and popped at the sound of his master. "That is Master Hibble! He is at the bottom of the hole!" His voice box crackled with static as he called back instinctively, "I AM COMING, MASTER HIBBLE! I SHALL BE THERE DIRECTLY!"

All of the robot's power was immediately rerouted to the sole task of reaching his master. Since Thaddeus had existed, Norman's primary directive was the boy's protection, and whenever the robot sensed Thaddeus was in danger, all other functions ceased immediately.

Unfortunately for Felix, who was dangling by the tip of his tail in the dark drain, this meant that Norman's hand was now needed for more important things. The cat's tail was immediately released, and the poor beast tumbled down the hole.

The fact that Norman was much too wide to fit into the drain was an unimportant detail to the robot. The shortest route to his endangered master was through the hole in the floor, so that was the way he intended to go. If it was too small, then he would simply have to make it bigger.

Like a huge piston, Norman rammed himself into the drain headfirst and began breaststroking his way down the hole. The lead pipe was no match for Norman's great strength. With each swipe of his powerful steel arms, Norman smashed steadily downward, sending chunks of rubble and pieces of pipe tumbling into the secret lab below.

CHAPTER 31

After Stenchley finished preparing the Friend for the operation, he opened the hatch of one of the sarcophaguslike tubes built into the large machine behind the gurney and slid the body inside. Next, he prepared his own body and climbed into the adjacent tube. An automatic timer would set the process in motion. The entire procedure would be complete in less than two hours.

Stenchley's puny brain was in fantasyland. He imagined how wonderful life would be when he was no longer trapped inside the scarred and deformed body that had always been his prison. People would no longer look at him with fear and repulsion. After the cell transferral, the Friend's features, so amazingly like the professor's, would be his. The madman would walk proudly out of the lab beside his revived master like the hunchless son he had always wanted to be. "Look!" he imagined people saying, "there goes Professor Celsius Hibble with his handsome son. What a handsome pair they are, with their handsome white hair and their handsome blue eyes! The lad is a chip off the old block!"

In Stenchley's twisted mind, no one would notice that the professor was a rotting, mumbling zombie. Everyone would be so entranced by the marvel of the well-fed youth at the famous man's side that they would forget that the professor had been dead for ten years and that he was missing several key body parts. He would be a famous boy with his famous father, admired by all. No one would ever lock Stenchley in an insane asylum again.

All these happy thoughts put Cynthia in the mood for a snack. The python noticed that the girl, lying slumped against the wall, was beginning to stir, making appetizing little murmurs as she regained consciousness.

Cynthia needs a bite, the python whispered, nosing her head into Stenchley's throat. *I let you have the boy to play your little games with, but now I want the girl!*

Stenchley felt a hunger begin rising inside him like a fever. He fell onto all fours and stalked over to the girl, his teeth bared. The hunchback sniffed his prey's delicate skin, saliva dripping from his lips. The aroma of her flesh made him dizzy with hunger.

An exposed inch of the girl's shoulder was too tempting for Stenchley to resist. *Let's start with that bit, dear*, Cynthia cooed. The madman's mouth snapped. As his yellow teeth bit at her skin, the girl's eyes popped open.

"Ow! Get away from me!" she screamed, clawing and kicking at him furiously. "Thaddeus! Help!"

But a twelve-year-old girl could not overpower Fetid Stenchley. Though she managed to scrape her nails across his face a couple of times, his apelike hands and feet held her down easily. Cynthia would gladly suffer a few nicks and scrapes to enjoy this meal.

Stenchley was so focused on his prey that he was unaware at first of the rubble and debris that began trickling from the open vent in the ceiling behind him. In seconds, however, the trickle became a cascade of rock raining down onto the floor. Stenchley turned to see a scrawny cat leap out of the old shipping crate just before a boulder smashed the box to splinters. He could have sworn the cat yelped a swear word as it scurried out of harm's way.

Instinctively, Stenchley crouched low over his victim as cracks began to open all around the hole. Then a huge section of the ceiling worked loose. With a loud boom, the chunk of rock hit the floor, followed immediately by a large, familiar robot.

☻ ☻ ☻

Norman found himself lying in a pile of rubble, unsure which way was up. He raised his head and tried to identify his location. The place looked familiar, and the robot suspected he had been there before, but could not recall the details. He tried moving his long arms and legs, which were sprawled awkwardly about him, and sensed that there was some malfunction. The gyroscope in his head whirred back online and he found his sense of balance. Slowly, he rose from the debris, rocks and dust cascading off his tuxedo. Norman methodically scanned his body, counting fingers and limbs, and immediately found a problem. Colored wires stuck out of his shoulder, their frayed ends sparking, where his left arm had been.

Felix appeared, gray with dust, and looked up at Norman. "Well, that was fun," he grumbled sarcastically, spitting a pebble from his mouth. "I'm gonna forget that you dropped me down the hole, even after I specifically asked you not to drop me down the hole, but only because I feel sorry for one-armed guys."

"Your sympathy is unnecessary," Norman stated. "I only hope my detached appendage will have no bearing on my ability to aid Master Hibble. I am sure I detected fear in his voice when he called."

Norman's steel head swiveled left and right, searching for some sign of the boy, until he spotted two people in the corner, half hidden behind a large broken piece of machinery. He identified one of the people as his master's female guest, the trespassing spy, but the other did not appear to be his master. The girl seemed to be engaged in a game of some kind—possibly wrestling—with the other person, whose back was turned.

"I beg your pardon, but is that you, Madame Prisoner?" Norman called politely, as if he were asking if she'd like some tea. "I am searching for Master Hibble. He called for me rather urgently a few moments ag—"

"Help me, Norman!" the girl yelled desperately. "He's biting me!"

"Biting? What type of game is that?"

"It's not a game, Norman! He's trying to kill me!"

"How rude!" Norman kicked the rubble away from his feet and stepped over of the pile of rock. "I am coming, madame. You may depend on me!"

Norman stomped toward the girl and her attacker. As he neared the two, the robot had a rare flash of recognition. The hunched back of the person holding her looked repulsively familiar, like a stain he had removed from valuable upholstery long ago, but that had somehow reappeared.

When the person turned to look at Norman, there was no doubt about who it was. Even with the man's head encased in the ridiculous helmet, with its mane of wires hanging down, the robot recognized his former enemy.

CHAPTER 32

The last time Norman and Fetid Stenchley had seen each other was the night of the professor's murder. Norman had been too late to save his master from the mad killer then, but had managed to keep the death toll that awful night to one. If the robot had arrived in the lab even a minute later, the Hibble family cemetery would have had two new residents.

If not for Norman's heroics that night, the police never would have dragged Stenchley away in shackles, screaming like a wildcat, to the Asylum for the Dangerously Insane. Now, somehow, the fiend had come back.

Fetid Stenchley and Norman had a long and bumpy past. When Professor Hibble first found his assistant and future murderer on the streets of Awkward Falls so long ago, Norman, still shiny and new, was at the wheel of the Rolls Royce they rode home in.

From the first moment they met, the robot and the hunchback rubbed each other the wrong way. Norman, with his regal posture, impeccable manners, and built-in revulsion toward anything less than spotlessly clean and orderly, was naturally annoyed by the grimy creature the professor brought into the robot's harmonious domain.

The professor had created Norman specifically to oversee all aspects of domestic life at Hibble Manor, and the robot was expert at his job. A tidier, more efficient household could not be found anywhere. Since the celebrated Professor Celsius Hibble loved to entertain his many notable acquaintances in those early days, Norman was accustomed to being surrounded by the erudite elite of society.

Until Fetid Stenchley arrived, all who entered Hibble Manor were bathed, groomed, and expensively dressed. No guests ate potatoes and gravy with their fingers, lapped up their soup like hounds, or blew their noses on the tablecloth. All preferred their meat cooked, at least a little. All slept in beds, rather than under them. All were, for the most part, sane.

When Norman realized the professor intended for Stenchley to stay at Hibble Manor permanently, he was appalled. To make matters worse, the professor decreed that it would be Norman's job to civilize the brutish creature. This was simply too much for the robot's logic circuits to handle, and they immediately shorted out, causing a small fire in his tuxedo. Several of Norman's key wiring bundles melted and had to be replaced.

The thought of Stenchley feeding at Norman's impeccable dining table, sleeping on Norman's crisply creased and ironed linens, traipsing about Norman's immaculate halls leaving footprints and fingerprints everywhere, and shedding on Norman's furniture, the foul creature's dander wafting about Norman's house like ragweed in springtime, was more than the robot could withstand.

But Norman accepted his task dutifully, for he was nothing if not professional. He followed the scruffy beast around like a frustrated mother whose toddler is more chimp than child. Norman found it constantly necessary to remind the little troll to remove his muddy boots before walking on the priceless twelfth-century carpet, to use the silverware to shovel his gourmet nine-course French meal down his gullet, to douse himself occasionally in one of the twenty-seven bathtubs the house possessed, to refrain from leaving droppings in the rose garden, and to do, or not do, a thousand other things.

After months of trying to force civility on Stenchley, Norman persuaded the professor that it was hopeless. A compromise was settled on, which satisfied everyone and brought harmony back to the house. Professor Hibble decided to allow Stenchley to create a living area for himself inside a small closet in the laboratory where Stenchley and the professor worked. A door to the outside was put in to allow the little hunchback easy access to the nearby forest to attend to his sanitary needs as well as his taste for raw game.

Since Stenchley preferred sleeping on straw instead of a bed, and had such crude dining habits, the closet soon resembled a stable more than a bedroom.

For a long time, this arrangement kept the peace at Hibble Manor. Even though rust and age eventually eroded Norman's built-in penchant for order and cleanliness, Norman never allowed him to enter again. As long as Stenchley confined himself to the lab and the outdoors, and Norman kept his nose out of Stenchley's closet, there were few confrontations. Even so, Stenchley had always despised the persnickety robot, and Norman had never trusted the beastly hunchback.

And then, of course, the uncivilized beast had committed the most unthinkable offense of all: murdering the professor.

CHAPTER 33

"Stedley Fenchid!" Norman said, as fragments of the madman's name found their way to the surface of his feeble memory banks. The old robot's inner alarm system jangled a warning. "Release the young lady immediately, sir!"

Stenchley had the girl's neck in the crook of his elbow and looked as if he could break her spine if he wanted to. The hunchback picked up the length of pipe that lay nearby. Holding the struggling girl with one arm and the pipe in the other hand, he leapt onto the catwalk and disappeared between the rows of glass cylinders. Norman clanked across the lab as swiftly as his elderly metal legs were able and went after him.

He found Stenchley crouched at the end of the row with his back to a tall bubbling cylinder. "You ain't sending me back to no asylum, tin man!" Stenchley grunted. "I ain't never going back!"

With Stenchley's attention focused on Norman, Josephine bit the madman's arm, hard. Felix, who had silently crept up onto an air duct above, leapt onto Stenchley's back and sank his claws into the hump.

"Run, girly!" Felix shouted, hissing and clawing at the killer's deformity.

Stenchley swore, and his grip loosened, giving Josephine the chance to wriggle free. She scurried quickly out of Stenchley's reach and jumped from the catwalk, splashing into the shallow lake of fluid covering the floor. She ran to safety behind a large gearbox and peered over the top to watch the conflict.

Now that the girl was out of the way, Norman charged up the short flight of steps and dove at the hunchback. Stenchley swung the pipe blindly, the steel clanging off Norman's thick metal chest and knocking him off balance. Before Norman could regain his footing, Stenchley swatted the cat off his back, sending it smacking into the wall, then scrambled away behind the next row of cylinders. Norman chased after him, knocking into pipes and valves, causing blasts of steam to shoot everywhere. Stenchley ran between the columns into a corner. With the wild killer trapped, Norman lunged at him. The one-armed robot snatched Stenchley up by his shirt and shook him like a rag doll.

"Where is Master Hibble?" Norman demanded.

Stenchley, eyes bulging and dizzy from being shaken, had managed to hang on to the pipe, which he now brought smashing down on the robot's head. Norman was momentarily dazed and staggered a bit, but did not let go of the madman. Before Norman could recover, Stenchley blindly swung the pipe again. This time, the blow glanced off the robot and hit the nearest cylinder dead center. The glass casing exploded, sending the noxious blue fluid inside blasting out at Norman. The robot tumbled over the railing and fell crashing to the floor, the gushing liquid pouring over him.

The moisture caused several of the robot's key circuit groups to short out, and he lay twitching and sparking, unable to get up.

Josephine ran over and tried to pull him to his feet, but the steel man was far too heavy.

"Norman, you have to get up!" she insisted. "He'll kill us all!"

"No-no-no need for concern, madame!" he answered, his voice mechanism sputtering. "I am only momentarily incapacitated . . . pacitated . . . pacitated. . . ."

"Oh, no!" she shrieked. "It's getting out!"

Norman looked up to see a large creature of unknown species climbing out of the shattered glass cylinder. The thing swayed unsteadily, dripping hoses and cables hanging from its body and neck. Then Stenchley stumbled over with the pipe and swung, breaking open the next cylinder. A waterfall of fluid gushed out and bowled Stenchley over. The creature that emerged this time was even larger and more dangerous looking than the previous one.

Laughing madly, Stenchley struggled to his feet, ran to the next cylinder, and smashed it as well, releasing another of the bizarre creatures in a flood of blue liquid. The hunchback went right down the line, slamming the pipe into the glass tanks, giggling like a child at each new monstrosity that emerged.

"Must find Master Hib . . . Hib . . . Hibble . . ." Norman said to Josephine.

"He's over there!" Josephine said. She pointed across the lab to the contraption behind the empty gurney. The boy's jacket and glasses lay strewn on the floor, his body just visible through a small window set into the machine's hatch.

"That ain't no tanning bed," said Felix. "We gotta get him out of there now!"

Felix and Josephine ran to the machine and tried to open the hatch, but found that it was locked tight. There wasn't even a handle or lever to pull on.

"Press a button or something!" said Felix. "There has to be a release catch somewhere."

Josephine pressed and punched and pulled every likely-looking button and switch on the control panel, but the door remained sealed tight.

"Break the glass!" Felix suggested.

Josephine pounded the window with her fists, but it was inches thick and reinforced with an embedded mesh of wire. She found a wrench and began hammering at the window, but wasn't strong enough to break the glass.

"It's too thick!" she grunted. The thought flashed through her mind that she should've done more push-ups in PE class.

"Rusty, we need you!" Felix shouted to the robot. "Can you walk?"

Norman struggled in vain to get to his feet. His internal damage control systems whirred and clicked, trying to reroute circuits and bypass malfunctioning parts, but the damage was too widespread.

"I regret to say I am rather discombob-bob-bobulated," Norman said, matter-of-factly. "My right arm appears to be my only working-king-king limb."

With great determination, the faithful old robot reached out his hand and tried to drag himself across the flooded floor toward his master. His heavy steel body was deadweight, however, and he was able to move only inches at a time.

Meanwhile, Stenchley completed his cylinder-bashing spree. When all the containers were shattered, their bizarre contents twisting and flopping around on the floor like newborn demons, he threw back his head and howled. A few of the creatures had already gotten to their feet and started moving around. They began sniffing and growling at each other like a pack of wild dogs, their strength building with each passing second.

Felix's eyes grew wide. "Don't look now, sister. I think the natives are getting restless."

As the creatures snapped their teeth hungrily, Josephine could see that it was only a matter of time before the things noticed them. She had to get Thaddeus out of the machine *now*.

Stenchley, cackling madly, seemed to have no fear of the creatures. He made an angry guttural bark and came splashing through the blue liquid toward Josephine, Felix, and Norman, knocking into a couple of the creatures as he came. The electrical leads on the helmet bounced wildly around his head like Medusa's snakes.

"Here comes trouble!" warned Felix, hopping onto the top of the console, readying himself for a fight.

Josephine glanced over her shoulder at Stenchley as she banged the locked hatch harder with the wrench, each swing sending a stab of pain into her shoulder where Stenchley's filthy teeth had pierced her skin. She could almost feel the army of bacteria that was surely swarming over the wound.

Finally, a crack appeared in the glass of the hatch's window. "It's starting to break!" she said. "Try to keep him away. I need a little more time!"

Felix arched his back and twitched his tail angrily. He snapped his claws out like switchblades and summoned up an impressive growl as the killer came his way.

Stenchley never made it that far. As he bounded over Norman's prone figure toward Josephine and Felix, the robot's steel claw shot up and clamped onto the madman's ankle. Stenchley crashed to the floor and the pipe flew out of his hands, rolling to a stop at the feet of the huge buffalo-headed creature.

Stenchley thrashed and twisted to try and free himself from the robot's iron grip, but Norman's remaining arm was as strong as ever. His claw squeezed the madman's ankle tighter and tighter, until Stenchley shrieked.

The huge buffalo-headed thing became interested in the tubular object that had clanged to the floor and landed at its feet, obviously trying to determine if it was edible. It nudged the pipe with its black muzzle, sniffing and licking at it. With every nudge, it moved the thing a little closer to Stenchley and Norman.

The hunchback stretched for the pipe, kicking at Norman's head with all his might, but the robot only squeezed harder. Stenchley got a finger on the pipe, then two fingers. The buffalo-headed beast bit at the pipe, moving it another inch in the madman's direction. In one swift motion, Stenchley's fingers grabbed the pipe and swung it hard at Norman's head.

In the split second it took for the pipe to swing through the air toward his head, the robot's mechanical brain calculated its speed and trajectory, and generated a probable damage assessment. Unless Norman released Stenchley's ankle and rolled away from the blow, there was a 98.6 percent chance that the robot's central control circuits would be destroyed and all his systems would shut down. On the other hand, if Norman released the killer's ankle, there was a 76 percent chance his master might be harmed.

The decision was simple. Even if it meant his own destruction, Norman would never allow the killer to endanger his master.

The robot squeezed harder.

Stenchley screamed in pain just as the pipe crashed into Norman's steel forehead.

CHAPTER 34

Norman lay forlorn and motionless on the lab floor, the red lights of his eyes now dark. Though his arm was missing and his head broken open like a steel melon, its jumble of wires and circuits now twisted and mangled, the noble machine-man still held the hunchback's ankle firmly in his grasp.

Fetid Stenchley pulled and kicked at the cold steel hand, trying to pry the robot's fingers from his leg. He banged on it with the pipe, but had no success. He may as well have been in leg irons.

The madman looked around and saw Josephine and Felix trying to open the hatch on the machine that held Thaddeus's body. Stenchley, with his leg now tethered to the heavy robot, was like a mad dog on a short leash. He grunted and swung the pipe as he stretched toward Josephine.

Felix dashed in and out of range, jabbing and slashing at Stenchley quickly, then jumping back to safety again. "Rusty!" he called to his old friend. "Speak to me, Rusty!" But Norman did not move.

"Felix, look out!" called Josephine.

The cat easily dodged a flurry of the madman's blows. "Don't worry, girl. I'll slice and dice this chump like a—"

Felix's eyes almost popped out of his head when he looked up and saw that Josephine's warning was not about Stenchley. The buffalo-headed beast was behind the madman, pawing at the floor. The huge, horned thing had found its legs and was eyeing the little group next to the gurney as if it badly wanted to crash their party. With a loud snort, the thing swatted Stenchley to the floor with a paw the size of a frying pan. It was a knockout blow, leaving Stenchley down for the count.

The beast seemed to briefly consider the hunchback's culinary merit, but stepped past him and instead took an interest in the bite-sized morsel that was Felix. The beast sniffed the scruffy cat as if it were trying to decide which end to eat first.

"Whoa, now, nice buffalo thingy," said Felix, his eyes wide. He began inching backward, away from the creature's large mouth. "You don't want me, I'm all gristle and bone. Empty calories. If you eat me now, you'll be hungry again in ten minutes!"

Josephine had to think of a way to distract the creature. She looked around frantically for anything that might be useful and saw something lying under the gurney. Josephine snatched the object from the shallow fluid and was shocked to find herself holding a rotted finger. There was no time to find anything else, so she swallowed her revulsion and eased over toward the hideous creature and his intended snack.

She crept forward carefully, holding the rotten finger out as if it were a delicious treat. Her heart skipped a beat as the thing noticed her approach and raised its awful black head. A low growl as deep as thunder rumbled from inside the beast.

"Here you go, big guy." She forced her voice to sound calm, even though she was terrified. "I've got a nice yummy finger for you. Mmmmm."

The buffalo-headed creature stuck its nose out toward the finger and sniffed. Josephine wondered if it was sniffing her or the finger.

"Felix?" she whispered, keeping her eyes trained on the beast's face. "Can you hear me?"

"Roger that," he whispered back.

"When I count to three, I'll give it this finger, and we'll back away slowly, okay?" she said, even softer than before.

"Good plan."

"One . . ."

The creature stuck its tongue out to taste the finger.

"Two . . ."

It liked it. Its eyes suddenly widened, and its nostrils flared. The creature's gaping red mouth flew open, giving Josephine a close look at its impressive teeth.

"Three." She tossed the finger into the thing's mouth.

Josephine and Felix tiptoed backward as softly as they could, watching the beast closely as they went. It swallowed the finger whole and was immediately ready for another. The creature bellowed insistently and began lumbering after them, snorting gusts of snot as it came.

"I hope you have some more corpse fingers in your pocket!" Felix muttered out of the side of his mouth. "Looks like feeding time at the petting zoo."

To her horror, Josephine saw that the rest of the mutated creatures were following expectantly behind the buffalo-headed beast. They all wanted a finger.

"I don't have anything else to give them! What do we do now?"

The buffalo-headed creature must have sensed that Josephine had no more treats to offer, for its demeanor suddenly darkened. It bared its teeth and snarled menacingly.

"Uh-oh," Felix said. "I think it wants more than a finger!"

All the horrifying creatures, now moving as a grunting, snorting herd, came alongside the buffalo-headed beast. Josephine felt their eyes scanning her, watching every move she made, as they stalked closer and closer.

Josephine backed into a wheeled table loaded with a tray of stainless-steel surgical tools with a clatter. The sudden noise was all it took to cause the mutant horde to charge. The beasts stampeded toward Josephine and Felix. The buffalo-headed beast, leading the pack, lunged at Josephine, its huge jaws snapping at her heels as she turned and ran. Another creature, one that resembled a six-legged

panther, swiped a massive paw at Felix, its knife-size claws slicing the cat's tail off at the root. The creatures now seemed mad for blood and seemed likely to get it any second.

"There's a door in the corner, over there!" Felix yelled.

Josephine saw it too, but suspected they'd never make it. The creatures were too big and fast. Still, it was their only hope, and she ran for it faster than she'd ever run before. With every step, she expected to feel teeth tear into her back.

Josephine was truly surprised when she reached the door untouched. She quickly turned the handle and slipped out into a dark corridor. She was about to slam the door behind her when she noticed that Felix was not with her. In fact, he was nowhere in sight.

"Felix!" she yelled. "Where are you?" There was no answer, nor was there time to call again. The creatures were still charging toward her, but not as closely as they should have been. Felix must have distracted them somehow. That had to be the only reason she was still in one piece.

Josephine hated the thought of leaving Thaddeus, Felix, and Norman inside the lab, but she had no choice. With the gang of huge, nightmarish beasts bearing down on her, it would have been suicide to go back inside.

"Felix, I'll be back. I promise!" she yelled quickly, then jerked the door shut just before the rampaging beasts caught up with her. There was no way to lock the door, nor anything available to barricade it with, so she ran up a long flight of stone steps, which seemed to be the only way out. She heard the creatures slamming repeatedly into the door behind her as she took the steps two at a time. Thankfully, the beasts did not have a clear understanding of how doorknobs worked. At the top of the steps was a heavy stone door, which she managed to shove open just wide enough to squeeze out.

Josephine found herself outside, behind the mansion in knee-deep snow. The storm had finally blown itself out, and now only an occasional snowflake drifted down. The sky showed signs of a cold gray dawn that was just beginning to break. She ran around to the side of the house toward her crossing place in the wall, certain that she had only seconds to climb to the other side before the awful things came tearing around the house after her. She bounded through the Hibble graveyard, past the crooked stones topped with snow, and scrambled up and over the wall.

She glanced over her shoulder as she raced through the trees on the other side and was glad to see she was not being followed yet. In a moment, she was at her own kitchen door. Josephine waited before going inside, even though she was half frozen, her coat and hat still in the parlor at Hibble Manor. She stood completely still and held her breath, shivering and listening carefully for the sickening sound of hooves and paws behind her.

But there was nothing, only the solemn hush of a place after a heavy snowfall.

CHAPTER 35

Josephine dashed through the kitchen door, feeling the blessed warmth of her own house envelop her as she skidded inside. How could it have been only a few hours ago that she walked out of this same door? It seemed like years.

For a moment, she was thrown off by the contrast between the cozy, peaceful world of her house and the bizarre place she had escaped from just minutes ago. She almost let herself believe that it was all going to be fine, that she was safe now. She could have a nice plate of pancakes with her mom and dad, and things would be normal again.

But things were not fine, and none of the people she cared about were safe, including her parents. The gruesome creatures from the lab were undoubtedly still after her and could easily track her to this very spot.

Josephine tore through the living room and up the stairs, yelling, "Mom! Dad! Wake up, wake up!"

She knew she had to tell her parents everything, immediately. She prayed they would believe her. At this point, it would be a good thing if they did call the police, since her family alone was no match for those monsters. She would figure out how to keep Thaddeus out of the orphanage later. First she had to keep him alive.

Howard, his hair all pointing northwest, appeared at the top of the stairs in his pajamas. "What is it, Jo? What's going on?"

"You guys have to get up!" she called. "It's a major emergency! We have to get in the car and get out of here, now. Hurry!"

Howard rubbed his eyes. "What on earth are you talking about?"

"I'll explain in the car while we're driving to the police station!" She ran back into the kitchen and picked up the phone. She quickly punched in 911 and waited impatiently for an operator. It took her a moment to realize there was no dial tone. The line was dead.

Howard came in and repeated, "What's going on, Jo?"

It was all so complicated, she didn't know where to start. All she could think of was Thaddeus and Felix and Norman back there, possibly dead or dying, and the raging horde of mutant creatures that would soon be attacking her family.

"Get the car started, Dad!" She jerked the keys off the hook by the door and slapped them into his hand. "We have to get help, right now! Where's Mom? Mom!" she yelled. "Come on!"

Howard grabbed Josephine's shoulders and made her stop for a second. "Now, hold on just a minute," he said, in his patient, fatherly way. "First, I want you to calm down and tell me what's wrong."

Josephine grimaced and pulled away from him when he touched her wounded shoulder. "Ouch!"

"Jo! You're hurt!" Howard saw the tear in her shirt and the red stain around it. "What happened?"

"Dad, it really is a long story, and I swear I'll tell you the whole thing as soon as we're in the car. We're in so much danger right now, my bite wound is the least of our problems. You have to believe me!"

"Bite wound? You have a bite wound?"

She heard her mother's footsteps coming down the stairs. "Howard? Is everything okay?" Barbara shuffled into the kitchen and yawned.

"Jo has just been telling me that we're in some kind of serious danger," Howard said. "And that she has a bite wound on her shoulder."

"Listen to me, you guys! We have to get out of here, now!"

"I believe you, Jo, but before we go speeding off to the police station at six o'clock in the morning—"

"Police station?" Barbara looked at them as if they were nuts.

"—in three feet of snow, you have to get me in the ballpark here," Howard went on. "Why are we in danger? What's so urgent?"

"Danger?" Barbara's voice rose an octave. "Oh, my gosh, Josephine, is that blood on your pj's? Are you hurt?" She immediately reached for Josephine's shoulder, but the girl pushed her hands away.

"No, Mom, it's nothing! I mean, it is, but we don't have time!" Josephine bit her lip and glanced anxiously out the window at the side yard. If the creatures followed her footprints, that's where they'd be coming from. A cardinal flitted in the trees, but she saw nothing else.

Josephine saw that she'd never get her parents out the door unless she told them the whole crazy story now. "Okay, here goes, and I swear this is all totally true." She took a deep breath and went for it, trying to tell only the important parts, as fast as possible. "There's this cloned kid named Thaddeus, who lives in the house next door with a cat and a robot, the one the librarian told us about. And Fetid Stenchley, the crazy murderer who escaped from the asylum, is over there too, but I think he's unconscious now, and all of them are in this weird lab, which is where I was too, until a few minutes ago when I escaped, and actually I was there all night, and the night before, and I'm really sorry I didn't tell you about it before, but anyway, the kid and the robot and the cat didn't escape, and they might be hurt, and we have to get the police or the army or somebody over there to help them, because there are these . . . things . . . with big teeth and claws and stuff you wouldn't believe, and they're after me, and they're probably going to show up right here any second now and try to kill us, because of all the stupid footprints I left in the snow, so can we get in the car and go get help now, please?"

Howard and Barbara's foreheads formed interesting wrinkles as they tried to digest what Josephine had just told them. They stared at her, then at each other, then back at her again.

Howard tapped his fingertips on his palm as if he were calling a time-out in a basketball game. "I'm sorry, dear, that's an awful lot of surprising information to swallow in one bite. Let's take it a little at a time. You say you've been in the old house next door all night?"

"Yes."

"And the night before?" Barbara asked, incredulously.

"Yes."

"And there's an injured boy in there?" continued Howard. "And he's a clone?"

"Right."

"And the escaped killer is there, too?" Barbara asked. "Are you sure?"

"I'm positive. It's all true!" Josephine pulled her torn sleeve up and showed them her wound. "See this? That's where the crazy guy bit me!"

Her parents gasped simultaneously. The madman's ugly teeth marks showed clearly on her shoulder.

"Oh, Jo!" cried Barb. "We have to get you to a doctor."

"I'll get the car started." Howard threw on his coat and ran out the door.

Barbara wanted to clean the wound before leaving the house, but Josephine refused, insisting that there wasn't time. They grabbed coats, hats, and gloves and hurried out the front door. The car was completely coated in a layer of ice topped with snow. It looked like an ice sculpture. When they cracked open the door and crawled inside with Howard, Josephine realized something was wrong. Her father was turning the key, but the engine wasn't making a sound.

"The engine block is frozen," Howard said. "It must be below zero out here."

"Maybe we can find a neighbor to drive us," Josephine suggested.

"Okay, we'll make a run for it." Howard pulled his Packers hat down as low as possible. "Let's move quickly, though. In this weather, it won't take long for frostbite to set in."

But before they could open their doors, a small animal fell onto the car's ice-caked windshield.

"What the heck is that?" Barbara said.

Howard wiped at the inside of the frozen windshield. "Looks like a squirrel."

But Josephine knew immediately that the animal was no squirrel.

"Felix!" She jumped out of the car and took the cat in her arms. "Oh, Felix, I'm so glad to see you! Are you all right?"

"P-p-peachy," he stammered, his teeth chattering in the frosty air.

"How did you get away? I was afraid they'd gotten you."

"N-n-no way," he bragged. "I s-s-still got a few m-moves."

"You're half frozen. Here, let's get you warmed up." Felix let Josephine tuck him inside her overcoat, with only his face peeking out between the top two buttons. "What about Thaddeus?" she asked hopefully.

The cat shook his head. "Couldn't get to him. Too many teeth snapping at me. But don't you worry, we'll get him out. We gotta get help fast, though. No tellin' what's goin' on over there."

The confidence in Felix's voice was comforting. Josephine wanted to believe him.

"Those are your folks, I presume?" He nodded at the two adults inside the Volvo.

"Yes, they are. Mom, Dad!" Josephine called to her parents as they got out of the car. "This is Felix, Thaddeus's cat I told you about!"

"Oh, how nice," said Barbara. "What an interesting-looking fellow he is!"

The cat's appearance was strange enough to make Howard and Barbara do a double take, with its mismatched parts stitched together like a crazy quilt. But their jaws dropped open in disbelief when it spoke to them in a gruff, manly voice that came straight from the streets of Brooklyn.

"Glad ta meetcha. You people got any weapons?"

Barbara and Howard looked at each other incredulously, too stunned by the talking cat to answer.

"You know," the cat continued, "flamethrowers, harpoons, bazookas, anything like that?"

"We were just going to get the police," Josephine said to Felix. "The car's dead, but we're going to try to make a run to the neighbor's house."

Felix shook his head. "You'll never make it. The bad guys are right on my tail."

Josephine turned toward Hibble Manor. Through the swirling clouds of snow, dark shapes were moving among the trunks of the hemlock trees.

"Oh, my God!" cried Barbara. "What are those things?"

Howard couldn't take his eyes off Felix. "Did that cat just speak? Or am I losing it?"

"We have to get back inside the house!" Josephine said. "If they catch us out here, we're dead!"

CHAPTER 36

The laboratory was quiet when Fetid Stenchley regained consciousness after being walloped by the paw of the buffalo-headed beast. His head throbbed in time with his pulse as he surveyed the wreckage around him. Although much of the lab's equipment had been destroyed during the mayhem he had caused as he freed the mutants from their enclosures, he was happy to see that the cell-transfer machine was still intact. The Friend was still sealed inside the sarcophagus, anesthetized and ready for the transforming operation.

Most importantly, his master was there, too. The revived corpse of Professor Celsius Hibble loomed crookedly nearby, watching his former assistant and murderer with one eye while the other looked elsewhere.

When Stenchley tried to get to his feet, a bolt of pain shot through his leg, reminding him that the troublesome robot's steel claw was still locked onto his ankle. After a half hour of frantic banging, wrenching, and filing, he finally resorted to a blowtorch to free himself.

The madman flung the robotic appendage aside and returned to his work, excitedly making final preparations for the operation. Nothing could stop him now. Stenchley took the dead man's hand and kissed it admiringly. "It won't be long now, Master. I will soon be a handsome Friend, and we will leave here forever."

Very soon, Stenchley and his Master would finally be the father-and-son team the hunchback had always dreamed of.

☠ ☠ ☠

It was a tribute to the professor's ingenious design that the cell-transfer machine could compensate for certain mistakes made by its operator. Thousands of things could have gone wrong during the procedure Stenchley undertook to transform himself into Thaddeus, yet only a few dozen actually did. As he turned the knobs to set the voltage levels, plugged wires into receptors, fixed the intricate settings on the synchro-pump, activated the automatic timer switches, and crawled inside the tube, he luckily guessed correctly more than he guessed incorrectly. When the machine reached full power, it sounded like a swarm of football-sized bumblebees, shook like a paint mixer, and belched smoke like an eighteen-wheeler, but nothing exploded; no fires broke out.

At lightning speed, the machine scanned the ten trillion or so cells that made up Thaddeus's body to locate its control cells, or CCs.

These were cells whose job it was to organize the accurate rejuvenation of skin, hair, organs, bones, and so forth, ensuring that a transformed person would look the same as the original. Every time the machine found CC clusters, the synchro-pump sucked them from the Friend's body and sent them into Stenchley's, routing them to the correct areas, where they picked up working right where they had left off. The only difference was, now they were working in the wrong body.

The madman's body vibrated inside the coffinlike tube as the imported CCs rapidly began building the Friend's features in place of Stenchley's. Without anesthesia, the process would have been unbearably painful for any normal person. But for Stenchley, whose nervous system was nearly prehistoric, it was no more than an annoyance. Even if he had been in excruciating pain, however, he would have been more than happy to bear it in exchange for the makeover he hoped to achieve.

In the flashing red light of the sarcophagus, the hunchback rolled his eyes down and watched as his crooked nose slowly changed shape. First it straightened, then became bulbous and round, with the distinctive wart and single protruding hair finally sprouting at the far end. He felt his flesh become plumper and softer, less leathery. His scalp tingled as cottony white hair sprouted on his head, overtaking the sparse, greasy stuff that had previously populated his pate. Even the hunchback's black eyes lightened and took on a bluish tinge.

It was working, at least on the surface. Bit by bit, Stenchley was beginning to look like the professor's favorite Friend.

In the adjacent tube, where Thaddeus lay unconscious, things were not going so swimmingly. Parts of the boy were beginning to look like Stenchley, but the changes were unstable. As clumps of the boy's own control cells left his body, some of Stenchley's did arrive to replace them. The problem was that not enough of the madman's cells were making the journey. Stenchley had erroneously set up the process to transfer cells mostly in one direction: from the Friend's body into his own. That was a big mistake.

If Stenchley had been a microbiophysicist instead of a deranged lunatic, he would have realized that he had just created a war zone inside Thaddeus's body. The two cellular armies, one composed of invaders from Stenchley's body, one of defenders from Thaddeus's, were evenly matched. The madman's cells were winning the battle for the moment, causing many of the boy's body parts to take on the ugly shape of Stenchley's. But the invading army would need reinforcements to hold the ground they had gained, reinforcements that were not coming. Even as Thaddeus's defeated cells retreated, their microscopic generals were planning a counterattack.

This was war, and like all other wars, it wouldn't be pretty.

CHAPTER 37

Felix paced to and fro on the back of the sofa, giving orders like Davy Crockett at the Alamo. "They could hit us any second now!" the cat warned, addressing his force of three. "Anything we can do to slow them down could save our gizzards. I want every door and window locked tight. Nail 'em shut if you can!"

"Right!" answered Josephine. "Dad, where's the hammer?"

Howard was still too awed by Felix's abilities to focus. "I don't get it, Jo. The cat can talk? How is that possible? Is this a trick or something?"

Felix marched over to Howard and looked right at him. "Get over it, Pops. I can whistle 'Dixie' and tap-dance, too, if you're interested. And if you think that's weird, wait'll you get a load of those hungry freaks outside. Now, where's that hammer?"

Howard looked more puzzled than ever, but he obediently went off to find the hammer. The scruffy cat, with its swollen black eye and the gnawed-off nub where its tail used to be, was not exactly inspiring to look at, but the voice that miraculously came out of its mouth was that of a leader. The cat was definitely in charge.

Howard quizzed his daughter as they worked. "Jo, I think it might be helpful to have a few more facts about what we're up against here. Can you tell me a little more about the physiology of those creatures out there? What are they like?"

"I think they're mutants of some kind," she said. "Different species all mixed together, with some mechanical stuff thrown in. One of them has kind of a buffalo head, but the body of something else."

Felix added gruffly, "Imagine grizzly bears, except bigger, uglier, and starved. Then imagine us as lunch, and you've got the idea. Where's the door to the basement?"

"Right over there." Josephine pointed.

"Good. Once we batten down the hatches, that's where we'll hunker down and make our stand, got it?" The cat hopped down and strode off to inspect the basement.

Howard and Barb watched in amazement as the cat reached up with its front paws, flung open the door, and disappeared down the stairs.

Josephine found some boards her mother had planned to make shelves with and began nailing them across the doorframe. As she hammered, she realized that her parents were in shock, still not fully accepting the reality of the situation. They wandered around looking dazed, hesitantly checking windows and doors, as if they still held out hope that this might turn out to be some crazy dream.

As Barbara closed the drapes she had hung on the parlor window the day before, she screamed, "Oh, my heavens, Howard, look!"

On the other side of the glass was the giant spiderlike creature Josephine had seen in the lab, its fierce baboon's head peering in at them. It raised one of its eight long arms and smacked the window with its mechanical pincer. The thing opened its mouth and made an angry guttural hiss, its steel fangs dripping fluid. Behind the spider creature, the buffalo-headed beast stamped around the driveway, butting the station wagon over and over again until the window of the old car was caved in. Then it rammed its head inside and began eating the upholstery.

Howard caught his terrified wife as she dove into his arms. He opened his mouth to speak, but no words came out.

Josephine's heart jumped into her throat. The intense fear she had felt earlier that morning flooded back into her system as if a dam had broken. Watching the old station wagon being attacked by the bizarre monster shook Josephine to the core. Seen in broad daylight, the awful creatures were all the more frightening now that they had crossed over from the surreal confines of the lab into the "real" world of cars and parents.

Howard became a man possessed. "Find some more boards! We have to hurry!"

He shoved a chair up to the wall and began madly hammering boards across the window. Nails skittered on the floor as he grabbed handfuls of them from a coffee can. On the other side of the glass, the spider creature snapped its pincers, confused and infuriated by the invisible barrier.

Felix appeared again and shouted, "Everybody down to the basement, pronto!"

Howard didn't want to stop now that he'd seen the creatures. Josephine and her mother had to pull him away from the window. "Come on, Howard!" cried Barbara. He hammered a final nail and reluctantly hopped down from the chair.

As they all ran across the room to the basement door, one of the spider's pincers crashed through the window and began swiping back and forth. Barbara, Howard, and Felix hurried down the stairs, with Josephine bringing up the rear. A second pane shattered just before she closed the door and followed everyone through the dark doorway.

In the basement, Howard found a pull string hanging from the low ceiling that turned on a bare lightbulb. The terror Josephine saw on her parents' faces in the dim light frightened her almost as much as the beasts gathering outside.

Thankfully, Felix started barking commands immediately, giving them no time to dwell on their fear. "Okay, Pops, get busy with your hammer, and nail that door shut. Use anything you can to reinforce it! Pull boards from the wall if you have to."

Felix paced in front of the terrified family. "I gotta feeling those things are chasing us just because we're running from 'em. Dogs are the same way. You run, they chase."

"It's true," said Howard. "Pursuit is often a reflexive reaction to fear. The creatures may be as frightened as we are."

Felix nodded. "Yeah, but they got fangs and claws. They might be so scared they'll slice us to shreds. Now that we riled 'em up, we gotta fight back. Sis, you look around for something flammable, like oil or paint thinner. Missus, I need brooms, mops, any kind of sticks you can find, and some rags."

"Torches?" guessed Howard.

"That's right," said Felix. "Those things are basically dumb animals. My hunch is that they will be afraid of fire. If they break in here, we may be able to hold them at bay with torches."

Josephine hurried around the basement, which was kept warm by the furnace rumbling in the center of the room. She looked through shelves stacked with a hundred years of junk. She found dozens of half-empty paint cans, jars, and coffee tins filled with nails; boxes of old magazines; lightbulbs; cleaning supplies; and, finally, a big jar of clear liquid labeled oil of turpentine.

Barbara quickly found two old mops hanging in a corner and used a handsaw to cut the handles off them. There was a box of dirty paint rags that she used to wrap the ends of the sticks.

"Perfect!" said Felix. "Now let's soak the rags in the turpentine and get them ready to light. We'll need matches, too."

Howard finished nailing some two-by-fours over the door and ran down the steps to help with the torch making. He opened a

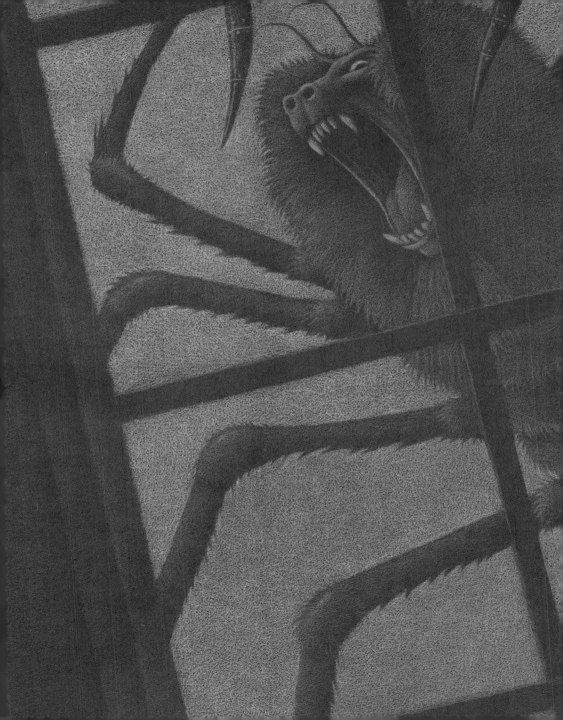

drawer in the worktable against the wall and found a rusty cigarette lighter that still worked.

Upstairs, it sounded as if a party for all the biggest, fiercest animals in the zoo was about to begin and the guests were all arriving at the same time. First, they heard a loud crash that sounded like the window had been completely knocked in and was now being used as a door. Then, a drumroll of heavy footsteps came stomping in the house upstairs. Felix and Josephine cringed when they heard the rumbling bellow of the buffalo-headed beast signaling his arrival. The house shuddered with several more crashes, as if the walls were being bashed in. The old floorboards cracked and popped under the massive weight of the things that were stampeding into the house. Josephine wondered if the floor itself was about to crash down on top of them.

Josephine was sure the things would soon sniff out their hiding place and come charging into the basement. Certainly no door was likely to stop them for long, if the huge things decided they wanted in. The basement suddenly felt more like a trap than a safe haven. With the creatures invading the house, the safest place to be was outside. She suggested as much, and Felix agreed.

"Good thinkin'," he said. "Everybody look around. See if there's a back door or a window anywhere."

They all fanned out into the dark corners of the basement. As they crept around, looking behind piles of dusty furniture and under tables stacked with boxes, the riot above their heads grew louder and louder. The beasts were snarling and growling angrily, slamming into the walls and floor. Josephine heard more glass breaking than seemed possible. It sounded like the creatures were literally ripping the house apart.

Josephine hurried around the basement, scanning the upper part of the walls for a window. It wasn't easy, since the walls were mostly covered by shelves and stacks of boxes. She noticed a sliver of light leaking in above the laundry area and climbed on top of the rusty washing machine. When she pushed aside a stack of ancient canned tomatoes on a high shelf, she found what she was looking for.

"There's a window over here," she called. The glass was iced over, and she couldn't see anything outside. "It's small, but maybe we can get out this way."

Felix hopped onto the shelf for a look, sizing up the opening. "It'll be a tight squeeze for your folks, but it's worth a try. Can you get it open?"

Josephine turned the small hand crank on the side of the window, and it slowly opened out like an awning. Snowflakes blew in on a gust of icy wind. The window was only intended as a vent, however, and stopped after about six inches.

"It doesn't open wide enough!" she said.

Howard climbed onto the washing machine with Josephine to have a look. "I could remove the window frame," he suggested. "Then we could climb out of the opening."

"No, that'll take too long!" Felix snapped. "We got minutes at the most. Just break the glass and get the heck out!"

Barbara tossed Howard the hammer, and he began knocking out the glass. Sheets of ice fell into the basement when the window-pane shattered.

"Hurry with the window, Howard!" Barbara called. "Something's growling on the other side of the door! I can hear it!"

Josephine heard it too. Whatever it was began slamming into the rickety door, making it very clear that it would be joining them shortly.

"I think we should light the torches now," said Barbara. "The door's going to give way any second."

"Light 'em up!" Felix yelled. "And get ready to stand your ground."

Howard passed the hammer to Josephine. "Here, Jo, you finish knocking out the glass. I'll help your mother." He jumped down from the washer and gathered the makeshift torches, holding out the ends for Barbara to light.

A huge paw plunged through the door, sending wood chips flying. The thing's claws slashed wildly, searching for a target.

Barbara picked up the lighter with trembling hands and flicked at the little steel wheel. Sparks jumped from the flint, but no flame appeared.

The paw crashed through the door again, widening the hole. A snarling black muzzle appeared in the opening. With another punch, the door was history. The buffalo-headed creature came blasting through like a freight train, splintering the door, the boards Howard had nailed up, and a large chunk of the surrounding wall into a cloud of tiny pieces. The massive beast's momentum sent it somersaulting down the stairs, crashing into a tall rack of shelves against the opposite wall. A half dozen cans of yellow house paint toppled down from the upper shelves onto the thing's head; one can broke open and spilled over the beast's black fur.

The huge creature lay sprawled on its back only a few feet away from Barbara, chomping a piece of the broken door. Her hands shook uncontrollably as she fumbled desperately with the lighter, and it clattered to the floor. The creature writhed and flailed. It would be up in a moment. Barbara picked up the lighter and flicked at it repeatedly, but it refused to light.

"We need those torches now, missus," Felix ordered. "Quick, before it gets up!"

Barbara's heart drummed in her throat. "I think the lighter's out of fuel!"

"Strike the flint close to the torch, dear," Howard said. "The sparks should be enough to ignite it."

The buffalo-headed creature grunted and shook its ugly head, flinging yellow paint this way and that. It rose to its feet. Barbara held the lighter next to the torch's turpentine-soaked rag and flicked the roller. At the instant the spark flew from the lighter, the rag burst into flames, singeing Howard's eyelashes in the process. He lit the other torch off the first one and handed it to Barbara. The beast reared up and bellowed as they thrust the flaming broomsticks at its face. It reluctantly began to back away from the fire.

Barbara shrieked as another creature smashed through the opening. It leapt through the hole into the basement, landing with a heavy thunk behind the buffalo-headed creature. The thing had the flat, wet snout of a boar and the remnants of a throw pillow speared on one of its long curved tusks. Two extra legs, ill formed and useless, hung from its front shoulders. Its wide red eyes looked panicked.

"How are you coming along with the window, Jo?" Howard called. "These rags won't burn for long!" The flames were already smaller than they had been just a few seconds ago.

"Almost done, Dad." Josephine found it nearly impossible to stay focused on her task of hammering out all the glass from the little window with such frightening mayhem taking place behind her. She frantically smashed the last of the jagged shards away and raked the bits to the side with the hammer. "Okay, the window is cleared, you guys. Let's get out of here!"

Howard took her torch. "Barbara, you and Jo go first, while I hold them at bay. I'll follow right behind you!"

Barbara quickly climbed up on the washer and boosted Josephine up to the window. Josephine reached through the small opening and pulled herself through on her belly. The window was just above ground level, so she crawled directly out onto the frozen earth of the backyard.

"Hurry, girls!" yelled Howard. "Get out, now!"

Barbara looked back and saw that Howard was in big trouble. The two torches were about to go out. The turpentine-soaked rags balled up on their ends had already burned down to small black cinders and were barely creating enough fire to keep the creatures from pouncing. The smaller the flames became, the bolder the beasts were.

Howard swung the torches back and forth at the creatures, who reacted by growling and stabbing their paws at him with little regard for the dying flames.

Felix prowled at Howard's feet, his back arched and fur on end, hissing at the creatures and shouting advice to Howard like a corner man in a prizefight. "Jab, Pops, jab! Give him the left! Watch out! Duck!"

More of the mutant creatures upstairs were now turning their attention to the commotion in the basement. They fought each other fang and claw to gain entrance. The hole in the wall and the bashed-in door quickly became one big gash, and the creatures dove in on top of each other. Hungry teeth flashed in the orange light of the flames, as the monstrous herd crept closer.

"Look out, Howard, there's one on your left!" Barbara called, as an ugly canine-ish creature tried to sneak up on Howard's flank. Howard spun quickly and smacked the beast's muzzle with the red-hot torch. It yelped and ducked away, but clearly would not be deterred for long.

Howard was losing ground fast. The buffalo-headed creature swiped a huge paw at him, ripping three parallel slices in his forearm with its claws. The blow knocked the torch from his hand, and it fell to the floor. Barbara panicked when she saw the blood begin to soak through Howard's shirt. With nothing to lose, and no other defense, she started throwing anything she could find at the creatures to hold them off. She bounced a full pickle jar off the buffalo creature's black head, temporarily causing it to step back. She flung cans of insecticide, books, rubber boots, spray paint, a baseball, a mirror, until she had emptied all the shelves within reach. The creature snapped at the missiles, swallowing the baseball whole.

Josephine could hardly bear to watch. Howard, down to one torch now, his gashed arm dripping blood, was moving a bit slower, his energy beginning to flag. She was starting to doubt that he would make it out of the basement before the creatures overcame him, when she spotted the jar of turpentine, still three-quarters full, sitting on the workbench. The smoldering torch her father had just dropped lay in perfect position on the floor.

"Felix, use the turpentine! It's on the workbench!"

"Right!" The cat hopped onto the table and kicked the glass jar off. It hit the cement floor and shattered, its flammable contents splashing across the floor under the buffalo creature's paws. When the pool of liquid touched the torch, a wall of flames exploded between the herd of creatures and their intended victims. The buffalo-headed beast bellowed madly as it danced in the fiery puddle.

"Time to go!" shouted Felix.

Howard climbed onto the washer and hurriedly boosted Barbara up to the window. He pushed on her feet as she worked her head and shoulders through the narrow space and went crawling out onto the snow. Howard managed to pull himself up far enough to reach through the window and take Barbara's and Josephine's hands. They braced their feet against the metal outer frame of the window and tugged with all their strength. Little by little, Howard inched his way out of the window and onto the snowy ground outside, where Josephine and Barbara lay trying to catch their breath.

Felix, his hind quarters smoking, yelled a particularly salty curse word as he came scratching his way out of the window and plunged his singed bottom in the snow. The creatures inside roared and howled as smoke poured out of the open window and the basement filled with flames.

Howard stumbled across the snow toward Josephine, Barbara, and Felix. "Get away from the house! The furnace is full of fuel. It could blow any second now."

Josephine quickly scooped up the dazed Felix, Howard pulled Barbara to her feet, and they all ran. They had hadn't taken ten steps when an earthshaking boom knocked them all to the ground again. A huge yellow fireball blew out the back of the house, leaving a gash in the wall. Fire and smoke poured out of the hole, and the entire house lurched backward.

Suddenly, like a circus lion leaping through a flaming hoop, the buffalo-headed creature crashed through the opening, bellowing madly, the fur on its back smoking. The other creatures came stampeding behind it, several of them in flames. The beasts wailed and shrieked furiously as they charged out into the snow in every direction. In the panicked confusion, several creatures smashed into each

other in a multibeast pileup, while others simply ran in circles trying to catch their smoldering tails. All were too busy to spot Josephine and the others, who would have been easy pickings now, lying on the ground not fifty feet away. Finally, the buffalo-headed creature seemed to find its bearings and loped off toward the tree line behind the house. The other creatures followed suit, and the entire herd thundered off down the slope into the dense forest.

Howard directed the group to a hiding spot behind a small pump shed. "Everyone stay down. There could be others nearby that we haven't seen yet."

Barbara went right into nurse mode. She quickly looked Josephine over but found no new injuries. Howard was next. She carefully pulled his sleeve up and frowned at his wound. "These lacerations are bleeding pretty badly, dear. They don't appear to be very deep, though." She ripped a swath of cloth from her skirt and began wrapping Howard's arm. "Thank goodness we've kept up with our tetanus boosters."

Josephine winced when she saw the blood on her father's shirt. "Oh, Dad, you're really hurt!"

"No, no," he said, with a shrug. "Your mother's right. It's a very superficial wound. How about you, Felix? Are you okay?"

Felix grimaced as he piled snow onto his blackened rear end. "My caboose is a charcoal briquette, but other than that, I'm swell."

Josephine peeked over the top of the small shed and watched the burning house. She had never seen such a big fire up close, and the violence of it was shocking. Towering orange and yellow flames leapt out of the windows, hungrily devouring the house's curlicued wooden trim and climbing quickly to the upper gables. The red-hot roof hissed and sizzled as snowflakes drifted down onto the shingles. The old house was completely ablaze. Any beastly creatures still inside were surely toast.

Now that they were safe for the moment, Josephine's mind turned to Thaddeus. It had been at least an hour since she had left the boy in the lab, locked inside the strange machine—plenty of time for awful things to occur.

CHAPTER 38

Waking up was not something Thaddeus enjoyed, even under normal circumstances. It seemed that the best, most luxuriously restful part of sleep, the only part that truly felt worthy of the word *slumber*, was the part that went on just before waking up. For this reason, there were strict rules in Hibble Manor regarding the manner in which the master was to be awakened. Every evening at precisely six o'clock, Norman arrived at the boy's bedside with a tray of perfectly heated, heavily sugared cocoa and a cookie. Only after the robot had rung a tiny silver bell three times and then put on an old gramophone recording titled *Songbirds of Appalachia* did Thaddeus's eyes open and his day (or night, actually, since he usually slept through the risky daytime hours) begin.

So it was with great dismay that Thaddeus found himself awakened by the rude sensation of having his pants stolen. When he opened his eyes, his head foggy from the anesthetic, he remembered in a nauseated rush where he was and who had put him there. He was still strapped to the operating gurney, the strange helmet still on his head, the tube still attached to his belly. He felt awful.

"Stop that," Thaddeus groaned. He attempted to kick at the person removing his pants, but the restraints on his legs kept him from it. "Those are my trousers, you barbarian!"

Thaddeus blinked and tried to focus, though it was hard without his glasses. The thief had taken those as well. He fought through the wooziness of the anesthetic, forcing his mind to sort out what was happening. Was the pants thief Fetid Stenchley? He must be, though even through the blur of Thaddeus's myopia, he could tell that the person did not possess the killer's unique hunched shape. In fact, generally speaking, the person rather resembled . . . Thaddeus himself.

But that was impossible.

Could it be one of Thaddeus's deformed clone siblings? That wasn't likely. None of them had appeared to be alive. Who, then?

The mysterious thief did not speak as he worked the pant legs off Thaddeus's feet, which were now shoeless. The boy noticed then that his shirt and jacket were gone as well. He was down to his undershirt and boxers. Thaddeus panicked when he realized that the dastardly pilferer might intend to relieve him of those, too. The thought of being naked at this moment was most unappealing.

"Why are you taking my clothes?" The blurry person did not answer, but appeared to be dressing himself in the white suit. "I demand to know who you are!"

The thief's snorting laugh, full of mockery and chronic nasal congestion, answered the question. Regardless of the thief's Thaddeus-shaped silhouette, the boy knew that only one person could produce that disgusting sound.

"Fetid Stenchley! What devious depravity are you up to now?"

Stenchley grunted. Thaddeus couldn't tell if he was smiling or grimacing.

The truth, though Thaddeus had not discovered it yet, was even worse than he imagined. At that moment, a commando force of Stenchley's cells was working inside Thaddeus, ambushing the boy's own CC cells and replacing them with Stenchley's.

If Thaddeus had been anywhere near a mirror, his own reflection would have terrified him. Hanks of thin, greasy hair had sprouted from his shaved scalp, his nose had begun losing its roundness, his eyes had become more mud brown than sky blue. Even worse, like a newborn volcano rising from the ocean floor, an ugly hump had begun bulging up from his shoulder. The person Thaddeus would have seen staring back at him from the mirror would have looked a lot like Fetid Stenchley.

CHAPTER 39

Stenchley was too caught up in the excitement of his own transformation to bother paying attention to the irate creature whose stolen cells had given him a new body.

He looked himself over and spoke to the python inside him. "Ain't we handsome now, sweet? Looky how the Master loves us now!"

Cynthia hissed. She was restless and irritable since the cell transfer had reduced Stenchley's hump, her den, to a fraction of its normal size. She had reluctantly taken up residence in his plump new belly, though it quaked and rumbled incessantly.

The professor's corpse, tottering nearby, did appear to be transfixed by the killer's altered appearance. A moan drifted up from the dead man's rotted throat as his hand reached out and stroked Stenchley's newly soft cheek.

Admiring his reflection in a shard of broken glass, Stenchley was thrilled to see that the operation had been a success. He now inhabited the handsome body of the Friend. The killer marveled at the old

Friend lying there whimpering and straining against the straps of the surgical gurney. The revolting features, the bulging eyes, the leathery scarred face, the greasy hair, the apelike arms that the madman had borne his whole life now belonged to that pathetic creature instead.

The former hunchback was so anxious to get out the door and greet the world in his glamorous new guise, he almost forgot to finish his work. Instinct told him the Friend should be disposed of.

Stenchley wasted no time. Since the victim was conveniently immobilized by the gurney's restraints, a few minutes should have been more than enough time to kill and run.

But things did not go as planned.

Stenchley's new hands were limp and soft, instead of knotty and powerful. They were hands built for the delicate stitching of spleens and for the tearing of chocolate bar wrappers, not for snapping ribs or ripping flesh. The plump, pink appendages failed even to tear the fabric of his victim's undershirt, much less affect the skin underneath. Undeterred, the madman bit hungrily at an exposed arm, but no blood came. He found his new jaws were weak, his teeth small and dull, unlike the jagged weapons that had lined his gums before. Instead of tearing flesh from bone, the best he could manage was an unsatisfying gnawing.

Thaddeus, on the other hand, had the distinct feeling that he had suddenly become very strong. He had no idea that his cells were being overrun by Fetid Stenchley's, and he was not able to see that his own features had grown to resemble those of the madman. All he knew was that he felt very strange. His bones and muscles, the majority of which he had never even been aware of, let alone used, were tingling with a feeling that was part itch and part sting. He was aware of the blood pumping through his arteries with a vigor he had never experienced before.

With astonishing ease, he broke the straps that had held him to the gurney. He flung the helmet aside and snapped the suction cup off his stomach, leaving a ring of tiny punctures in his skin where the device's connection points had been.

Thaddeus leapt from the gurney and attacked Stenchley, his body acting almost on its own without consulting the boy's mind at all. It was a strange feeling, tackling what appeared to be himself, seeing fear in what appeared to be his own face.

A wave of nausea washed over Thaddeus as his insides continued to shift and churn. He fell to his knees and nearly retched, giving the killer a chance to wriggle free. When the sick moment passed, he saw that Stenchley had run out the lab door.

The professor's corpse had appeared as well and was ascending the stairs in Stenchley's wake. The dead man reached out after the killer as he climbed, moaning as if trying to call him back.

An aggressive new instinct told Thaddeus to pursue the madman, but what he saw on the floor of the lab kept him from obeying it.

"Norman!" He shoved his way through the debris until he came to his faithful servant's broken steel body, looking like so much useless junk.

Thaddeus fell to his knees and laid his hands gently on Norman's dented silver face. "Norman, what has happened to you? I command you to speak to me this instant!"

But the domed top of Norman's head was bashed in and dislocated, with wires spilling out the sides—his circuits were smashed to bits. His steel hand was gone from his one remaining arm, its connectors twisted and frayed. Desperately, Thaddeus opened a small panel in the robot's chest and began twisting and turning the knobs and switches inside, trying to restart his servant. Norman remained motionless, however, the red lights of his eyes dark.

Thaddeus had never considered the possibility of Norman's demise. The robot had always been with him, seemingly indestructible, his only purpose to attend to the boy's every whim. Every sugary morsel of food Thaddeus had ever eaten had been served to him on a silver platter by the robot. Every mug of cocoa that had ever touched his lips had been prepared and heated to exactly the right temperature (126 degrees Fahrenheit) by Norman. Every time Thaddeus had ever been woken by a nightmare, Norman's steel claws had been there to soothe him to sleep again with a gentle back scratch. The doddering old contraption had been mother, father, friend, valet, teacher, toolbox, and Candyland opponent since Thaddeus had entered the world.

And now he was gone, destroyed by the mad killer who had stolen Thaddeus's body.

A pitiful expression appeared on the boy's awful new face. His bottom lip quivered, the outsized teeth of Fetid Stenchley overhanging it like shovel blades. He backhanded a tear off his cheek as a towering rage grew inside him. Some new part of the boy wanted revenge.

Thaddeus flew after the madman. He was surprised to find himself galloping on all fours at an unprecedented speed, like some beast from the African savanna. It felt so natural, he wondered why he had never tried running this way before.

CHAPTER 40

Felix heard the sirens in the distance first.

He put his sensitive bat ear to the ground. "Listen! The cavalry's comin', I can hear 'em . . . two fire trucks and a police car . . . and it sounds like the police car needs a new muffler."

"Finally!" said Josephine. "The police can rescue Thaddeus. I hope it's not too late."

The Cravitzes and Felix hurried around to the front of the house, keeping well back from the raging fire. They reached the street just as two very old fire trucks with men hanging off the sideboards rumbled into Oleander Alley, plowing their way through the snow that covered the street, sirens screeching. The trucks were closely followed by a black and white Awkward Falls Police car, its bubble light flashing on the roof.

All of them, including Felix, jumped up and down in the middle of the street, waving their arms over their heads and shouting, as if there might be some doubt as to where the emergency was. Josephine had to remind Felix that he should probably act like a normal cat when other people were around.

"Oops, sorry," he said. "Meow."

As the fire trucks pulled up in front of the house, a gang of oddly dressed firemen piled off and began scrambling to unroll hoses and unload ladders. The men, some in ties and dress shoes, some in workers' coveralls, two in hockey uniforms, were obviously volunteers, not professional firefighters. Still, they set to work with their axes and hose nozzles, blasting jets of water at the blaze and hacking at doors as if they knew what they were doing.

Josephine dashed straight to the police car as it came to a stop next to the fire engines. There was no time to lose.

"Officers, come quickly!" she yelled as the two policemen stepped out of the vehicle and came toward her. "The escaped killer Fetid Stenchley is right next door!"

Instead of uniforms, the officers wore jeans and flannel shirts, and each had a badge clipped to his pocket. Ball caps with the letters *AFPD* emblazoned on the front served as their official headgear.

The senior officer, a potato of a man with enormous red eyebrows that resembled fox pelts, looked Josephine over with unhurried curiosity. He hiked his gun belt up so that the buckle sat on top of his large belly. The holster, which held a half-finished sports drink instead of a gun, slid right back down as soon as he let go.

"Morning, folks," said the officer. "Sergeant Cole and Deputy Flange, Awkward Falls PD. We were in the area and saw the smoke from the conflagration. Thought we'd best check it out."

Deputy Flange, who was much younger and many waist sizes smaller than Sergeant Cole, whistled when he got a good look at the burning house. "That's some fire ya got there, eh. Five alarmer, I'd say."

"Yes, it's awful," Barbara said. "But I believe there is a more urgent emergency next door."

"So you've seen the escapee, have ya?" Sergeant Cole asked Josephine, who was squirming with impatience.

"Yes, it was definitely him," she exclaimed. "He's at the house next door right now!"

"He bit our daughter!" said Barbara.

"And he's holding a boy hostage!" added Howard.

Flange pushed his hat up and read slowly from the form on the clipboard he carried. "I'll need to get your legal names, folks, for the record."

"Um, Josephine. Cravitz."

"I'm Barbara Cravitz, and this is my husband, Howard."

"Howard what?" Flange asked.

"He would obviously be a Cravitz, too, wouldn't he, Clarence?" said the sergeant. "Now, put the blasted clipboard away. We've got a code periwinkle on our hands here."

"Should I call for backup, Sarge?" Flange reached for his walkie-talkie. "I think the Mounties are still in town. Maybe they could bring a couple o' helicopters or a tank or something."

"Don't be a hoser, Clarence. This is the chance we've been waiting for to show those big-city boys how the AFPD handles a situation. Now get the SWAT gear, on the double."

"Aye, roger that." Flange paused and scratched his head. "Where'd we put the SWAT gear again?"

Cole nodded toward the rear of the car. "It's under the spare tire, Clarence, right where it always is."

"You really should hurry, officers!" Josephine pleaded. She started toward Hibble Manor and motioned at them to follow her. "He could be hurting Thaddeus!"

Flange returned from the car with a large fishing net, a tranquilizer gun, and two goalie masks. They each put on a mask, with Cole grabbing the gun and Flange wielding the net.

"You folks stay here, and don't worry about a thing," said the sergeant. "Let us trained professionals handle this."

As the policemen strode off in the direction of Hibble Manor, a short boy in a white suit came stumbling toward them across the side yard.

"Look!" Barbara pointed at the runner.

"It's him!" Josephine shouted to the officers. "It's Thaddeus!" The boy was moving faster through the deep snow than she would have guessed he was capable of. Then she saw why.

He was being chased by Fetid Stenchley.

CHAPTER 41

Of course, the short boy in the white suit was really Fetid Stenchley, not Thaddeus, and the hunchback chasing him was Thaddeus, not Fetid Stenchley, but there was no way for Josephine or anyone other than Thaddeus and Fetid Stenchley themselves to know this.

"Thaddeus!" yelled Josephine, incorrectly, jumping and waving her arms. "Run!"

The chubby boy looked terrified as he hustled awkwardly through the snowy side yard. The loping hunchback, clothed only in a pair of boxer shorts, charged behind him, yelling crazily. As if the awful sight of Stenchley in the light of day weren't scary enough by itself, it sounded as if he was yelling Josephine's name.

Cole slid a moose-tranquilizer dart into the chamber of his weapon and took aim. "Prepare to apprehend the fugitive, Clarence."

Deputy Flange crouched low with the fishing net poised over his head. "Aye aye, Sarge."

"Be careful!" called Josephine. "Don't hit Thaddeus!"

The sergeant laid a furry eyebrow on the gun's scope and leveled the barrel at the hunchback. The tranquilizer gun popped and the target yelped, a small dart punching him squarely in the shoulder. Flange whipped the net down over the criminal's head as he stumbled past, his eyes already glazing over. The hunchback teetered, the dart's narcotic swiftly shutting down his nervous system.

"Jos—," he began, as his ugly bulging eyes met Josephine's for an instant, then he pirouetted and plopped down in the snow.

"We got him, Sarge!" yelled Flange. The deputy began to do a little jig around the netted fugitive. "Yahoo!"

"Of course we did," said Cole. "Who needs Mounties and helicopters when you got moose darts? Now, stop that silly dancin' and get him in the car before he comes to. I can't wait to see the looks on those big-city boys' faces when they find out we caught Stenchley."

In no time, Flange had the unconscious hunchback cuffed and stowed in the backseat of the cruiser.

With the person who appeared to be Stenchley captured, the sergeant scooped up the dazed person who appeared to be Thaddeus and carried him like a watermelon toward the Cravitzes.

"I gotcha, lad," the policeman said. "You're safe now."

Josephine ran over as the policeman set him down.

"Thaddeus! Thank goodness you got away," Josephine said. "Did Stenchley hurt you?" She stepped back and looked him over quickly.

There were no obvious signs of injuries, though he had several bald spots on his normally heavily thatched head. The boy, still panting from the exertion of his narrow escape, just stared at her, his eyes wild and wide.

Felix rubbed against Thaddeus's legs, looking up at him happily.

"So, is this laddie your brother, then?" asked Sergeant Cole.

"No, he's . . . he's actually my friend." Josephine put her arm around Thaddeus. She hoped he wouldn't choose this moment to reject her again. The boy stiffened at her touch, but said nothing. "He's, um, staying with us."

Barbara shook both policemen's hands. "Thank you, officers. It's such a relief to know that awful man is in custody again."

Sergeant Cole's belly swelled with pride, causing his holster to slide toward his ankles. He caught the buckle quickly and pulled it up again. "All in a day's work, missus. It's what we get paid for."

"What will happen to Stenchley now?" Howard asked the sergeant.

"We're taking him straight back to the Asylum for the Dangerously Insane, where he belongs," said Sergeant Cole. "If we leave now, he'll be jacketed and locked in his cell by the time the tranquilizer wears off."

"Wait," said Josephine. "What about the monsters?"

Cole and Flange paused. "Monsters?"

"Yes, I know it sounds strange, but there were these . . . huge beasts," Howard began, "a whole herd of them. They broke into the house, and we had to fight them off, which is how the fire got started in the first place. The whole bunch just ran off into the woods over there a few minutes ago. You might want to call someone from animal control. They're extremely dangerous!"

The police officers perked up at this unexpected information. Deputy Flange took out his clipboard again and began writing everything down.

"What kind of beasts were they, sir?" asked Cole. "Wolves? Bears?"

"Not exactly," Howard said, choosing his words carefully. "The species was hard to determine. They may have been mutations or crossbreeds of some kind."

"Mutations?" The sergeant looked puzzled.

"How do you spell *mutations*?" asked Clarence.

"Sound it out, Clarence," said the sergeant. "What kinds of mutations, sir?"

"I . . . I'm not really sure. Look, officer, the point is, the things are very large and dangerous, and still on the loose. They tore holes in the walls!"

The officers looked at each other with raised eyebrows. "Tore holes in the walls, you say. With what? Their paws? Hooves? Teeth?"

"All of the above, yes. One of them clawed me." Howard showed them his bandaged arm.

"That's certainly a nasty scratch. What did these animals look like, sir?"

"Well, one of them resembled a buffalo, but its body was more like that of a big cat. It had paws, not hooves."

The sergeant scratched his head. "You're sure it wasn't a grizzly? We get those around here every now and then."

The deputy snickered. "Bet it was a moose. Yanks always get spooked by the moose, eh."

Howard shook his head. "Definitely not a bear or a moose. Another one was more spiderlike, with eight legs, although its head appeared to be simian."

"What's *simian* mean?" asked the deputy.

"Look it up, Clarence!" said the sergeant, scowling at the deputy. He turned back to Howard. "And this 'simian' spider tore a hole in the wall, sir?"

"Well, yes. It was a giant spider, actually," Howard explained.

"A giant simian spider."

"Yes, I'd say about seven feet tall. With fangs."

"It's true!" Josephine insisted. She could see the policemen were beginning to think they were a bunch of crackpots. "It chased us around and tried to kill us!"

Barbara weighed in at this point. "We all saw it, officer! And I'm a nurse, by the way," she added, hoping that might make her sound less crazy.

"How do you spell *simian*?" asked the deputy.

"Never mind, Clarence." The sergeant closed the deputy's clipboard for him. "I think we have enough to go on here."

He put his hand on Howard's shoulder in a fatherly way. "Mr. Cravitz, you and your family have been through a terrible experience. You're cold and tired. I suggest you let one of the fire trucks take you to the doc to get your injuries looked at, then get yourselves a nice meal and a warm hotel room and try to forget the whole thing. Leave the giant spiders and buffalo-lions to us, eh?"

"But . . . but . . . you have to do something!" shouted Josephine as the policemen climbed into their car. "They could hurt someone!" But the doors slammed shut and the car sped away, its lights flashing and siren whining.

Josephine stomped her foot with frustration. "What are we going to do now, Dad? They thought we were nuts."

Howard shook his head. "For the time being, there isn't much we can do. At least the creatures were headed north into the wilderness, away from town."

Josephine gazed toward the tree line behind the house. The forest appeared as still and quiet as always. "I hope they stay there."

☠ ☠ ☠

In spite of the danger being finally over, Josephine noticed Thaddeus was still ill at ease. As Barbara took his pulse and checked other vital signs, his eyes darted left and right nervously. He seemed ready to bolt at any moment.

"It's all right, Thaddeus," Josephine said, trying to calm him down.

She really wished he would say something. His silence was beginning to worry her. "My mom's a great nurse. She won't hurt you."

"Let's give him a little space," said Howard. "The poor guy's been through heck."

The boy said nothing. He looked at them all as if they were complete strangers, which of course they were.

CHAPTER 42

Twittington House was little more than a pile of cinders and scorched beams by mid-afternoon, when the motley crew of firefighters had finally doused the last of the flames. The fire chief/chef was unimpressed by the blaze, saying that they were used to old homes like this going up in flames every so often. The houses were real firetraps, he complained, with nothing built to modern safety codes. He never even bothered to ask how the blaze started, though Josephine and her parents tried to tell him. Unfortunately, he was even less interested in killer mutant creatures than the policemen were.

As the firefighters coiled their hoses and stowed their equipment, Barbara was allowed to use the supplies in the fire truck's medical kit to sterilize and bandage Howard's clawed forearm and Josephine's bitten shoulder. Luckily, the kit also contained vials of rabies vaccine, which she used to give each of them an injection to ward off the deadly disease.

"Do you think this stuff works on mutant monster scratches and cannibal bites?" asked Howard.

She shrugged. "They didn't teach us that in nursing school."

Josephine was much more concerned with Thaddeus's condition than her own. He looked unhurt on the outside, but under the surface he was not himself. She tried to get him to talk, but he would not even make eye contact. What had happened in that lab to cause him to shut down so completely? Standing apart from them, shivering and mute, he seemed like an entirely different person.

Felix made his concern plain. "I'm no bloodhound, but the kid smells funny," he said to Josephine, away from Thaddeus's ears. "My nose is tellin' me somethin's fishy."

The firemen offered the family a ride into town on the bumper of one of their trucks, but Howard declined, asking for a jump start for the old Volvo instead.

Howard revved the engine gently as the trucks drove away. "Can't leave this old girl behind. She's just about all we have left after the fire. It's too bad about the sofa, though. Naps will never be the same."

"Forget it, Howard," said Barbara. "It's time we replaced that ancient thing anyway. The important thing is we're all safe."

They piled into the car, with Josephine and Thaddeus in the back and Felix curled on the seat between them.

"We really should get Thaddeus to a hospital," Barbara said quietly to Howard. "He needs a thorough examination."

Josephine overheard her. "No, we can't do that, Mom! You promised."

"I know," said Barbara. "But he could really be hurt, dear. There could be internal injuries, hidden wounds, who knows what else. We have no way of knowing if he's all right until he gets a complete physical by a doctor."

The boy's eyes went wide as saucers. He wasn't talking, but it was obvious that he did not like the idea of going to the hospital at all.

"But, he's a clone, Mom, remember?" she whispered. "When the doctors find out, they'll turn him into a guinea pig. You know they will. They'll see him as some kind of science experiment. He's never even been outside that spooky old house in his whole life, except to buy junk food at a gas station. A hospital would terrify him!"

"I think Josephine may be right, dear," said Howard. "The boy seems to be stable enough at the moment, with no obvious problems. Maybe peace and quiet and a good night's sleep would be the best thing for him at this point. Given his . . . unique . . . characteristics, the stress of going to a hospital for the first time might do him more harm than good. What do you say we get some food in him, watch him closely overnight, and see how he does? If symptoms develop, we can always take him in then."

Barbara finally agreed, though reluctantly. They stopped at a pharmacy in town, and Barbara bought a thermometer, a blood pressure gauge, and various medicines and supplies to help monitor his condition through the night.

"If his temperature goes up so much as one degree, if his blood pressure does anything remotely abnormal, or if he even so much as coughs," she declared, looking very much like she meant it, "we're taking him to a doctor, stat. Does everyone understand?"

Everyone did.

☻ ☻ ☻

They found a room at the Hook, Line, and Sinker Lodge, a creaky old fisherman's inn whose leaning sign proudly proclaimed it had been in operation since 1928. Since the place was mostly empty, the severe weather having deterred all but the hard-core anglers from driving up from the south, the desk clerk put them in the Trophy Suite. The suite was made up of two pine-paneled rooms on the ground floor, decorated profusely with mounted pike and boat paddles arranged in artistic formations. A clanging radiator made the place blessedly warm.

They were all starved by this time, so Howard went across the street to a Chinese restaurant for takeout. He came back minutes later with veggie lo mein, sweet and sour tofu, and two or three other meatless dishes, and dinner was served. The boy looked at the plate Barbara fixed for him as if it were piled with rocks instead of food. A red spatter of sweet and sour sauce interested him briefly, until he put a bit on his finger and tasted it. He frowned and spat. No amount of Barbara's motherly coaxing could make him eat.

"Maybe he doesn't like Chinese food," said Howard.

"He likes sweets," Josephine said.

"For dinner?" asked Barbara.

"He's got a sweet tooth the size of France," said Felix. "Dinner, breakfast, brunch, whenever. He never met a candy he didn't like."

Howard found a few chocolate mints in a dish on top of the dresser and offered the boy a few. Thaddeus sniffed the candies, then tossed them all into his mouth, not even bothering to remove the wrappers.

"Whoa," said the cat." Guess the kid was hungry after all."

For the rest of the meal, while the Cravitzes and Felix ate, Thaddeus sat still as a stone, becoming animated only when a fly buzzed near his chair. Out of the corner of her eye, Josephine thought she saw him catch the fly and pop it into his mouth in one swift gesture.

Since the old black-and-white television in the room picked up only one channel, devoted exclusively to lake temperatures and weather forecasts, the group began to yawn not long after dinner. Barbara thought it best that Thaddeus be given one of the bedrooms to himself. A good night's sleep, she knew from experience, often worked wonders.

The beds were squeaky and old, but were layered with soft quilts. Josephine and Barbara watched with curiosity as Thaddeus climbed between the sheets fully clothed, not even bothering to remove his shoes or glasses, but neither said anything. He was bound to have some odd habits, Josephine thought, having grown up the way he had. She put a glass of water on the nightstand, and Barbara tucked him in. A final temperature reading showed 98.6, and Barbara deemed him well enough to be out of her sight for a few hours.

"Good night, Thaddeus," said Josephine. The boy barely glanced at her as she turned out the light and closed the door.

"I wish he'd eaten something besides candy," said Barbara. "He looks like he could really use some protein."

CHAPTER 43

Just as a shark has no interest in fruit salad, cannibals generally eschew vegetarian Chinese food. Fetid Stenchley, a strict cannibal whenever possible, was famished, and had every intention of enjoying a late dinner. The candies, which would normally have repulsed him, had gone down surprisingly easily, but they were not nearly enough. Other than that, a cockroach and few flies were all he had managed to slip between his brand-new lips since escaping from the lab. Now he was ready for something more likely to stick to his ribs.

Cynthia was beside herself with hunger. In the gray moonlight, the python slid from the madman's mouth and curled her scaly head around to his ear. She began singing a hissing lullaby that Stenchley found irresistible, her forked tongue tickling his earlobe as she crooned.

A father for me, a mother for you, she lilted, *a girl for dessert, and a kitty pie, too. . . .*

The hypnotic rhyme possessed Stenchley's weak mind, urging him up and out of bed. The snake had to be fed. The people in the next room would all be asleep by now, he was sure, which would make things easier. He knew what to do.

He opened the door silently, tiptoed into the main room, and froze, watching to see if anyone had awoken. The girl lay between her parents in the big bed, all three making quiet sleep sounds. The cat was a furry puddle purring on the quilt at their feet. None of them would wake up in time to stop him.

A floorboard squeaked beneath his clumsy new feet, something he could have prevented in his old body, the body so skilled in night-time hunting. The mistake reminded him of the difficulty he had had with the Friend, when it had overpowered him. His new hands and teeth had not been enough to subdue the friend. He needed a weapon. Glancing around in the darkness, he saw the remains of the revolting takeout meal they had tried to feed him on the coffee table at his knees. Utensils lay next to the boxes. Stenchley took a fork and knife, one in each hand, and moved closer to the man's side of the bed. He would eliminate the strongest of them first. The females would be easier to handle with the big male out of the way.

Stenchley loomed over the man, mumbling under his breath, "A father for me, a mother for you . . ." The black serpent inside him hissed madly as he raised the fork and knife high over his head, directly over the man's heart. His mouth watered, and his jaw dropped open as he stabbed with all his might.

Which was not much.

Once again, Stenchley found that his might was not what it used to be. Also, he had overlooked the fact that the fork and knife he had chosen as his tools of death were plastic. Instead of plunging into the victim's heart, the dinky utensils snapped into pieces when they struck the man's chest and merely woke him up.

Howard, Barbara, and Josephine all screamed simultaneously and leapt out of the bed. Howard pushed the chubby attacker away, sending him spinning across the floor.

"Thaddeus!" Josephine shouted. "What the heck are you doing?"

"Everyone stay back!" Howard said. He used a chair like a lion tamer to keep the boy away.

The boy was drooling and panting, and a low hissing came from deep inside him. He looked completely mad.

"He must be delirious!" said Barbara, turning on the bedside light. "We have to get him to a hospital. Howard, he needs a doctor!"

Howard slowly began to approach the wild-eyed boy. "Now, calm down, buddy. No one's going to hurt you," he said.

Stenchley backed up to the wall and crouched like a cornered animal, still holding the broken nubs of the plastic knife and fork as if they were deadly weapons.

"I ain't goin' to no hospital!" he said, in a horrible voice that had no business coming from Thaddeus's mouth.

"What did you say?" Josephine asked, confused. "Why does your voice sound like . . . like that?"

The boy hissed again and bared his teeth like an animal.

"Thaddeus? What's wrong?" asked Josephine.

"No doctors. No surgeons. No asylum," the boy growled. "Cynthia don't like it!"

"Wait a minute, he's not Thaddeus. He's Stenchley!" Felix's bald tail twitched and the hair stood up along his spine. "I knew somethin' was rotten in the state of Miami!"

It seemed impossible, but Josephine saw that Felix had to be right. This looked like Thaddeus, but wasn't. She took her mom's hand and pulled her away from the boy. "I think Felix is right, guys! That's Fetid Stenchley!"

"Stenchley?" stammered Howard and Barbara at the same time.

"You mean this isn't Thaddeus?" asked Barbara.

"What are you talking about, Jo?" Howard asked. "He's just a sick kid. He can't be Stenchley."

Felix hopped down from the bed and cautiously approached the white-haired person in question. "He must've done something in the lab to make himself look like the kid," said the cat. "With all the weird equipment in there, there's no telling what he did. Believe me, I know the boss, and that ain't him!"

"It's true," said Josephine, her voice quivering. "I'm sure that's Fetid Stenchley!"

Barbara reached for the phone on the nightstand.

"I'm calling the police," she said.

"No!" snarled Stenchley. He grabbed the coatrack by the door and ran at the window. Holding the stand like a jousting lance, he bashed out the window, then dove through the opening.

They all hurried to the window and saw him roll down the snowbank outside, then run off into the freezing darkness.

Josephine figured she could catch him if she got a quick start. She began to climb out the window after him, trying to avoid the sharp shards of glass. "Come on! We have to catch him!" she said.

Howard held her back. "No, Josephine, it's too dangerous! If that's Stenchley, we'd better let the police handle it."

"But he's getting away!" she pleaded. "I could've caught him!"

"He won't get far," said Howard.

Josephine reluctantly came back inside. She found Thaddeus's glasses on the floor where they had fallen from Stenchley's face during the scuffle. One of the thick lenses was cracked. Wherever the real Thaddeus was, he was probably in a panic without the spectacles. She had to find him.

Barbara had already dialed 911 and was talking rapidly into the phone, trying her best to relay the outlandish information to Deputy Flange on the other end without sounding like a complete nut.

"She's a complete nut, eh?" said Deputy Flange as he hung up the phone. "First, spider monsters attack their house, and now the boy isn't really the boy, he's really Stenchley, the escapee."

"They're a kooky bunch, all right," said Sergeant Cole.

"Do we have to go out and investigate?"

The sergeant leaned back in his chair and turned his attention back to the hockey game on the portable television on his desk. "Investigate what? We captured the fella and delivered him to the asylum ourselves, didn't we? With no help from the Mounties, I might add!"

Flange grinned and high-fived him.

"What kind of medal do ya think they'll give us, Sarge? The Cross of Valor, maybe?"

"Oh, I wouldn't be surprised if we ended up with the CV, Clarence. I wouldn't be surprised a bit."

CHAPTER 44

Squatting next to a Dumpster behind the Wily Walleye Restaurant, gnawing a discarded fish head, Fetid Stenchley pondered his situation. In the piercing arctic wind, he pulled the shag carpet remnant he had found tighter around his shoulders and the paper bag on his head lower. Somehow, he thought, his beautiful plan had gone wrong. He had expected that he and the Master would be enjoying a posh new life as celebrity father and son by now. But that had not happened. He didn't even know where his master was now. He had not seen him since being chased from the laboratory.

He crunched another walleye head, slurping the slippery eyeballs out with his lips, and decided that he should find the professor. That seemed like a good idea. And maybe along the way he could murder something fresh for the grumbling Cynthia. It would have to be a creature weak enough for him to overpower with his soft new body, of course. He wondered what that might be. A cat? No, the claws would be a problem. Maybe a mouse. That was better.

They were small, not much meat on their bones, but they were weak. Surely he could manage to murder one of those.

And maybe he could scrounge up a chocolate something or other to go along with it. Since the transformation operation, the madman had found himself fishing candy wrappers and ice cream tubs out of trash cans for any smear of the brown substance that still clung to them. He suddenly couldn't imagine a raw meal without it.

The old Stenchley would have galloped off right then into the freezing night without a thought for comfort had he still inhabited his tough killer's body. But now, with his soft, round belly full of walleye heads and potato scraps, as well as a large female python, he found he really just wanted to curl up somewhere cozy and nap for a while.

He burrowed deep into the layers of greasy newspapers, plastic trash bags, and pungent odds and ends of refuse and got comfortable in the warm core of the garbage. In minutes he was dreaming the macabre dreams of a lunatic killer and snoring like a polar bear.

CHAPTER 45

—————⟶⟩⟨⟨⟵—————

On the long, long list of places one would not like to find oneself after being darted with moose tranquilizer, the inside of a tiny, dark, windowless, locked steel cell would be very near the top. Unfortunately, this is just where Thaddeus was when he regained consciousness. He tried to move but found it almost impossible, because of the straitjacket he was encased in. Also, he didn't have his glasses, which made the situation not only dire, but blurry as well.

"Help!" he called. "Where am I?"

Silence.

"HEEEELLP!" More silence.

Thaddeus tried to recall just how he had gotten here, wherever "here" was. He remembered being in the laboratory and having his clothes stolen by Stenchley, who had somehow made himself look like Thaddeus. He remembered chasing Stenchley out of the lab on all fours, seeing Josephine in the street outside, trying to call to her, seeing a policeman aiming a weapon at him, then blackness.

Thankfully, the nausea he had felt in the lab seemed to have passed, though he was anything but comfortable now. His mouth was parched, and he was intensely hungry. Before he could think about it, he found himself picking up a fat centipede from the floor with his teeth and munching it. It was the stinging kind, he noticed, just before devouring it, and his brain told him it should have been disgusting, yet somehow it wasn't. In fact, it was good, and he immediately wanted another. He saw a small trough of water jutting out from the wall in the corner and waddled over to it.

Leaning over carefully, he could touch his lips to the liquid. With his arms pinned inside the straitjacket, he had no choice but to lap the water up the way Felix did. After drinking his fill, he watched the ripples on the surface as they smoothed and saw something that made him gasp. In the dim light of the cell, he was just able to see his reflection in the water. Even without glasses, he could tell it was the wrong face.

His mind reeled at the horrible thought of such a nightmare. Thaddeus paced the cell and yelled for help again, louder than before, more desperately than before. Even though he had no rational hope of being rescued, he continued to call out to anyone, even those who had put him here. Yelling turned into howling, howling into a hoarse wail. But his cries did not penetrate the gray walls surrounding him. The merciless cell swallowed every sound.

He rolled on the floor, twisting, biting, and jerking to try to escape the straitjacket, but could not loosen the bindings even the tiniest bit. He tried scraping the canvas against the rough stone walls, but the material was too tough to tear. Spots danced in front of his eyes from the effort.

Finally, fatigue caused his panic to quell a bit and his rational mind regained some small measure of control. Logic began to offer possible answers for what was going on. He knew that he now looked like Stenchley and that Stenchley looked like him. Even Josephine and Felix had failed to recognize him when he ran out of the lab in pursuit of Stenchley. The police had obviously arrested him because he appeared to be the escaped murderer, which meant that he was now either in a jail cell, or . . . no. Not that other place. He couldn't be there.

He had to find a way out.

With his hands bound inside the straitjacket, he used his bare feet to search the dark cell for cracks in the wall or hidden panels. Hibble Manor had several secret passages he liked to use as short-cuts, and he thought maybe this place might have one too. A catch might be hidden somewhere that would release the lock. He ran his bare foot over the cell's iron door, feeling for openings or levers, but found none. The cell was sealed as tight as a tomb.

He did discover something of interest near the bottom of the door, however. His toes felt three raised letters embossed in the steel, like the Braille text in books for blind people. It was too dark for his weak eyes to see the letters, but his toes were able to read them one at a time: *A. D. I.* With Thaddeus's broad vocabulary, he was able to imagine many things the letters *ADI* might stand for, such as Absolutely Dreadful Igloo, or Amusingly Droll Iguana, but he knew better.

His heart sank like a stone in a well. He was inside the Asylum for the Dangerously Insane.

All of Thaddeus's yelling had been pointless. Even if someone came to see about him, nothing would change. No one would look at him and see an innocent boy. They would see Fetid Stenchley, notorious murderer.

He sat down on the hard, damp floor and moaned.

Thaddeus had never known real despair before. His emotions had always ranged between "not bad" and "pretty good" with occasional dips and spikes to "fairly gloomy" and "reasonably agreeable." There had been moments of anxiety, of course, when he had caught sight of the man in the black suit lurking around the edges of the estate, and he did worry about being sent to the orphanage. But what he experienced now was much worse. His stomach seemed to be made of cement; his eyes leaked streams of tears; his chin quivered uncontrollably.

Worst of all, he was alone. He had never realized how much he valued the company of Norman and Felix until now. If his two friends had been here, he had no doubt they could find a way out. With Felix's ingenuity and Norman's strength, they would be free in no time. But they were not here.

That nosy girl, Josephine, had been the start of all this. If only she had minded her own business, and stayed on her side of the fence, perhaps none of this would have happened. Before her rude intrusion into Hibble Manor, his life had been peaceful and predictable. Then she had barged into his world and turned it upside down. After spending just two evenings with her, he had lost everything that mattered most to him. His parents no longer existed, his "grandfather" was nothing of the sort—he had very likely been mad, and possibly evil to boot—his faithful robot was demolished, his freedom had been taken away, and there were now serious doubts as to whether Thaddeus himself was even fully human.

It was all her fault.

Thaddeus should have been angry. He should have wanted to yell loud, insulting things at her, have Norman tie her up and lock her in the closet again. Part of him was, and did.

But mostly he wished she were there. He had no earthly idea why, and was supremely annoyed by the fact, but he knew it was true. He missed her, which made him feel even worse. *Botheration!*

He cried harder.

If ever there had ever been a moment when Thaddeus needed a break, this was it. Having been saddled with the hideous body of a murderer and wrongly tossed into an asylum packed with real murderers, a stroke of good luck just then would have been very welcome.

And one came. The problem was, it seemed an awful lot like bad luck at first.

The debilitating sickness he had felt earlier came back in full force. His head began to throb, his stomach gurgled, and his skin itched. He didn't know if it was possible for veins to hurt, but if it was, his did. *What is happening to me now?* he wondered. *What more must I endure? Am I dying?* He was almost relieved to think the end might be near.

But Thaddeus was not dying. The good news, which he could not have known, was that the cellular army of his immune system had just launched a massive counterattack all over his body against the madman's tiny invaders.

A new battle was in full swing in locations like his nose, his skin, his hump, certain organs, and other places. Strategic skirmishes were being won. The boy's own forces were routing entire regiments of foreign cells. The result was that many body parts which an hour or two earlier had been very Stenchley-ish were being restored to their original Thaddeus-like state.

Thaddeus was starting to look like himself again.

But the sound of footsteps outside the door signaled the end of his brief run of good luck. Keys jangled, heavy hinges screeched, and the cell door opened. There loomed five wide, thick-armed orderlies in white tunics, surgical masks, and black rubber gloves.

"Hello, Mr. Stenchley," said the orderly in front. The man's voice was unexpectedly soft, but his muscles looked as if they were dying to rip their way out of his tunic and begin breaking things. "So glad you are safely back with us again. You've been a very naughty fellow!"

Thaddeus tried to speak. He wanted to say, "I'm not Stenchley, I'm Thaddeus Hibble! I don't belong here!" but the battle going on inside his body had turned his tongue into a petrified log, allowing only a hoarse squeak to come out.

The man said, "We're here to escort you to the Treatment Chamber. Of course, since you've fallen behind, we'll be giving you two per day to catch up. Won't that be fun?" The men chuckled as they reached for him.

☠ ☠ ☠

The Treatment Chamber was kept at a nippy 46 degrees Fahrenheit. The frigid temperature was perfect for the delicate circuitry of the room's controls, ideal for the generator motor, optimum for maintaining the viscosity of the volatile chemicals in the tall glass reservoirs of the dehydration unit, but most uncomfortable for Thaddeus or any other human dressed only in his underwear.

As the boy lay shivering, strapped tightly to the table, the cell war inside his body gave him the itchy sensation of ants crawling just under his skin. His head felt hot and cold simultaneously, and his eyeballs danced, each to a different tune. He groaned desperately and tried to free his hands for scratching.

"Help me!" he tried to say. "I'm itching!" but his swollen tongue still would not cooperate and only got in the way when he spoke.

The masked technicians working busily around Thaddeus to prepare the machinery for the Treatment paid the mumbling patient little attention. This was their last procedure of the day and they were in a hurry to go to the Sauerkraut Appreciation Day parade. Besides, their job was only to set things up for the surgeons who would do the actual procedure, not to interact with the subject. If the technicians had taken a moment to examine the wriggling patient, they would have noticed something very strange. Parts of the subject's body were transforming. His skin rippled, blotches of pale pink blooming here and there on his leathery hide. His face contorted; his features shifted. The hump on his back had begun shrinking like a punctured beach ball.

Even as they hurriedly draped a splatter cloth over Thaddeus's face, the technicians did not notice that he was a bit young for an insane murderer. When they had connected all the cables and hoses, brought the enormous rumbling, sparking electrical generator up to speed, the men filed out of the chilly chamber, speculating excitedly about who would be chosen as this year's Sauerkraut Queen.

Now alone, Thaddeus wondered what awful thing would happen next. He had heard the technicians mention that surgeons would be there shortly. Apparently, he was going to receive a treatment of some kind, whatever that was. He hoped it wouldn't be painful, but the ominous machinery all around him led him to expect otherwise.

☻ ☻ ☻

The surgeons bustled into the Treatment Chamber, their stiffly starched white coats swishing with static electricity and their rubber soled shoes squeaking on the cold floor. In their surgical masks, scrub hats, goggles, and gloves, the doctors were impossible to tell apart, except by size. There were two tall ones, a short one, and a round one. One of the tall ones shone a light into Thaddeus's eyes and ears, while another measured the boy's head with a pair of calipers.

Thaddeus was frozen with fear, as well as from the freezing cold room. He tried again to speak, but still could not. He was helpless.

"Open the skull and insert the microwave heat probes into the frontal lobe, Dr. Smoot," Thaddeus heard the head surgeon say.

"I can't seem to locate the skull seam, Dr. Penrose," answered another.

"Don't be silly, Smoot. We've opened this patient's head more times than I can count."

"See for yourself, sir. There isn't even a scalp flap."

Thaddeus could feel their gloved fingers searching the perimeter of his head. Did they really intend to open his skull and insert probes? Adrenaline shot through his body at the thought. He strained mightily against the restraints, but could not loosen them even the slightest bit.

The head surgeon sighed with irritation. "How inconvenient! The seams must have grown back somehow while he was at large. Get the skull saw, we'll have to recut."

Thaddeus's heart pounded, and his breathing became a desperate pant. The familiar whizzing noise of the saw came next, and though Thaddeus could not see it, he could picture its round diamond-toothed blade whizzing. It was a tool he had used himself many times in his work on damaged pets, and now it was about to be used on his own head. He knew that once his brain had been altered, he might never be the same again. He could lose his memories, his knowledge, everything that made Thaddeus Thaddeus.

CHAPTER 46

This is what it must feel like to be buried alive, thought Josephine as she and her parents followed Dr. Herringbone deeper and deeper into the heart of the Asylum for the Dangerously Insane. They took an elevator down an unknown number of floors, then descended several flights of stairs. Josephine had no idea how far underground they were, but it felt like a mile. She shivered to think of Thaddeus locked up in this place.

After the attack and escape of the other Thaddeus, who was really Fetid Stenchley, Josephine had put two and two together. If the person who looked like Thaddeus was really Stenchley, that meant that the hunchback who had been moose-darted and taken away by the police was actually Thaddeus. And since the police thought he was Stenchley, they would have taken him . . . back to the Asylum for the Dangerously Insane.

Once she arrived at this horrifying conclusion, she had alerted her parents and Felix, and they had come straight to the asylum. She was angry with herself for not recognizing Thaddeus in spite of the physical differences. She realized now that he had been trying to call to her just as he was shot with the dart. This whole thing felt like her fault.

She hoped they were not too late.

Convincing the security staff to allow them inside the asylum had taken some very insistent explaining mixed with sympathetic begging. It also didn't hurt that Howard was a scientist with university credentials and Barbara was a licensed nurse. In the end, the gates had opened and they had been shown to Dr. Herringbone's office. The man was appalled. He, of all people, was most unlikely to misidentify Stenchley, having been brutally attacked by the madman only days before during his escape. The doctor still wore bandages on his arms, head, and leg from the bites and scratches Stenchley had inflicted. He assured the Cravitzes their outlandish claim could only be incorrect, but they were adamant. Finally, the doctor was persuaded that they should at least be allowed to see the patient very briefly for themselves.

The cold stone floor in the surgical block slanted downward, its center grooved from years of dangerous inmates being marched to and from the Treatment Chamber. Josephine's pulse quickened when they turned into a narrow, low-ceilinged corridor where the air was sour with the smell of chemicals. Machines hummed and buzzed behind the locked steel doors, and muffled sounds that might have been screams leaked out into the hall.

Dr. Herringbone unlocked a door marked with a red lightning bolt and strode in. "This is all highly irregular, not to mention dangerous," he protested as he reluctantly led the Cravitzes into the Treatment Chamber. "The administering of the Treatment is a delicate business. Interrupting the process could cause both the patient and the equipment irreparable harm!"

As the group entered, the surgeon operating the skull saw paused and turned to see what the ruckus was about, the spinning blade only inches from the flesh and bone of the person on the table.

The director squinted at the chart on the clipboard at the foot of the operating table where the patient lay surrounded by surgeons. "As I expected, there has been no mistake," he said, over the whine of the saw. He pointed emphatically to the name on the sheet. "The official chart states very clearly that the patient's name is Mr. Fetid Stenchley. You can see for yourself."

Josephine was not interested in what was on the clipboard. She looked over the table's steel side rail at the person strapped to the table. A small sheet covered most of his face.

"May I uncover his face, please?" she asked.

Herringbone nodded, and she lifted the veil.

Josephine was confused by what she saw. The patient looked like a bald version of Thaddeus.

"This isn't right," she murmured. " He should look like Stenchley."

"He looks just like the guy who was in our hotel room, Jo," said Howard. "Can you tell the difference?"

Josephine moved closer, gnawing her pinkie nail. She could see that the boy, if that was what he was, looked mostly like Thaddeus, but a little like Stenchley as well. This made things even harder to figure out. A pair of jagged teeth stuck ominously out of his mouth. His skin was weird, too, as if it were part leather.

"Is that him, dear?" asked Barbara.

Josephine did not know. She had been fooled before and did not completely trust what her eyes were telling her.

"Thaddeus?" she whispered, leaning in close to his ear. But not too close. "Is that you?"

The person on the table turned his head slightly toward her. His eyes, which were blue like Thaddeus's, yet tainted yellow like Stenchley's jaundiced orbs, lolled in her direction.

☻ ☻ ☻

Thaddeus had given up all hope of escape. His head was about to be sliced open like a coconut and his brain barbecued, and there was nothing he could do about it. He wondered if it really mattered in the end. Who was he, anyway? An experiment gone wrong, a creature that had no right to exist in the first place, discarded and soon to be forgotten. Even orphans were better than he was. At least they had had families once.

As he waited for the saw to begin its work, he let his mind conjure up his favorite fantasy. It was a scene Thaddeus had pictured many times before. He was sitting at the table of the dining room at Hibble Manor between his parents, who were finally home from their travels. The long-planned homecoming celebration was under way. Everyone, even Norman and Felix, was wearing party hats and laughing while playing a game of Candyland. Overflowing tureens of exotic candies, platters of fried pies, and a large pot of cocoa were set out within easy reach.

His mother was winning the game, and her laugh filled the room. In his dreams, Thaddeus had envisioned many different faces for his mother, and he kept them in a kind of portrait gallery in his mind. He chose the most angelic one of all for her now as she moved her plastic gingerbread man down the rainbow path of the game board.

The surgeons could not hurt him now.

Suddenly his imaginary mother's perfect face began to change into the much plainer one of Josephine Cravitz.

"Thaddeus, is that you?" she asked. "Thaddeus?"

The entire fantasy faded. Just like that, his parents were gone again, and he was back in the Asylum for the Dangerously Insane. Once again Josephine had intruded into his world, uninvited, and shattered his dreams.

This would normally have been an undesirable development, resulting in a major tantrum, a dangerous spike in blood pressure, and yells for Norman to do something. But this time Thaddeus was thrilled. He had never been so happy to see anyone in his life.

Josephine, who was real flesh and blood, not just a misty dream, had not forgotten him.

The girl's large ears, one slightly lower than the other, were as beautiful as the sails on a rescue ship to Thaddeus. Even her oblong, hairless nostrils, which the boy had found curiously irritating at their first meeting, filled him with happiness.

Thaddeus was so overjoyed to see her, so overcome with emotions, he was actually glad he was strapped down. Otherwise, he suspected he might have leapt up and hugged her, or heaven forbid, done something even more repugnant.

☠ ☠ ☠

Josephine pulled the thick-lensed eyeglasses from her sweater pocket and took a deep breath. Either she would prove that the person was Thaddeus, or she would get a finger bitten off, verifying that the patient was Fetid Stenchley. She dug deep inside herself for courage and quickly slid the glasses onto his face.

The person's mouth snapped open, displaying the two large teeth in their ugly, jagged entirety. Josephine recoiled instinctively, but the mouth did not try to bite her. Instead, it spoke two words.

"Mizz . . . Cravitz." The voice was barely loud enough to be heard. "I mean . . . Josephine."

A relieved smile spread across Josephine's face. "Thaddeus!" she exclaimed. "It's you!"

"Are you sure it's really him, dear? It could be a trick of some kind," warned Barbara.

"No doubt about it," Josephine said confidently. "Dr. Herringbone, this is my friend Thaddeus, not Fetid Stenchley! Please set him free!"

"But the official chart is very clear on this matter," the doctor began.

"Then the official chart is wrong!" said Josephine. "Don't you see? He's a boy. He couldn't possibly be Stenchley!"

"The chart is never wrong, young lady," he said. "This is a pre-eminent institution, not some backwater outpost."

"Can't you forget about the dumb chart and just look at him?" she insisted.

With a sigh, the director leaned over the operating table and looked carefully at the patient.

Dr. Herringbone raised his eyebrows. "I . . . I don't understand. This is not Fetid Stenchley at all!"

Even with a couple of yellow overgrown teeth here and a leathery patch of hide there, the doctor could not deny that the person on the table was obviously a boy and not the grizzled murderer he remembered.

He turned to the head surgeon and fumed, "I demand a new official chart on my desk this afternoon, Dr. Penrose! And turn that saw off!" He snapped his fingers at the orderlies by the door. "Have this boy discharged immediately!"

While technicians disconnected the wires and leads from Thaddeus's head and chest, Howard took off his coat and covered the shivering boy. Josephine could see that he was still cold, however. Thaddeus's head, without its full topping of white hair, seemed naked. She immediately knew what she should do and was surprised to find she had no qualms about it. Josephine pulled Eggplant off her own head and put it on Thaddeus's, tugging it down snugly over his ears.

The boy looked goofy, but grateful. Josephine smiled. Somehow it felt good to give away her prized possession. She told herself it was no big deal, just the right thing to do for someone with a cold head.

CHAPTER 47

When Fetid Stenchley crawled out of his cozy nest in the Dumpster, he found that the sun had risen a good while earlier and had thawed the icy streets nicely since the night's gale. The madman headed off in what he thought to be the general direction of Hibble Manor with his plan to find the professor still floating around in his mind. The bustling village streets were gaily decorated with banners and flags for the big SAD parade scheduled for later in the day, and the Awkward Falls High Fighting Pike marching band, their tall hats modified to look like cans of sauerkraut, were gathered in the square practicing their rendition of "Wooly Bully." More than one member of the decoration committee gave Stenchley an odd look as he shuffled along in his carpet wrap and paper bag hat. He did appear to be a child, after all, if a very dirty and fragrant one.

Stenchley turned a corner and strolled into the park in the center of town hoping that a young mouse or rat, preferably an injured one, might present itself. As if by magic, a small furry creature skittered onto the path directly in front of him. Without the glasses he had left behind in the hotel room, Stenchley couldn't make out the details of the animal's features. He fell to the ground, catlike, and readied himself to pounce. When the creature was close enough, the madman snarled and leapt at it. The animal easily sidestepped him at the last second and watched as Stenchley did a face plant into a snowbank.

The madman scrambled to his feet, shaking snow from his hair, and was about to leap at the creature again when he saw that his prey was on a long leash. Heading toward him at the other end of the leash was a heavily bundled elderly woman who was waving at him excitedly. Even if Stenchley had seen her clearly, he would have had no idea who the woman was. She was accompanied by a group of equally senior females all trailing a troop of yipping pets on leashes.

"Yooo-hooo, Mr. Hibble!" she trilled. " Hello, Mr. Hibble! It is I, Mrs. Gladstone. How nice to see you!"

Her companions followed her over with their animals. Stenchley found himself surrounded by small, yapping, jumping, sniffing creatures that were extremely interested in his pant legs. Many of the beasts seemed to be comprised of mismatched parts. One of them locked its jaws onto the carpet remnant the madman wore and tore it off his shoulders, angrily ripping mouthfuls of shag material from it.

The widow Gladstone waved a hand at the women. "You know the other ladies of the poker club, of course."

The women all tittered like birds.

"And look! Coco remembers you as well." Her own animal, the quick, rodentish beast Stenchley had failed to nab, nipped at his trouser seat. "Don't you, Coco? Yes, you do! This is the young man who made you all better after that nasty old Zamboni squashed you!"

Stenchley backed away from the animals nervously. There were too many of them. His natural fear of dogs made him want to run, but the sight of a mounted policeman down the snowy path ahead kept him nervously in check.

"Will Mr. Norman will be attending the festivities today as well?" The woman appeared to blush beneath her thick makeup. She craned her neck this way and that to see if the robot was nearby.

Stenchley did not bother to answer. The gaggle of beasts had begun to force him backward until he had to turn and run to get away from them. He was finally cornered at the granite base of a large statue. The creatures became increasingly excited, spurred into a frenzy by the fishy Dumpster-stink of his clothes. The ladies were in a tizzy, tugging on the leashes and trying to pull the animals off the white-suited boy.

Stenchley scrambled up the base of the statue and jumped off the other side. Panicked, he ran across the smooth snow that covered the lawn, dodging from tree to tree. The animals, which had pulled free from their masters, were now chasing him freely, their leashes dragging behind them. The madman ducked behind the Tomb of the Unknown Angler, then made a beeline for the black wrought-iron fence that enclosed the park. Once he made it to the other side, he would be safe.

Stenchley had jumped many fences in his day; tall ones, wide ones, electrified ones. A skilled murderer of some stealth, he was in fact something of a fence-jumping expert. This particular enclosure was nothing special outside of its spike-topped posts. Without really thinking, he knew from experience that he would leap onto the upper section of the fence, then vault over, landing on all fours on the other side. It should be easy.

It was not easy. Again he failed to consider the fact that he was depending on Thaddeus's soft, plump body to get the job done. His leap was not high enough. His grip was not strong enough. Stenchley flopped against the fence and fell backward into the snow as if he were a very large toddler. He got back up quickly and began climbing hand over hand, inch by inch, up the fence as the relentless animals reached him. Up he went, ever so slowly, the nip of tiny teeth sinking into his calves and thighs repeatedly.

Finally, as he climbed beyond the reach of the beasts, he flung his legs over the top and dropped to the ground on the other side. He lay on his back in the snow, panting, just happy to be away from the crazed pets. When he caught his breath, he hurried toward a large, safe-looking building nearby. The granite front steps were broad, just like those at Hibble Manor, the front door similarly tall and formal. The familiar style of the building, its pointed arches, multiple gables, ornate columns, all reminded him of the mansion as well. When

Stenchley took the brass knocker in his hand and tapped the front door, he almost expected Norman to answer.

Instead, a man, impeccably dressed in a midnight-black suit, opened the door. To Stenchley's surprise, the man smiled as if he knew him.

"Well, well," said the man in the black suit. "So you're not a phantom after all. Come in. You're just in time for porridge."

Fetid Stenchley could not guess what the man was talking about, but stepped inside anyway, drawn by the smell of food. The madman's intuition about the similarities between Hibble Manor and this place had been more accurate than he could have imagined. The two buildings looked alike because they were built by the same architect at almost the same time and were financed by the same man.

Had Stenchley known how to read, and if he had bothered to look up as fate guided him inside, he would have seen above the entrance of the building a row of tarnished brass letters that read C. T. HIBBLE ORPHANAGE.

CHAPTER 48

A Formula 1 race car could not have carried the Cravitzes, Thaddeus, and Felix away from the Asylum for the Dangerously Insane fast enough to suit them, much less an elderly station wagon with a top speed of fifty-three miles per hour. Plans were yet to be made about where they were going and the more thorny issue of what they should do with Thaddeus. For the moment, simply being out of the asylum was enough. Everyone, most of all Thaddeus, breathed easier once the gray walls of the monolithic madhouse were out of sight.

He was stationed in the backseat between Josephine and Barbara, with Felix curled on his lap, purring heavily. Peering out from beneath Eggplant's fuzzy wool, and wrapped snugly in blankets, he had finally stopped shivering. Josephine had still not made up her mind whether the hat was going to be a loan or a gift. She felt somewhat exposed without it, but also unexpectedly liberated. She realized Thaddeus was the first person other than herself ever to wear it.

Every few minutes, Barbara felt his cheeks for fever or took his hand in hers to check his pulse. Josephine was surprised that the normally grumpy boy did not recoil at her mom's motherly attention. On the contrary, his eyes became almost starry every time Barbara touched him. If she hadn't known better, Josephine might have thought he was smitten.

"How are you feeling, Thaddeus?" Barbara asked. "Are you warm enough?"

"Quite." He gazed into her eyes like a puppy hoping for a scratch. "Though I seem to be a bit light-headed. No doubt the result of having missed several meals during my incarceration. Perhaps something chocolate would set me right again." He paused thoughtfully, then added, "Oddly, I have a craving for raw meat as well."

EPILOGUE

A funeral at any time of year is an unpleasant event, even in otherwise pleasant places such as Florida, or Waikiki. Sunny days lose a great deal of their allure when they are spent burying the dead. But a winter funeral in northern Manitoba is especially grim. The weather is so cold and miserable that the ground is frozen solid, requiring the use of heavy machinery just to dig the hole. It is not unusual for mourners themselves to die from exposure, which leads only to more winter funerals, which lead to more deceased mourners, and so on, until it is a wonder that any northern Manitobans are still alive when spring arrives.

Even still, when the notice of Sally Twittington's death appeared in the *Awkward Falls Chronicle*, the Cravitzes decided to brave the elements in order to pay their respects. Josephine had expected a crowd at the cemetery, but only a handful of mourners besides the Cravitzes and Thaddeus attended the funeral. Sally's nurse, Olga, was there, as was O. R. MacManus, the librarian, who arrived at the last minute in a rattling pickup truck that may have been older than she was. *It seemed a shame for so few people to be there to say good-bye,* Josephine thought. *She must have outlived her friends and family.*

The graveside funeral began at noon, though the sun was nowhere to be seen. A priest in an orange hunting cap read something in Latin, the freezing wind scattering his words like leaves the second they left his mouth. Josephine shivered as she teetered against the gale, her feet so cold she had to look at them to make sure they were still there. Barbara and Howard were huddled to one side of her, with Thaddeus between them, resembling a stack of inner tubes in his huge new coat.

Josephine was glad Thaddeus had come along despite his fear of being outside the new house he now shared with her family. He still had nightmares about Fetid Stenchley. The madman had not been heard from since the night he had attacked the Cravitzes in the Hook, Line, and Sinker motel. Although the authorities had lowered the threat level all the way down to brown, the boy was sure the killer was still lurking nearby, disguised as Thaddeus himself, just waiting for an opportunity to do something horrible.

But Stenchley wasn't Thaddeus's only worry. He was still plagued by the random transformations that caused his features to morph back and forth between Stenchley's and his own, and he feared a public display. Even on a normal day, Josephine would have had to coax Thaddeus out the door, but today he was especially reluctant. A full moon was due to rise that evening, bringing with it the

possibility of what the family had come to refer to as a "Full Stenchley."
When the previous full moon had appeared, it had triggered a major
transformation. On that memorable evening, Thaddeus had suddenly morphed into a near twin of the killer hunchback while grocery shopping. As he, Josephine, and Barbara browsed the aisles of
the A&P, a replica of the madman's ugly hump rose on his shoulder.
At the same time, a group of dangerously jagged incisors crowded
their way into his mouth, his eyes dilated and bulged, and the backs
of his knuckles hit the floor. With a hair-raising howl, he broke for
the meat case and belly flopped into a stack of prepackaged ham-
burger. Luckily, the natural modesty of the other Awkward Fallsian
shoppers had caused them to avert their eyes from the ill-behaved
child and his family. It was a good thing, since the sight of the boy-
turned-cannibal cramming bloody, cellophane-wrapped beef into
his mouth could have resulted in someone dialing 911 and getting
him sent to the asylum again. They were lucky to have been tossed
out of the store with only an admonishment and a large meat bill.
For two days afterward, *Sesame Street* reruns and saucers of raw
meat were the only things that kept the toothy boy's snapping jaws
at bay.

The risk of a Full Stenchley occurring in the middle of the day
was small, however, and Howard assessed that it was safe for him
to venture out. They would be home long before the moon made
its late-night appearance, in plenty of time to stock up on red meat
and lock all the doors. Still, they parked the Volvo as close to the

gravesite as possible and left the motor running, in case a speedy getaway was required.

Aside from the transformations, having Thaddeus around the house for the last few weeks had been mostly a good thing. Glancing over at him now, his nose protruding like a tomato from beneath Eggplant, Josephine wondered how long he would stay with them. Her parents seemed to have pretty much accepted him as a member of the family. Felix had become an honorary Cravitz as well, and was content to be wherever Thaddeus was, as long as it wasn't out of doors on a freezing day. The cat had called them all nuts for going out in such weather, preferring to stay in the car. While it was true that Josephine had always wanted a sibling, Thaddeus wasn't exactly what she'd had in mind. He was sort of endearing in his curmudgeonly way, but he didn't really fit in with the family. If the Cravitzes had been an unusual family before, they were downright outlandish with Thaddeus and Felix in the mix.

On the other hand, thanks to Thaddeus, Josephine's prediction that her life would descend into bottomless boredom in Awkward Falls could not have been more wrong. Thaddeus seemed to be the epicenter of bizarre occurrences. Since meeting him, she had been bagged by a robot, bitten by a cannibal, attacked by mutant monsters, and chased by a dead guy. She had helped burn her own house down, rescued Thaddeus from the Asylum for the Dangerously Insane, and fed the finger of a deceased Nobel Prize winner to a buffalo-panther, and now she was attending the funeral of a formerly famous actress and sauerkraut heiress in subarctic weather. With Thaddeus stationed in the room across the hall, boredom might be banished from her life entirely. And although that probably meant safety would be banished as well, the bad driver part of Josephine's brain decided it was, all in all, an acceptable trade-off.

☠ ☠ ☠

Curiosity about the human burial ritual was the only thing that got Thaddeus out of the car. The cemetery, with its hundreds of tombstones and vaults, was filled with places Stenchley could be hiding. The boy was somewhat comforted by the Cravitz parents, who flanked him as they stood at the grave, each holding one of his hands, though he was disappointed that they had refused to carry weapons of some kind. As an added precaution, Felix was stationed inside the Volvo with a pair of binoculars with which he promised to scan the area for any sign of the killer. Two beeps on the car's horn would signal a sighting.

Thaddeus also held out hope that he might see the professor. The boy speculated that there was a slight chance the wandering corpse could be in the vicinity, since it had been heading in roughly this direction when Thaddeus had last seen it. There was unfinished business between the boy and his creator. Thaddeus knew he was the professor's clone, an exact genetic copy; but did that mean he was doomed to do the same terrible things Celsius Hibble had? Was

Thaddeus inherently evil? It was a long shot, but he hoped that seeing the professor again, looking into his eyes, might provide insight of some kind.

The funeral began, turning Thaddeus's attention to the odd scene at the gravesite. The ceremony, with the corpse locked in an ornate box suspended over the hole where it would be interred, and the clergyman reciting words in a language no one spoke, struck him as theatrical and inefficient. It seemed such a waste of both the box, which would have made a nice coffee table, and the body, to simply toss them into the earth and cover them up the way a dog might bury a bone. Surely a few of the woman's organs were reusable, despite her age. In many species, the spleen in particular tended to hold up quite well in elderly specimens. And why was the hole so deep? Was there a concern that the corpse might escape? It was baffling.

If only Norman were here, thought Thaddeus, *he could explain it.* Norman could explain nearly anything. Thaddeus's happiest memories were of sitting on the sofa with a perfect cup of cocoa as the ditzy robot rattled on and on, scribbling explanatory diagrams and notes on a chalkboard. He missed the old robot. In the days after his rescue from the asylum, Thaddeus had badly wanted to return to his former home to retrieve Norman's remains for repair. This had proven too risky as Officer Cole had decided to declare the place a crime scene, and had cordoned off the entire estate with yellow police tape. They had driven by a few times and seen Deputy Flange's cruiser parked at the gate. The rebuilding of Norman would have to wait.

Now that Thaddeus was living with the Cravitzes, Josephine's parents performed many of the functions that Norman had at Hibble Manor, though Howard and Barbara were far less obedient to Thaddeus's demands. Barbara only laughed when he announced that he would have his breakfast in bed. And despite his assurance that he was clean enough, she required Thaddeus to engage in a ridiculously inconvenient and unnecessary amount of washing daily. In her favor, she had tried to make cocoa for him using her bland, organic ingredients, though the result always fell far short of Norman's sweet, creamy confection.

The family's vegetarian meals were even worse. At their first supper together, Thaddeus realized that normal food was unheard of by these strange people. On his plate were piled several varieties of horrid things that seemed to be shrubbery clippings. Some were little more than raw leaves, others were thin and twiggy, some orange and cigar-shaped. A slice of yellow-and-green-speckled pie offered hope, until he found it contained only more clippings and not a molecule of whipped cream or butterscotch.

It was only the discovery of ketchup that saved Thaddeus from starvation. He had been pillaging the pantry for anything that might satisfy his sweet tooth when Howard pointed out a substance he claimed often improved the taste of certain things. Thaddeus tried a squirt and found it delicious. From that moment on, the bottle of tangy red goop became his constant companion at mealtimes. He slathered mounds of it on everything from salad to oatmeal. As long as it was buried under ketchup, he had found he could eat any fiber-rich, vitamin-packed, chlorophyll-crammed concoction Barbara foisted on him.

Thaddeus forgave the Cravitz woman's many shortcomings, however, when he discovered that she, too, was a board game enthusiast. In many ways she reminded Thaddeus of his own mother, the one he had created in his fantasies, when they played. Barbara was not as glamorous or as beautiful as the mother who had lived in his dreams, of course. But he had to admit there was something pleasing about the ratio of gums to teeth when Barbara smiled. Plus she was a satisfyingly formidable opponent at Candyland, and was nearly unbeatable when the game was Mousetrap.

Howard Cravitz assumed the role of Thaddeus's tutor once Josephine started at Awkward Falls Junior High. To Thaddeus's chagrin, Howard insisted on spending ridiculous amounts of time on such useless piffle as social studies and poetry. But his science lessons made it tolerable, and their discussions on physics, chemistry, and biology often went on for hours. Thaddeus wished they were having one now, over a pot of hot cocoa.

When the clergyman came to the end of his reading, the undertaker began turning the crank on a squeaky contraption that lowered Sally's casket into the freshly dug hole. The priest took a handful of dirt from a pile next to the grave and tossed it onto the coffin as it descended, then crossed himself. Olga did the same, followed by Howard, Barbara, and Josephine. Thaddeus tossed a handful as well, but felt silly doing it. Instead of dirt, O. R. MacManus dropped a fishing lure onto the coffin. The priest said a few more words, then turned and headed for the parking lot.

Just like that, the funeral was over.

As everyone hurried for the shelter of their vehicles, Olga caught up to Josephine and Thaddeus. She pressed an envelope into the boy's gloved hand.

"I expected you might be here. I found this among Ms. Twittington's possessions. It is addressed to you." With no further explanation, the nurse spun and walked away.

"Wait, what is this all about?" He started to run after her, but she was already closing the taxi door. A second later, she was gone.

"Wow," said Josephine. "Pretty weird."

Once inside the relative warmth of the Volvo, Thaddeus took his gloves off and fingered the envelope. In swishy cursive lettering was written *Thaddeus Hibble, Esq.*

He had never received a letter before, and tore it open carefully. The paper was thick and creamy-white, covered with neat handwriting that was almost too pretty to read.

Dear Thaddeus,

I write this as I wait in the wings before my final Parisian performance. I will be brief, as my entrance is nigh. Since your recent visit, I have come to realize that you are the most innocent player of all in this macabre tragedy and the least deserving of the role fate has dealt you. Seeing your face that night, so perfect a copy of Celsius's own, stirred dark memories I have spent a lifetime trying to forget. Yet there is one scene I feel I must recount, for your sake.

I received a note from Celsius some years ago, our first communication in decades, beseeching me to come to Hibble Manor and meet with him. He had made a major breakthrough in his work that he wanted me to see. Although I had sworn never to enter Hibble Manor again, the desperation I sensed in his note led me to break my vow.

Upon my arrival, the robot led me into the underground laboratory where I saw Celsius. Though I had tried to prepare myself for this moment, I was taken aback. Some sixty-three years after our last encounter, my former fiancé's face was unchanged—there was not even the tiniest sign of aging. I felt embarrassed by my wrinkles and gray hair, which stood in such stark contrast to his unending, virile youth.

But the man inside the impossibly youthful body had changed in other ways. His sparkling blue eyes, though as piercing as ever, were now furtive and unfocused. His hands fidgeted and swiped at invisible things in the air. He laughed at odd moments, and when he spoke, words poured out in torrents, many of them senseless. It was clear that Celsius was insane.

After leading me past enormous test tubes containing things too bizarre to describe, we came to a smaller set of containers separate from all the rest. Celsius stopped and pointed proudly. Inside each bubbling tube was something so small, I would have missed it had he not shown me where to look. They were human embryos. I was appalled. He was cultivating human beings as if they were tadpoles. Yet, despite the macabre nature of the endeavor, it was obvious that, for Celsius, this was no mere experiment. The look in his eyes as he gazed at the tiny beings in those tubes was as innocent and as full of love as a parent's.

"These are my sons," he said, his voice trembling, "my babies."

One of them was you, Thaddeus.

Celsius, though immortal in body, had become mad with loneliness over the years, cloistered in his laboratory with only the robot and a madman for company. His damaged mind foolishly fantasized that I might rejoin him and together we would rear his new "family." But I was more convinced than ever that my decision all those years ago to leave him was correct. Celsius's use of his talent was wrong, immoral, and unforgivable. He created many monsters in his quest for immortality, but you were not one of them. In his way, I believe Celsius loved you as much as he could love anything. Alas, the curtain rises. My public calls.

Adieu,

Sally Twittington

It would have been nice if the northern Manitoban sun had peeked out from behind the clouds at that moment, giving Thaddeus a sign from above that even a parentless boy cloned by a mad professor had reason to feel good about himself, but it did not. The sky actually became darker, and the wind blew harder and colder than ever. Still, he felt a degree or two warmer when he read Sally's words.

Josephine tugged anxiously on his puffy coat. "Come on, what does the letter say?"

Thaddeus folded the pages and stuffed them in his pocket. "It says . . . that I am not a monster."

A small smile on the boy's face exposed a gaggle of teeth that had begun to extrude beyond their normal positions. The Full Stenchley was ahead of schedule.

Josephine rolled her eyes and punched his shoulder. "Well, duh. I could've told you that."

Keith Graves is the author and illustrator of many picture books, including *Frank Was a Monster Who Wanted to Dance* and *Chicken Big*, which was a Junior Library Guild Selection, BookPage Best Children's Book of 2010, and E.B. White Read-Aloud Award Honor Book. His own children, thirteen-year-old twins, inspired this story, his first novel. Keith lives in Austin, Texas.

Copyright © 2011 by Keith Graves.
All rights reserved. No part of this book may be reproduced in
any form without written permission from the publisher.

Library of Congress Cataloging-in-Publication Data
Graves, Keith.
The orphan of Awkward Falls / by Keith Graves.
p. cm.
Summary: Josephine Cravitz, the new girl in Awkward Falls, and her neighbor
Thaddeus Hibble, a reclusive and orphaned boy inventor, become the targets
of a mad cannibal from the local asylum for the criminally insane.
ISBN 978-0-8118-7814-2 (alk. paper)
1. Science—Experiments—Juvenile fiction. 2. Dangerously mentally ill—
Juvenile fiction. 3. Murderers—Juvenile fiction. 4. Orphans—Juvenile fiction.
5. Inventors—Juvenile fiction. [1. Mystery and detective stories. 2. Science—
Experiments—Fiction. 3. Mental illness—Fiction. 4. Murder—Fiction.
5. Orphans—Fiction. 6. Inventors—Fiction.] I. Title.
PZ7.G77524Or 2011
813.54—dc22
2011008008

Book design by Kristine Brogno.
Typeset in Adobe Jenson.
The illustrations in this book were rendered in colored pencil and acrylic paint.

Manufactured by Toppan Leefung, Da Ling Shan Town,
Dongguan, China, in August 2011.

1 3 5 7 9 10 8 6 4 2

This product conforms to CPSIA 2008.

Chronicle Books LLC
680 Second Street, San Francisco, California 94107

www.chroniclekids.com

GRAVE   HVINX

Graves, Keith.

The orphan of Awkward Falls /

 VINSON
 11/11